RUNNING IN BED

RUNNING IN BED

JEFFREY SHARLACH

TO VERNON
WITH ALL MY BEST WISHES

[signature]

DENVER 7/9/2012

TWOHARBORS
WWW.TWOHARBORSPRESS.COM

Two Harbors Press
212 3rd Avenue North, Suite 290
Minneapolis, MN 55401
612.455.2293
www.TwoHarborsPress.com

ISBN: 978-1-937293-48-2
LCCN: 2011940196

Cover Design: John Kneapler
Cover Photographer: Leo Diaz
Cover Model: Pablo Hernandez

Printed in the United States of America

For Ken and all the others

whose beauty and promise ended too soon

The dreams began that first night after he returned to the city. There was the grid, the plan that kept everything in order. First Avenue, Second Avenue, Third, Lex, Park, and Madison crossed by the numerical streets; all neatly rectangular. But in these nocturnal wanderings, there was always the unexpected. Hills and sharp white cliffs while walking across 37th Street. A gigantic stairway at the north end of Central Park, dovetailed around like the steps to a forest ranger tower and then reaching a wooded plateau that began at 110th Street. (And he had never even been to 110th Street, nor to that northern end of the park.)

The flat geography of New York during waking hours was transformed into an unusually varied landscape. There were winding highways that flew out of the park with those massive green-and-white directional signs like one might encounter on a long boring stretch of I-95. And small clapboard cottages had sprung up on hilly country lanes just off Central Park West.

The disarray startled him. Sometimes it even awakened him as he puzzled over his surroundings, scared at feeling disoriented. How much more frightening to be lost in someplace so familiar than in a place one doesn't know.

❧ 1 ❧

Sitting on the American Airlines jet as it flew up along the Hudson River, I looked out at the Manhattan skyline. It was dusk, and the headlights from the rush-hour traffic illuminated the crisscross of the city streets as the sun set on the opposite side of the plane. It still looked like a magical place, the Emerald City at the end of the yellow brick road.

With that view, the memories of my first autumn in New York ten years before, in 1977, flooded back. Those days, I certainly wouldn't have recognized the man I'd become today. Back then I was trying not to be that person.

I remembered how my skin felt like it was on fire that fall. The burning sensation lasted only an instant, probably less than a second. And when I left the doctor's office there were no marks. He had asked me to bring in a photo of Jerry. I didn't really have very many, considering all the time we had spent together at Cornell until graduation that spring. There was one of him in gray T-shirt and jeans that I had used as a bookmark, often staring at his handsome face and broad shoulders before I drifted off to sleep.

"That'll do," the doctor said when I described it to him. "Bring that."

And there was Jerry, projected on the white wall across the room. With that cute smile of his, he looked like he was happy to see me. Which was strange because every time I saw his picture, the doctor turned the dial to give me another shock. The electricity surged through my body, pulsing with an instant flash of heat.

There were pictures of other guys, all with their shirts off and some in even less. But Dr. Radofsky said the therapy would be much more effective if I actually had the behavior modification treatment while using an image with the object of my affection.

Dr. Bruce Radofsky's office was on Park Avenue and 67th Street. The entrance was actually on 67th Street, but it had a Park Avenue address. The first floor of the building had a number of doctors' offices, but Radofsky didn't have a nurse or a secretary or anyone else there with him. The doorman checked my name on an appointment list, and I would let myself into the waiting room.

This was already my sixth weekly session. The first had been at the end of September, not long after my first full month of work at Carlton Bennett Associates—CBA—the big advertising agency. Fresh out of Cornell with my degree in marketing, I considered myself very fortunate to start my career at CBA. And not only that, I was working as a junior account executive on the General Motors account, the agency's largest.

I was making $21,000 a year, which was a good starting salary in '77 and more than enough to pay the $300 rent on my one-bedroom apartment, with plenty left over for Radofsky's $55-an-hour fee each week. He wasn't really a medical doctor, so I couldn't claim it on my insurance. But he had a PhD in psychology; hence, he was called "doctor."

After all those years of being supported through school by my parents, I finally didn't have to answer to anyone about where I was spending my money. I had read about Radofsky in the *New York Times* in an article describing his success at changing homosexual men into women-loving heterosexuals.

"Look at your friend Jerry," he instructed. And then he turned the dial. "It makes you feel bad, right?"

Actually, I loved that picture of Jerry, with his wide grin and hair that curled down over his forehead. And getting the shock, or the jolt, or whatever the electric charge was called only made it more erotic for me.

But more than anything, I wanted the therapy to work. So I tried not to look at Jerry's smile and his brown eyes.

There were pictures of women, pictures of the seashore, and mountains, and tall pine trees with the sun filtering through. And then there would be a few men in tight bathing suits, and that's when the amperage would be turned up—and for Jerry's photo, the same.

Jerry was only the latest in a long line of candidates for my attention. My earliest sexual thoughts about other boys came early in elementary school in Scarsdale, a sleepy suburb about twenty-five minutes from Manhattan.

By junior high I was getting turned on watching the guys in gym class. It was terror mixed with excitement in that musty locker room, and the desire got me more overheated than the steam and sweat that seemed to suck up most of the breathable air. But I hid those feelings deep inside. High school was even more complicated. I was on the swimming team and was expected to go out with girls, but the emotions inside always betrayed me as I began to develop crushes on other guys from the team. I didn't know what I was feeling, though, and the sensations that kept coming to the surface in these relationships startled and scared me—and even more so, the guys I dreamed about who were mostly just puzzled by the overflowing abundance of attention I showered on them.

I never said anything. Not once, all through high school and college, had I acted upon those feelings. I was too frightened of them. And school was school; I figured that once I got out in the real world, maybe everything would change. Maybe it *was* just a phase, something that I'd leave behind after graduation. So in the meantime I used my fantasies to climax on my own, often two, sometimes three times a day.

Before Radofsky, I had tried my own behavior modification experiment for a while: seeing if I grabbed a *Playboy* magazine right before ejaculation that might change the scenes I replayed in my head. It didn't work.

I tried to learn what I could on my own, but it wasn't easy in those days. I furtively bought a copy of *Everything You Always Wanted to Know About Sex (But Were Afraid to Ask)* at the off-campus bookstore in Ithaca. Inside, I read as Dr. David Reuben explained in question-and-answer format that homosexual encounters are generally impersonal bathroom sex, where guys exchange notes on toilet paper and then go at it. "No feeling, no sentiment, no nothing." But "are all homosexual contacts as impersonal as that?" he wrote. "No," he answered, "most are much more impersonal." And then another question: "But all homosexuals aren't like that, are they?" Yes, Dr. Reuben answered, "unfortunately, they are just like that."

That was definitely not the life I dreamed about having. And I had already been pretty sure I wasn't really a homosexual anyway. I wasn't like the people I'd been seeing stories about on TV. I had zero interest in having sex in public bathrooms and certainly wasn't interested in the children that the homosexuals on TV seemed to get arrested for preying upon.

And I didn't have anything in common with men I assumed were homosexuals that I'd pass in Greenwich Village, near my walkup apartment on the top floor of a brownstone on Ninth Street, just off Fifth Avenue. I'd see them in the neighborhood with their mustaches, leather boots, and black jackets, and the more I saw, the more I was convinced that I didn't want to be like them.

I was sure Radofsky would be the answer. He was going to finally get me to stop dreaming about men, forget about Jerry, leave behind thoughts of all those other guys, and be the happy heterosexual I wanted to be.

At CBA, I had my own office and just outside sat Rita, my secretary. Even then we didn't call them secretaries; Rita was my administrative assistant, or "admin" for short. Not "an admin," but "my admin." The office was tiny, with no windows, but like every other account person, I was assigned an admin to take dictation, type letters, and arrange meeting and appointments for me by calling back and forth with the other girls who lined the hallways with their L-shaped desks and Dictaphone machines. It was the perfect setting for the images of heterosexual life I had in my mind from watching Rock Hudson and Doris Day together in the movies.

When I went for my interview at CBA during spring break from senior year at Cornell, I remember I couldn't even sit still without knocking my knees together from a combination of nervousness and excitement.

"I'm Josh Silver," I announced at the front desk, tightly holding on with both hands to the leather portfolio I had bought just for the occasion. The receptionist nodded toward one of the two white leather couches in the reception area as she talked on the phone, apparently to a friend, and simultaneously applied nail polish.

She had light skin, which looked even paler with her red-orange hair and matching lipstick. "Carole Rubino" the nameplate gleamed.

On the way out, I said good-bye. "Hopefully, I'll be seeing you again soon."

She asked me how the interview went, and I told her it had gone pretty well. Or at least I thought it had. Carole tapped her cigarette on the glass ashtray on the counter.

"Remember, it's Carole with an *e*," she said as she winked. "I'm sure it will work out fine."

And now after three months on the job, it seemed to be, except for this one little nagging problem I was seeing Radofsky to fix. After each session, I would leave his office and take the subway down to Union Square, less than a five-minute walk from my apartment. Even more exciting for me than working at CBA was having my own place in Manhattan, something I had dreamed about for as long as I could remember while I was growing up in the suburbs. It had been less than a month after graduation that my parents, Herb and Lillian, drove me into the city in our faux wood-paneled station wagon loaded with some old furniture from my childhood bedroom and the old white Formica table from the pre-renovation Silver family kitchen that would be my desk.

At forty-seven, my dad was five years older than my mom, but they both helped me haul my belongings up the four flights of stairs that steamy Sunday afternoon. When they left a couple of hours later, I double-locked the door and went to the window to watch them drive away, just to be sure I was really on my own. The apartment was in a brownstone, an old single-family house that the landlord told me had been built in 1840. Before being converted into apartments it had been a boarding house; each landing on the stairs had numerous doors that had been sealed shut for years and painted over with so many coats they appeared like a reverse trompe l'oeil.

There were a few friends I knew from Cornell in the city, and occasionally I got together with them in those first couple of months. Carole had introduced me to some of the other young people at CBA, but I was still pretty sure that I was the only twenty-two-year-old virgin in the city.

I wasn't sure how much progress I was making with Radofsky, but when I questioned it at the end of the sixth session, he reminded me that it was going to take a while to reverse all the positive reinforcement I had given myself over the years from ejaculating to my homoerotic fantasies.

That seemed to make sense to me; I remembered enough from my one intro psychology class that people can be conditioned to respond to certain stimuli. Still, I was beginning to have my doubts about it all. I didn't feel the slightest dissipation in my attraction to men or the slightest arousal toward women. And then there was Dr. Bruce. He didn't seem particularly happy to me; as a matter of fact, lots of times he looked pretty miserable when I arrived. There were diplomas and news articles around the office but no pictures of his own girlfriend, wife, or any other human for that matter. Not even a dog photo. I supposed I could have asked, but I never did.

Two months later CBA sent me on my first business trip, to Detroit. There was the guy at the meeting who sat across from me at the conference table all the first day and kept locking his eyes on mine. This time I wasn't in the high school locker room; I was an adult staying alone in my own hotel room, in a place where no one really knew me, and still didn't do anything—even after a long drunken dinner with him at the hotel's rooftop restaurant that revolved seventy-two floors above downtown Detroit.

But on the flight back the next morning to LaGuardia, that was all I could think about. Why hadn't I said something? Why didn't I just invite him to stop by my room, just a few floors down in the same hotel, and at least invite him to smoke a joint?

That trip changed me. It was the first time I'd ever been on a plane when my parents didn't pay for the ticket. Finally, it was starting to dawn on me that I didn't have to answer to anyone. I decided before the flight home landed in New York that I was done with Radofsky.

❧ 2 ❧

Just on the other side of Sixth Avenue, right at the beginning of Christopher Street, I passed the Oscar Wilde Bookshop. I knew it was a gay bookstore from the posters in the window, and I had wanted to go in before and once, just days after I moved to the city, had come within seconds of walking up the steps and ringing the buzzer but got scared at the last minute and turned away.

This time I turned around and went inside. The store was cramped and filled with five customers besides me—literally filled; there really wasn't room for anyone else to fit.

On the top of the nonfiction shelves, the *Gay Yellow Pages* was displayed with a red-and-blue cover displaying the familiar "Let Your Fingers Do the Walking" logo. In addition to the yellow paper, it stood out prominently because of its large dimensions; the pages were the size of a traditional phonebook but much thinner than the regular New York City tome, less than a hundred pages.

Inside, a directory, arranged state by state and then city by city, listed various categories of establishments—bars, discothèques, hotels, restaurants, accountants, lawyers, and others—that were either gay-owned or welcomed gay clientele. The pages were broken up with some display ads, but mostly there were columns of names, addresses, and phone numbers.

While I was at the counter, a guy younger than me, probably not even eighteen, came in and asked if they had any books about "coming out." Hearing someone say the words aloud startled me, although I wasn't exactly sure why. I paid cash; that way I was sure there was no record I had ever been there.

The spontaneous part of the day was deciding that I'd actually go to a gay bar that night. But for me, like everything else, it was carefully planned. I lay down in bed, thumbing through the *Gay Yellow Pages*. There were lots of ads for the various bars, but one caught my eye because, relative to those that surrounded it, this one looked more respectable. There were no drawings of cowboys or sailors, just the word "Company" in a logo that looked like a Broadway theater marquee with bulbs spelling out each of the letters. And it was only about a mile from the apartment on 29th and Third; by foot, less than a half-hour walk.

It was just after ten as I headed east over to Third Avenue, avoiding Union Square, which was virtually empty and notoriously dangerous at night. Even the police were said to be afraid to go into Union Square Park after dark. It had pretty much been taken over by drug dealers and the homeless.

As I crossed 23rd Street, I started to get nervous, but I never thought about turning back. I was determined to go through with it. When I got there, the illuminated sign in front flashed "Company" in the same bold typeface as the ad in the *Gay Yellow Pages*.

I pushed open the door. The bar was on the left. Two older heavyset balding men sat where it curved around a corner in front of the window, and there were six stools to their right, all empty. There was a song I recognized from some old movie on the sound system. The bartender smiled at me and came over.

"Hi, there. I'm Tony. What can I get you?"

Tony. The first gay man I had ever met in a gay bar. Or at least I guessed he must have been gay.

I wasn't much of a drinker; when I was growing up the only alcohol in the Silver home were the bottles of Manischewitz Concord Grape accumulated for Passover. Bottles that weren't finished were saved for the following year. And this was when it cost less than two dollars a bottle. In college my friends and I mostly smoked pot and drank beer. And at the ad agency, it seemed most of the people drank Jack Daniel's or Black Label on the rocks—and that was at lunchtime or during the afternoon at their desks.

"I'll take a Black Label on the rocks," I said.

Tony put down a napkin and turned around to grab the bottle of Johnnie Walker off the backlit shelves. I smiled back at him in the mirror. Did I look that nervous, I wondered? Why did he keep smiling at me? Maybe no one drinks Black Label at gay bars.

"Is this your first time here?"

"Yeah," I said. "I've gone by before, but this is the first time I've come in."

"You're here alone?" he asked.

"No, waiting to meet some friends." Which, after I said it, I realized was actually accurate.

It wasn't long before all the stools were occupied, and a crowd started to gather behind me. Tiny spotlights overhead shining down on the counter accentuated the cigarette smoke as I looked down the bar toward the door. That's when I first caught sight of Randy Starke coming out of the restaurant section with a group of three other people headed for the door—and right for me.

I put down the drink and tried desperately to find a pocket of fresh air to inhale among the smoke. *It can't be*, I told myself. This seemed like an impossibility, after only the first twenty minutes of my entire life in a gay bar. But there he was, Randy Starke, with a big grin on his face. Randy worked at CBA as an admin, the only male with that job, at least on my floor. And he worked for Harriet Burns, the only woman VP at the agency. It was hard to imagine that here, on the first night of my life in a gay bar, after less than an hour, someone was here that I knew. Maybe if I had turned around right away, I could have just stared down into my drink and miraculously avoided an encounter.

But here he was, life-size, right in front of my face.

"Come here often?" he asked. It wasn't until a few years later that I realized Randy had been making a joke with world's oldest standard pick-up line.

"No, this is the first time," I said. "Actually it's the first time I've been in a gay bar. Ever."

Randy smiled and looked down at the floor.

"So you're not really gay; you're just here to meet a friend."

"Umm. Well, I guess I'm gay. I think ... I'm pretty sure I'm gay. But I've never been to a gay bar before." I think it was the first night I had used the word with anyone other than a so-called health care professional.

"Yeah. Right. Me too," Randy said as he and his three companions all laughed.

I didn't. I sat there, still somewhat shocked that the conversation was even taking place at all. I was mostly worried about what it was going to mean that one of my coworkers knew me as gay, totally oblivious to the fact that now I knew he was gay, and not only that, he seemed pretty happy about it.

"You're serious about that, aren't you?" Randy said. "This is my lover, Gerard. And these are our friends, Sam and Marc."

Randy and I started to talk about other people at the agency: who was definitely gay, who might be gay, and who we wished would be gay. We went on for an hour; Gerard kept stopping back after talking with other people. Just before midnight Randy asked if I wanted to come back to their apartment for a nightcap. It was only a couple of blocks away on 36th and Second Avenue, he explained.

The three of us walked out the door, and the cold air felt great on my face, especially after the cigarette smoke of the past two hours. It was only minutes away to their building, and Randy pointed out local landmarks. "That's Uncle Charlie's Restaurant there, another gay restaurant like Company," he said.

"Only the food is much worse," Gerard said.

We turned on to 36th Street, walked past the doorman, and took the elevator to Randy and Gerard's place. I was used to student apartments, so I was impressed when we walked through the door. Theirs looked like a magazine photo spread to me: artwork, statues, and all the colors matched. Presumably, none of it was leftover furniture carted in from childhood bedrooms.

We sat down on the sofa, and Randy put on an album of jazz. He still had the cigarette in his mouth that he'd had from the street. "Do you want to smoke a joint?" Randy asked as he stubbed out the cigarette in the ashtray.

"Sure," I said and watched as he opened a small marble box on the glass table next to the sofa and pulled out a perfectly rolled joint. He lit it and took a deep breath before passing it to me.

"Take another hit. Just relax." He put his hand on my leg. I was wondering how to react, since I had certainly dreamed of touching Jerry's thighs when we had sat around in college smoking weed. Maybe that was just the way gay men acted with their friends.

Gerard stood up. "I'm going to open the bottle of wine so we can celebrate your coming out," he said.

"Coming out?" I asked. "I don't know." Despite my confidence of earlier in the night, it was still hard to say it.

"Not only is this the first night I've ever been in a gay bar, but this is the first time I've even talked to anyone about it."

"It?" Randy asked.

"Being gay."

"Have you ever been with another guy?" Randy asked.

"No."

"Shit. Are you serious?" Randy asked as he pulled his hand back from my leg and reached for another cigarette.

"No. I mean, I've been turned on by my best friends since junior high school," I said. "But no, I've never kissed another guy."

"My God, Gerard, we've got a lot of work to do with this one!" Randy said with a laugh. "Okay, well, at twenty-two, I'd say you're ready for some action."

"Yes, I'm definitely ready."

"Have you ever been to Uncle Charlie's South?" Randy asked.

"No, where's that?"

"It's right up the street on 38th Street and Third Avenue. It's where a lot of guys go when they first come out," Randy said. "Kind of a young and preppy crowd."

Randy went to the kitchen and pulled out a small pad of paper. "You can take your *Gay Yellow Pages* book back for a refund on Monday," he told me. "I'm going to make a list of places for you to go."

"And he's put many nights of extensive research into screening each of them, just in case he ever ran into someone like you who needed the information," Gerard said.

Randy wrote out six or seven names along with the addresses from memory. "Listen, we're having some friends over on Wednesday night for a little pre-Thanksgiving dinner," he said. "Why don't you join us? It will be early, around eight, and then if you want, you can go walk over to Uncle Charlie's and look for trouble afterwards."

"Okay, that sounds great."

The lights were dim and three candles burned in the windowsill. All three of us relaxed, listening to George Benson, as Saturday night eased into Sunday morning.

The next Wednesday was the day before Thanksgiving, and we all had the afternoon off at Carlton Bennett. Randy and I worked at totally opposite ends of the floor and by shortly after noon, the place had pretty much come to a standstill, everyone looking at the clocks for the next hours, waiting to leave. Most of the executives, nearly all men, would soon rush the few blocks over to Grand Central to take commuter trains home to meet their families in the suburbs of Westchester and Fairfield counties. The secretaries would take the subway to Queens or Yonkers.

Later that evening I waited in the entrance of Randy and Gerard's white-brick building as the doorman called upstairs to announce my arrival. Randy greeted me at the door with a more affected accent than I heard him use at CBA, a blend of someone descended from some distant British house of royalty mixed with his actual southern Louisiana ancestry. He held a cigarette in one hand and drink in the other.

Randy was shorter than me, probably about five-foot-eight or so, and in his jeans and cable-knit sweater, he seemed a lot better-looking than I was used to seeing him at CBA with his white shirt and tie. He had a handsome face, in a rugged sort of way; I suppose it could be called a ruddy complexion, but some of that was due to acne scars.

The friends who came over that night were all pretty much mid-thirties; Sam and Marc, both of whom I had met before at Company, another couple, and two singles who had previously been living together. Actually, from listening to the conversation, it was unsettling to realize that each of the eight had, at one point, slept with one or more of the others.

I was the focus of much of the attention—first, purely by being the new one in attendance, and second, the fact that Randy had apparently advised everyone in advance of my virginal status. It was certainly fun being the youngest one in the room, but like most things in my life that I experienced early on, I didn't enjoy it nearly as much as I would have if I had the chance to do it over again, later on, when I'd have been able to appreciate it so much more.

Joints were passed around between courses, and by the time we finished with dessert, I was high and feeling trapped. I needed to get some fresh air and move around, so at about 10:30 I left to walk over to Uncle Charlie's. Having dispensed considerable advice from their own personal experiences over the years, all of them smiled and wished me well on my adventure.

"Maybe we'll even see you there later on," Randy said, with his arm now wrapped around Marc, "if you haven't already gone home for sex with someone by the time we arrive." That shocked me. I definitely wasn't ready for that and hadn't even considered the possibility. Maybe if I got lucky, I'd meet someone and plan a date.

Unlike Company, which was primarily a restaurant, Uncle Charlie's had no other reason for its existence than for gay men to meet, drink, and socialize. I guess if I hadn't been high from the alcohol and the pot, I would have been a lot more nervous, but I couldn't have been more eager and excited as I pushed open the door.

The place was dimly lit, with walls covered in wood paneling, the kind I remembered from our Westchester basement rec room. On the left, a long bar lined the wall, and opposite that were two openings into a separate room, which was set up with a floor and lights for dancing, although signs warned that none was allowed due to city licensing regulations.

Behind the dance floor was another room with a large pool table and an alcove in the rear that had two doors leading to men's and women's bathrooms. I watched as various people sauntered up to a chalkboard on the wall to write their name before heading for one of the two bathroom doors.

Fuck. Why hadn't Randy told me about that? I figured that gay bars like Uncle Charlie's had normal men's rooms, like at Company. What was with the names on the chalkboard?

I got a drink and stood by the pool table as I considered the possibilities, wondering how long I might actually be able to last without urinating and having to figure out the names on the chalkboard. Although I never played pool and wasn't exactly sure how it was played, I stood there paying rapt attention to the game in progress.

At eleven o 'clock the jukebox was shut off and a live DJ took over from a small raised wooden booth with two turntables. I leaned against the wall and looked around the room. The crowd was a real mix: effeminate skinny boys, the ones who had before always managed to convince me that I must not be gay since I wasn't like them; older guys with their leather jackets and flannel shirts and lots of mustaches.

I had been hoping for Randy to show up and explain the chalkboard system to me but now, Randy or not, I needed to go the bathroom. I walked back to the opening, passed the chalkboard, and went into the one labeled "Men," although both appeared to be used interchangeably by the patrons. It was uneventful, and I was relieved: I hadn't been accosted in the bathroom, no one confronted me about not putting my name on the chalkboard, and my bladder was empty.

I went back to the disco room and tried imitating the various postures I saw around the room. Randy's friends had advised me to look as casual and disinterested in the surroundings as possible, while still standing up tall. I finally settled on right leg bent at the knee and pressed back, heel against the wall, with the hand not holding the drink firmly planted in the front pocket of my jeans. Randy's friend Sam had set out the routine for me: look at someone, wait longingly for him to look back at me, and then look down or away and anywhere else in the room, and then repeat.

The bar had started to fill up quickly after eleven. People were looking at me, mostly, I suppose, because I was a new face in a place that, I quickly learned, prized such a novelty. It was fun to have the attention, and I scanned the room.

Besides being new to the scene, I had thankfully inherited some decent genes from Herb and Lillian. At six feet, I had my father's height and his honey-colored eyes. Lillian was tall, too; she had done some modeling for a local department store when she first got out of high school, and I had her well-angled facial features and dark curly hair. I had hated the curly hair most of my childhood, envious of the boys with the long straight hair that looked so shiny and straight when coated with Vitalis. But now my hair was longer, too, and the curls looked good; I liked it.

The rest of the crowd was another story. Too old. Too short. Too fat.

But there was one, over near the front door, tall like me, with long blond hair that fell down in front of his eyes. It wasn't a California blond, more like a New York dirty blond. He had on a sweater so it was hard to tell exactly how he was shaped, but he seemed to have a nice body. I looked up; the guy looked down. He looked over; I looked away. Three times and then we caught one another's eyes head-on. He walked over.

"Hi, I'm Robert," he said, sticking out his hand.

"I'm Josh."

"Are you from out of town?" Robert asked.

"No, I live in the city. In the Village. Why did you think that?"

"It was just the way you were looking around," Robert replied. "Kind of like a tourist."

"It's one of the first times I've been here," I told him. Robert looked up and smiled but didn't say anything. "Actually, it's the first time I've been here," I said.

"You have a boyfriend?"

"No," I said. "I'm kind of new at this."

"You're just coming out?"

"Well, sort of," I said. "Yeah, I guess I am."

Robert looked at my beer and played with the lime stuck on top of the bottle of Corona.

"Why do people write their names on the chalkboard there by the bathrooms?"

"That's the list for playing pool," he said without skipping a beat. I smiled. That had been a lot of worry about nothing, a pattern I seemed to have inherited from Lillian.

Robert was twenty-six and lived on Staten Island with his parents. He worked as a nurse at a hospital there.

"Do you want to go back to your place so we can talk more?" he asked.

"My place?" It came up out of the blue. I had thought maybe we might plan a date, like when I went out with girls in high school.

"We can't go back to Staten Island; it would take more than an hour and besides, I live with my mother. You're only five minutes away," Robert said.

I was thinking maybe I should just go for it and get the first time out of the way right then and there. I thought about how worried I'd been about the names on the chalkboard and that turned out fine. After that, and still being high from all the pot at Randy's, I decided Robert didn't appear to be very threatening.

We took a taxi back to Ninth Street; the stairway had never seemed longer, but I had warned him about the four flights of steps before we left Uncle Charlie's. Robert pulled out a partially smoked joint and held it up. I nodded, and we each took a couple of hits as we sat down on the large brown sofa. I leaned over and lit a candle on the table.

If I was going for it, the first time I had sex with a man was not going to be in the men's room at Grand Central. Or the high school locker room. I had waited a long time, and now I was going to get it right— MGM Technicolor right. The first kiss came pretty naturally, and soon we were touching one another, lying next to each other on the couch. Robert pulled off his sweater, I opened my shirt, and Robert ran his hands over my chest. It felt great.

After years of kissing women and pretending they were men, doing the real thing came a lot more naturally. I felt Robert's lips against mine, our tongues wrapped around one another. I reached down and rubbed my hand against Robert's jeans, feeling his thighs. The rest of our clothes came off, and we went to the bedroom.

It was a throbbing, pulsating thirty minutes that I can still remember ten years later, although I'm not sure how I even knew exactly what to do. Robert took the lead, and I managed to follow along. I guess all those years of fantasizing had prepared me better than I realized, though Robert looked slightly bored as he pulled away and lay next to me on the sweat-covered sheets.

He fell asleep seconds later. I got up and went in the bathroom and stood in the shower. I left the door open, worried that Robert might try to leave and take something on the way out, although I had no reason to suspect that, other than years of past warnings from my mother about strangers. I scrubbed myself clean and stood with the hot water of the shower running over my body for a long time.

My throat was dry and even standing there wet, I was still hot. Now what was I supposed to do? After I dried off, Robert was still asleep. I lay down and when he felt me next to him again, he reached out and wrapped his arm around my stomach, just below the chest. I couldn't sleep, marveling at how much my life had changed in less than a week and thinking back on how long I had been avoiding what had happened this night.

The next thing I remember was the light beginning to seep in around the window shade above the air conditioner in the bedroom. I looked at the clock. It was 6:00 a.m. I felt like I hadn't slept at all. I looked over at Robert and put my hand on his chest.

"What time is it?"

"Six."

"When did we go to bed?"

"I guess around 2:30 or so," I said.

"Man, I'm tired."

"We can sleep more if you want," I said. "I have to take the train up to Westchester at noon."

"Yeah, but set the alarm for nine," Robert said. "I've got to get back to Staten Island."

"This was the first time I ever spent the night with a guy," I said excitedly.

"But not the first time you've had sex with a man?" Robert asked.

"Yeah, actually it was," I said.

"You didn't tell me that last night."

"Well, I told you I was new at it," I said.

"Hmm," Robert said as he rolled over and fell back to sleep.

We were both asleep when the alarm went off a few hours later. I started to kiss Robert again, but he gently pushed me away.

"I've really gotta go," Robert said.

"Do you want to take a shower?"

"No, that's okay," Robert said. He was already sliding on his jeans.

I went to the bathroom and wrapped the towel around myself. I tried to fix my hair in the mirror.

"Do you want some orange juice or anything?" I asked. Lillian had me well trained in the finer points of hospitality.

"No, I'm fine." Robert wasn't nearly as talkative as he'd been at the bar or even when we had first gotten to the apartment. "Thanks for the beer," he said, walking toward the door.

"Can I get your phone number?" I asked.

"I live with my mother so I can't have guys call me there," Robert said.

"What about at work?"

"At the hospital?" Robert asked. "No, I don't really have a phone there. Give me your number, and I'll call you."

"Promise?"

"For sure."

❧ 3 ❧

The grin on my face went from ear to ear on the train up to Scarsdale that Thanksgiving morning, and for nearly the entire trip I sat with my eyes closed, thinking about the night with Robert. I could never remember feeling happier at my parents' house than I felt that day. On the train back to the city that evening, I wondered if anyone had noticed.

I called Randy when I got home to thank him for the dinner and give him a full report on the night before.

"So our lessons must have paid off," Randy said. "Let me tell Gerard."

"It was exciting," I said. "And he was a really nice guy. You'll meet him some day."

"I wouldn't sit by the phone waiting for him to call," Randy said.

"No, he will," I said. "He promised. He's a nice guy."

"Hmm" was all Randy managed to get out before wishing me a happy Thanksgiving.

Monday morning I was still thinking about Robert as I stood on the subway platform, until the screeching noise of the approaching train brought me back to reality. It wasn't a great way to start the day, jammed into the subway car, the fans whirring at both ends, blowing the warm fetid air, even in November. At least it was quick, and five minutes later I was upstairs at Grand Central walking toward the CBA office at 380 Madison.

"What's with the big smile?" Carole asked me as I walked in. Half a cigarette was still burning in the ashtray next to her.

"You'd better be careful with the cigarette and the nail polish," I told her. "You could burn the place down."

"Worse things could happen," she said. "Someone looks like he had a good weekend."

I wondered whether it was really unusual for me to be smiling so much. "It was good," I told her.

As I got to my office, the phone rang. No, it wasn't Robert. Nor were any of the other phone calls that day from him.

Back at home, it was the same apartment but, except for the stairs, I felt like I was living somewhere new. Every walk down the street became an adventure. Each night was full of possibilities waiting to be discovered.

Robert never did call, which probably would have bothered me more if Randy hadn't fixed the odds that I'd hear from him at 100-to-1 against. Robert got me through that first night unscathed, physically or emotionally, and for that I was eternally grateful. Even today, I think how it could have gone differently and sent my life in another direction.

The months after that evening with Robert crammed my mind full of memories, a blur of different men. Sometimes, the brief romance from an out-of-town business trip was memorialized on multiple tiny pages of a hotel notepad, an arrow at the bottom of each to signify continuation of the tale on a subsequent sheet. Other times, I wrote on whatever paper was available on the flight back, so there were fragments of these romantic moments captured on the back of in-flight menus and occasionally motion sickness bags. I saved all the little crumpled slips of paper, napkin corners, and matchstick covers that were filled with the phone numbers of the men I had met and kept them in a teddy-bear shaped cookie jar on the kitchen counter that my mother had given me shortly after I moved in, with the word "TREATS" embossed across the bear's tummy. The men were all fleeting, in most cases gone long before the light of the next morning, so this way I was able to preserve the memories intact, my fantasies frozen at a moment in time.

At the office, I'd sit at my typewriter and sometimes, after a particularly quixotic evening, I would close the door and instead of writing about the latest and greatest new Pontiac models, I would muse about the night before, trying to hold on to the intimacy and the companionship, even though it was unlikely I would ever see the person again. I learned quickly over those months why Randy had been skeptical that Robert would ever call me after that first night.

I had grown a mustache, my first facial hair ever, to fit in with my new life, as nearly all the young gay men had one. Other than that, though, and the fact that I suppose I came to work with a smile on my face more frequently, my coworkers probably noticed little difference.

One Saturday night at the beginning of February, Randy took me to 12 West when Gerard was away for the weekend. On the phone he had explained that 12 West was the largest of the new gay clubs that had opened in Manhattan as businesses catering to homosexuals became less secretive about their existence.

"You can't imagine what it's like for us to actually see these places advertised on posters and ads," Randy explained.

At 12 West, I stared in wide-eyed wonderment as we walked into the cavernous warehouse on West Street, opposite the recently closed elevated West Side Highway at 12th Street. It was in the meatpacking district; almost all the buildings in the neighborhood were dedicated to the processing and preparation of meat that took place during daytime hours. After six o 'clock it was totally deserted, except for a few bars facing the piers along the river.

As we walked in, the music blared with Gloria Gaynor's "I Will Survive." I stood there, mesmerized by the sight of more than a thousand men, most with mustaches but without shirts, filling the giant high-ceilinged room, illuminated by flashing colored lights and a giant mirrored ball in the ceiling. A large bar ran along the right side of the room, and there were multi-tiered carpeted platforms built up along the other three sides. There were men kissing, lying next to one another, and some sitting alone, while hundreds more were out on the dance floor. Everything was bathed in a haze of smoke from tobacco and marijuana.

Spring was slow in coming to the streets of Greenwich Village that year. The trees really never lost all of their leaves over the winter, their natural cycles disrupted by the bright streetlamps that never gave them any moments of darkness. I was getting compliments for my work at Carlton Bennett and besides Carole and Randy, I had gotten to know some of the other younger people there. I didn't tell them I was gay but also didn't pretend I had a girlfriend.

On Fridays and usually one or two other afternoons during the week, I walked with Randy over to Third Avenue and down to Company for the two-for-one happy hour. Just about everyone left the office by five or 5:30, even the most ambitious executives. After five o 'clock there was no one to call on the phone, and it was past the 4:45 postal service cut-off, so there wasn't much point to staying later. The Telex machine, used for urgent text communications, required an operator who also left for the day at five. Nearly all offices were the same, so by 5:30 it wasn't too unusual for the bar at Company to be packed with men and smoke. In addition to Randy's usual drinking pals, I had started to build my own circle of bar buddies—people who were regulars at the Company happy hour. They weren't friends in the traditional sense, in that I knew very little about their lives before they got to Company and less after they left. Oftentimes, people would show up, we'd see them regularly for a few months, and then they'd disappear, and we'd never hear from them again.

"Married or dead," Randy would say.

Most of the after-work crowd was older than me, in their thirties and forties. Tony was still there, with the same T-shirt and the same smile, and we usually gathered at his end of the bar, away from the front door.

As the happy hour wrapped up after seven, occasionally Gerard would show up, and he would join me, Randy, and anyone else from the group who wanted to stay for dinner there at Company or another nearby place in the neighborhood. Other nights I would stop for some take-out food on the way home and eat it while I watched TV and made plans for that night's cruising—the hunt for love, or at least sex, to ease the loneliness. There was never work to take home; no one ever expected that any of us would show up in the morning having accomplished anything since having left the office the night before.

So by about ten o 'clock I would usually make my way back to one of the usual hunting grounds, either Uncle Charlie's South or the Barefoot Boy, which was around the corner on 39th Street. I kept a record of how many nights I would go without meeting someone with whom I would head back to either his place or mine, and I rarely got past five. Even that was only because I was being more selective than most people; otherwise, having a different partner every night wouldn't have been difficult to arrange. I had heard about the bathhouses, with their easy, anonymous sex, but had never gone and had no interest in going. What possibility was there for romance with no names?

I was looking for someone to fall in love with and the random sex was only a means to that end. In New York, each block held out the promise of that possibility. With the warmer weather, people slowed their usual rush down the sidewalk. They now stopped under trees for a moment of shade, paused to gaze in store windows, and so even changing a usual walking route could mean the chance for two pair of hungry eyes to meet and whatever might follow from that.

It wasn't that all these escapades didn't make me worried at times. A story in the *Times* mentioned that a man had been stabbed in his apartment after being robbed by someone he willingly invited. The dilapidated old piers in the Hudson, where men supposedly went to have sex in the dark, hulking shells, had deteriorated to a point that people sometimes fell through the floor into the filthy river. I hadn't believed the tales at first, but then there was story on the news, complete with a photo of the victim, a former TV weathercaster.

There was always the risk of VD—venereal disease, gonorrhea and syphilis. I had read about both of them in *The Joy of Gay Sex*, which I had bought at the Oscar Wilde right after it was published. It replaced *The Joy of Sex* on my bookshelf, the original heterosexual version that I had bought years before in the hopes that maybe being more familiar with the different practices of straight sex might somehow induce a desire to actually engage in it. I had thrown Dr. Reuben's *Everything You Always Wanted to Know About Sex* in the trash months before.

In March, I noticed signs of a murky discharge on my underwear. Randy told me to relax. "I'll give you the name of a doctor, he'll give you two shots of penicillin in your ass, and poof, it's gone," he said, holding up one hand and then opening it quickly to dramatize the speed. "It's nothing; it's like taking aspirin to get rid of a headache."

Hmm. I wasn't sure that's exactly how Lillian would have taken it back in Scarsdale. At lunchtime I walked over to the bookstore at Grand Central, which was my general source for information those days. I started to read about all the various possible horrible things that could develop from VD and then decided that maybe they should probably be treated with the same skepticism as Dr. Reuben's *Everything You Wanted to Know About Sex*, which I had gotten at the same bookstore.

And indeed, Randy was right; it wasn't much more complicated than taking a pill for headache. He gave me the name of a physician on Sheridan Square who specialized in treating gay men for VD. "He's a real quack," Randy said. "I wouldn't trust him with anything more serious than VD, but for that he's quick and painless; plus, you don't have to worry about damaging your reputation as a nice Jewish boy from Scarsdale with your regular doctor."

By the next night, I was back at Uncle Charlie's but just to look around. The doctor had told me to wait at least seventy-two hours before having sex with anyone.

Saturday nights almost always meant an invitation to a dinner party at Randy and Gerard's and, although Gerard never went out afterwards, Randy, along with a couple of the other guests, might venture along with me to one of the clubs, like Flamingo or Paradise Garage.

I had learned that by dressing right—which meant like everyone else—I could usually fit in and not be stuck outside with the dreaded "Bridge and Tunnel Crowd"—the "B&T crowd"—from Brooklyn, Queens, and the other boroughs.

"It's a very fixed pattern, followed for years" Randy explained one night. "First, some fabulously connected person opens a place that draws the gays, the artists who actually have money, beautiful people from Manhattan—the A-crowd. They are soon joined by the less trendy straights—a more varied group but still from Manhattan—as word of mouth starts to spread."

He propped the hand holding his cigarette on his elbow as he leaned over and explained that next, the B&T crowd took over, which usually forced the A-crowd off to the next new place. Then the Long Island and New Jersey crowd moved in, and the B&T people replaced the A-crowd at the next place down the line. At the bottom rung on the ladder, a club might hold out for a final year or two, coasting on its past reputation, holding private affairs and corporate events before closing for renovation and starting the process all over again with a new name and new décor to welcome the A-crowd once again.

I liked these clubs. They were a lot larger, with a generally a more attractive crowd and less smoke. And, unlike Uncle Charlie's, here it was possible to meet someone and embrace, kiss, and touch in one of the dark corners—or even in the light—and no one cared. Sometimes I might go to another guy's apartment or take someone home with me, which I usually preferred. This way, if they did end up spending the night, I was in my own bed with my own pillows, toothbrush, and contact lens case.

But lots of nights, I didn't go home with anyone. I might end up making out with someone I met on the dance floor, but I had already learned that for all its millions of inhabitants, gay New York, especially the group that was out at the bars and clubs, could feel like an incredibly small town.

❧ 4 ❧

In mid-April Randy grabbed me in the hall at CBA one morning and said, "Really, dear, you should start thinking about what you're going to do for the summer." I still cringed when Randy used "dear" and other similar affectations, especially at the office. After six months I still hadn't gotten used to it.

He was all excited about the coming weekend, because the water was being turned on for the season so he and Gerard could start using the house they owned on Fire Island. "Once we get settled in, I'm sure we'll have a spare bedroom one weekend, and you can visit," Randy told me. "Everyone who's anyone leaves town on the weekends for the summer," Randy said. "You'll just be bored silly stuck here with the tourists and the poor people who can't afford to leave."

I wasn't too concerned. I was still mesmerized by the thrill of going out on the hunt most nights, and being in the city, with the possibility of love right around the corner, seemed more exciting than spending the weekend in a house with Randy, Gerard, and their friends. I imagined it probably be would be just an extended version of one of their Saturday night dinner parties.

But the next month when Randy invited me to tag along, I was ready to give it a try. The weather was getting warmer, and I could already see that it was going to be nice to get out of town occasionally on hot summer weekends.

"We're going to have an empty bedroom at the house this weekend—I checked with everyone—and we'd love to have you come join us," Randy said.

I was pretty excited about it; like so many other aspects of gay life that Randy had introduced me to, this seemed like the perfect way to make my first visit.

I had seen pictures of Fire Island, and Randy had spent hours at Company after work, explaining the terrain and the rituals, which were observed with the fervor one might normally associate with a religious sect.

"Our house is in the Pines," Randy explained. "That's one of fourteen communities on the island. Everyone thinks of Fire Island as being totally gay, but really only two of the communities are mostly homosexual, the Pines and Cherry Grove." At the mere mention of those last two words, his face contorted into a sneer. "Cherry Grove." He tightened his neck while both corners of his mouth pointed to the floor. "You wouldn't go there except for quick, anonymous sex or to dance at the Ice Palace. People from Manhattan just don't go—except the lesbians, of course," he said as he flicked his cigarette on the side of the ashtray. "It's all a protected barrier island, a national treasure," and then, laughing at his own mistake, corrected himself: "I mean a national seashore. That's it, a national seashore."

The two of us took the bus together from Manhattan. The trip was about two hours to the ferry dock in Sayville, but the time passed quickly; the bus was filled with gay men, disco music, and an attendant in shorts and tank top dispensing rum punch. It was early May, and the sun was just setting by the time we arrived; the ferry was already boarding. Randy and I headed for the upper deck, which was open and, like the lower, had rows of white benches all facing front, with a center aisle.

"A month from now it will be overflowing with people," Randy said. "Especially at this hour, it will be packed." Randy and Gerard had been coming to the Pines for six years now, and Randy knew many of the men on the boat. He kissed some hello, nodded to others, and ignored the rest. Once the engines started up, he gave me a snippet of background on the kiss-or-nod recipients. "That one was just fired at Halston. The one in the red shirt just broke up with the one in the blue striped shirt because he was sleeping with the one in the yellow, who is the ex-lover of the one in the green."

Luckily, they had made it easy by all wearing different colored shirts.

There were still some shreds of daylight left in the sky, but the lights in the harbor had already come on, and Tea Dance was in full swing when the ferry pulled into the Pines harbor. It all looked a bit ramshackle to me, not at all the fantasy isle that had been promised. Randy explained that the tea dance took place at the Blue Whale, which was in a 1950s-era motel called the Botel. Along the left side were two floors of rooms, with cinder block walls and tiny bathrooms with metal stall showers. "Simply dreadful," Randy said.

That didn't sound too inviting, and I was already feeling a bit overwhelmed by all the various routines I was expected to follow.

"You'll have to have a Blue Whale to drink; it's a tradition," Randy told me. "It actually is this horrible blue color that stays—at least for a while—on your lips and on your tongue. When the place first opened ten years ago, the idea was to show everyone how many people came to the Blue Whale for cocktails every day."

We walked over to the deck and left our bags along the wall, where others had already been piled. "Young Hearts Run Free" was playing, and with the sun gone, it had cooled down. Most of the people had moved inside, although there were still about two dozen people along the rail by the water.

"Imagine it at midsummer, with the sun still up and more than a thousand men standing here," Randy told me. "You won't be able to move." That sounded more promising.

At seven, as Tea Dance ended, Randy led me around from the harbor to the right and onto Fire Island Boulevard, which was the main wooden boardwalk that ran the entire length of the community. We walked past more than a dozen grown men pulling little red wagons, like the one I had as a kid in Scarsdale, back and forth to the grocery store at the harbor. We turned off on Driftwood, another wooden walkway, to the house. "South of the Boulevard," a marker, Randy pointed out, as being on the right side of the tracks. Gerard greeted us wearing a beige, oversized caftan— cigarette in one hand, scotch in the other, posed like an Erté statue.

The other housemates were already there on the deck. I had met all four of them before. There were Sam and Marc, whom I had seen that first night at Company. Sam was a fashion designer like Gerard, and the two of them could gossip for hours about that world, like a secret society whose rituals were incomprehensible to the uninitiated. Sam was in his mid-forties, about ten years older than Marc, who worked for a small-time theater producer in the city.

The other couple wasn't really a couple at all, just one of those pairings that I was learning was not atypical among those of a certain age in Manhattan: two people who appeared to be a couple, attended parties, and went on vacations together, but were not, in fact, married, in love, or otherwise attached to one another.

In this case, Bernice and Gary were probably one of the better-known non-couples about town. Gary had been married and living in Connecticut with his wife, two children, the station wagon, dog, and other accoutrements of suburban life, all of which had come to a crashing end when he was arrested in the men's room at the train station after propositioning an undercover policeman. He was one of those people my mother had always warned me about at the train station.

Randy explained to me how Gary had left Connecticut and moved to Manhattan, a more apropos locale for the life of sin he had been pursuing. Fortunately, his father-in-law kept him employed and continued grooming him to take over the family's dress-manufacturing business.

Bernice was a women's dress buyer for Associated Merchandisers, Inc., known as AMI, which acted as a New York buying office for the dozens of smaller department stores and regional chains spread throughout the U.S., like Dillard's, Burdines, and Jordan Marsh, who couldn't afford to have their own buyers. According to Randy, Bernice was an important figure in the fashion world; her orders could make or break a designer's career in some cases, particularly if one wasn't successful at the big Manhattan stores.

We had more cocktails at the house, and Gerard made an elaborate dinner of shrimp remoulade. We smoked a joint, and I went to bed.

That next morning dawned clear, and I got up early to walk to the beach by myself. It was an incredibly beautiful stretch of white sand, extending to the horizon in both directions. There were no buildings along the beach, only contemporary wood-and-glass houses of one or two stories, and these were set back behind dunes of sand covered with sea oats and other vegetation. Being close to the water felt nourishing. I had always loved being near water.

Saturday dinner was another elegant affair prepared by Gerard. I took a nap until around one in the morning and then walked back to the Sandpiper, the one nighttime bar and club at the Pines. Gerard slept, but Randy joined me on the nighttime walk back to the harbor, only to keep me company, he claimed. The tables and chairs had been cleared away, and the windows at the restaurant had been covered with wooden shutters so neighbors wouldn't be bothered by the noise.

It was warm and crowded inside, and the smoke and lack of ventilation made it feel difficult to breathe when we first walked in. Randy and I had smoked a joint on the walk over, and pretty soon I was caught up in the music and the sight of all the men dancing under the mirrored ball, which made me forget about the need for fresh air. The place shut down at four, but Randy had warned me that we needed to clear out before then. "You certainly don't want to be there when the lights come on; it's not a pretty picture," he said.

Later, the boardwalks were crowded with men walking home and others headed to the "meat rack," the dirt paths that carved through the stretch of woods and brush between the Pines and Cherry Grove. Although I didn't have any desire to go, Randy insisted on giving me a tour. "Like I'm sure your mother used to tell you about eating your vegetables, you won't know if you like it unless you try."

On the paths there with Randy, I saw the shadows and heard the sounds of men having sex, but I was disgusted, not turned on. There were cans of Crisco, the lubricant of choice, nestled in tree limbs and sitting on the ground. It reminded me of what I thought all homosexuals were like before I knew better—and what had kept me from even considering the possibility that I might be one of them.

I wanted romance with candles and flowers and longing glances into each other's eyes. What I wanted I knew I wasn't going to find there amid the brush and trees, so I walked back to the house and left Randy on his own. Finally in bed, I lay awake thinking about the evening, whether I really fit in or even belonged there on Fire Island.

Having trouble falling asleep was nothing new to me. Since I was a kid, whenever I was anxious about anything, even the first day of summer camp, I'd always rub my feet against each other in bed. Not softly but back and forth pretty quickly, almost like I was running in bed.

But Sunday morning dawned bright and sunny, and a walk on the beach put me in a more accepting mood for the rest of the day. That evening we took our bags with us for a short stop at Tea Dance and then boarded the ferry for the trip back to the city right before the music stopped.

"You really should get a share for the summer," Randy told me after we got on the bus at Sayville. "It would be perfect for someone like you, just coming out." I told him I'd think about it. Except for the voyeuristic tour of the outdoor sex scene, I had enjoyed pretty much the entire weekend. The beach was beautiful and as one of the younger people in the place— and one whom no one had slept with yet—I had gotten a lot of attention. I liked that too.

Randy told me to look in the classifieds section of the *Village Voice* for summer shares, as the *Voice* was the only paper that would carry ads mentioning the word gay or the abbreviation "GWM," for gay white male. That Wednesday I bought a copy and took it with me to Company so Randy could help me look through the share listings.

"This one looks interesting," Randy told me as I pointed to one in the middle of more than thirty ads.

"FI Pines: 4 GWM have one open BR in 3 BR house, WBMD-WALD," it read.

"Weekend before Memorial Day to Weekend after Labor Day," Randy told me. "I know your anxious mind. Don't get nervous that they're abbreviations for some deviant sexual practices."

"It's good that there's four of them because they probably all know one another," Randy said. "It won't just be a group of strangers all meeting for the first time. And that's a good phone exchange in the city—367—Dorset—somewhere on the Upper East Side." I tore out the ad and stuck it in my wallet.

When I got home I smoked half a joint left over from the night before. Then, fortified by that and the two glasses of scotch from happy hour, I dialed the number.

"I'm calling about the ad for the share on Fire Island."

"Oh, hi, this is Jim. What's your name?"

"Josh."

"Hey, Josh. How are you?" Jim said. He sounded like a regular guy.

"I wanted to find out how much the bedrooms were."

"The one we have left is fifteen hundred for the season."

We talked a little about what I did, and Jim explained that he was a part-time model and actor and that his lover, John, was a financial consultant. The other guys in the house were Rick and Elliot, college friends from Notre Dame. At the end of the call we made plans to meet for a drink at Jim and John's apartment the next night. "Rick will be over here earlier that night for dinner, so you'll have a chance to meet him, too," Jim told me.

The next evening, I took the subway uptown and then walked the short blocks over to 320 East 84th. The good part of the Upper East Side, the part that looked like pictures of a nice neighborhood in Paris, was along Madison and Park Avenues. This was farther east but still a whole different feel from the Village—less bohemian and more aristocratic.

I rang the buzzer, and Jim greeted me at the door.

"Hi, Josh. C'mon in," he said.

Jim was a handsome man, probably in his early forties, with a deep tan and wavy black hair streaked with silver gray. About six feet tall, too, he did look like someone who could actually earn money from modeling, unlike most of the so-called models I had met.

The apartment was neat, which I immediately took as a good sign. It had been decorated, which to me, in those days, meant matching furniture.

Rick had a nice body, as was evident from the tight white tank top he wore, and although he had shaved the hair on his head, which seemed unusual for such a young guy, I thought he was kind of sexy-looking. He was in the kitchen cleaning up after dinner, which also seemed strange, as Jim had made it sound as though Rick was going to be there as a guest.

The more Rick talked, the less attractive I found him, which was turning out to be a common experience for me with a lot of the men I met. He was smart—he had a degree in religious studies from Notre Dame—but I cringed at the way he moved his eyelids when he talked, and his hand movements were definitely too effeminate for me.

"John's in the bedroom on a call," Jim told me. "He'll be right out."

I told them the story about my much-delayed introduction to the gay world back in November and about my first trip to Fire Island the weekend before. Jim and Rick asked me about the house where I had stayed, but neither of them seemed to know Randy or Gerard or any of their friends.

We made small talk about movies and bars, and finally John came out of the bedroom. He was the oldest of the three, balding but a tall, good-looking man with a trim beard. Jim explained that he and John would use one bedroom, and Rick was going to share the other bedroom with Elliot, a friend of his from Notre Dame.

"So what do you think?" Jim asked me.

I was surprised; I thought they would be the ones evaluating me. "I think it sounds great," I told him. They all seemed nice enough, they were an attractive bunch, and they didn't smoke cigarettes.

It seemed like a decision I should have agonized about more—I had often spent more time deciding whether or not to buy a pair of shoes. But I had become an adventurer in the past six months and was ready for a new expedition.

❧ 5 ❧

Like most of the advertising agencies in New York, CBA closed at one o'clock on Fridays during the summer, and I headed over to Penn Station, taking the train to the ferry terminal in Sayville. It wasn't easy to find a seat on the Long Island Railroad train on any afternoon, but summer Fridays were particularly tough.

Fortunately, I found one at the end of the car, facing backwards, which I then worried might bring on a bout of motion sickness. *Better not to chance it by reading anything,* I thought. I hadn't become that adventurous. So instead, I spent the nearly hour and half to Sayville looking at the rest of the passengers. These days, anyone might be a potential partner, and I scanned the crowd, deciding who might be gay or straight, trying to see if someone's eyes met mine. After six months of spending nearly every night at either Company, Uncle Charlie's, or both, I had gotten the technique down pretty well. Randy had instructed me that most men were only interested if they thought you were unavailable or not interested in them.

"They all want the challenge of the pursuit," Randy had told me at happy hour one night, with his scotch in one hand and a cigarette in the other. "It's a primal male character trait: hunt and conquer. Just stand there, hold in your stomach, and look as attractive as possible," he continued. "Look around like you're looking for a friend. Check your watch. Look toward the door. Then, if you notice someone checking you out, that's it; don't look back at him again," he told me. "You need to wait for him to approach. The moment you look like you're interested in him, he'll lose interest in you. You've got to present a challenge."

As the boat pulled into the Pines harbor that Friday afternoon, the scene was already much livelier than it been the time two weeks before. Like most of the houses, there was a fence in front of #10 Seaview that blocked the view from the walk. Jim had showed me Polaroid photos of the outside of the house and one of the living room, so I had a pretty good idea of what to expect. As the homes went in the Pines, it was probably at the lower end of the scale, without a single interesting architectural detail. It was a simple rectangle on a single floor, surrounded by a wood deck.

I opened the gate and walked up to the sliding glass door. Jim was sitting inside at a round table, drinking a beer and reading a magazine.

"Hey there, welcome," he said. "How was it?"

I told him about the train and taxi adventure.

"Do you want a beer?"

"Sure."

Jim stood up and got a Bud Light from the refrigerator. In his tank top and with the bright sunlight reflecting off the deck, Jim looked even more handsome than I remembered from that night we met in the city.

He showed me my bedroom off the living area, and it was pretty much as I pictured it from Jim's initial description over the phone. It was small, but the lack of furniture made it not seem as confining as I had imagined it might. The bed, somewhat larger than a twin but not quite a full, was pushed up against one wall. The other wall had a closet that apparently at one time had sliding doors to hide the rod with dozens of empty wire hangers of varying colors, sizes, and shapes.

"Throw your bag on the bed, and I'll give you a tour," Jim said.

In the back of the living room was an open kitchen and off to the side, the dining alcove had been walled off and made into another bedroom. "This is where Elliot and Rick will be," Jim said. "And John and I are here in the back." There was one bathroom, kind of rustic with no tile, just unfinished wood on the walls. The two-by-four framing held various containers of shampoo, conditioner, moisturizer, and other necessities. It was neat but definitely not up to Lillian Silver standards.

I went to my room. It was warm and smelled musty from being closed up all winter. I unpacked the bag and threw the clothes into the three drawers. For all my fastidiousness in other aspects of my life, I did a miserable job of keeping my clothes organized. At home, my shirts were hung without being buttoned, pants were not properly aligned on the hangers, and T-shirts were barely folded in the drawers. Maybe it was more assertion of my independence from Lillian's insistence on having everything neatly arranged, even behind closed doors.

Jim had gone back to his magazine, and I joined him at the table. "How are we going to work the food?" I asked him. I was surprised that in my excitement and in the speed with which the whole transaction was consummated, I had never raised the subject that first night we met. It wasn't like me to leave something like this unplanned.

"Usually we'll have dinner together—we can rotate cooking and those receipts and anything else for the group we'll put on the fridge under the magnet," he said, pointing to a miniature disco ball on the door. "We just take turns at the liquor store, and anything you want for yourself, just buy it and keep it on one shelf in the refrigerator."

I nodded. "I guess I'm going to head down to the store then, so I can buy food and get ready for Tea Dance." When I got to the harbor, another ferry was pulling in. It was 4:30; the lunch tables had been cleared away at the Blue Whale and "Ring My Bell" was blaring from the speakers, but no one other than the bartenders was there that early.

The liquor store was expensive, as I had expected, but I bought a bottle of Black Label to share with the group and then went to the Pantry, which seemed ever more overpriced. As Randy had explained to me that first weekend, everything needed to be brought over by boat from the mainland, and there was no competition.

When I got back to the house, I had hoped one or two of the others would have arrived, but Jim was still the only one there.

"John is on a business trip to Toronto and won't be here until tomorrow," Jim told me. "And Rick is coming out later after work with Elliot."

"What does Elliot do?" I asked.

"Something at the Whitney Museum. I think he's in the membership department," Jim said. "You'll have to ask him."

I looked at Jim and was trying to decide the color of his eyes. Steel blue, I'd say. *He's definitely handsome*, I thought.

There was a knock on the screen door. An older man in blue work clothes stood there with a toolbox.

"This must be the phone guy," Jim told me as I went to open the door. "John does a lot of work out here, and we needed to get an extra line installed."

I nodded. There was already the one phone line there with the famous KY-7 Fire Island prefix, which was the number I had given to my friends—and also to my parents, in case they needed to reach me in an emergency. I had told them I was sharing a weekend house on Fire Island and hadn't mentioned it was in the Pines, although I wasn't sure that would have meant anything to them anyway. And I also still hadn't told them I was dating men instead of women now.

Those first weeks back in the fall had been so exciting, I felt like I wanted to stand on the corner and shout.

Randy had loads of advice on the subject. "You tell each person when you're ready," he had told me. "And believe me, you're not ready to tell anyone yet."

At six I got ready to head out for my first official tea dance of the season. The phone guy was still there, his work interrupted just before I left when Rick called from one of the pay phones at the ferry dock to let Jim know that he and Elliot were getting on the next boat. Jim stayed with the installer, and I stopped off on the walk back to the harbor to see if Randy and Gerard had arrived yet.

They were on the deck with Gary and Bernice, already well into their own happy hour.

"They're going to stay here, but I'll go over with you for an hour," Randy said. "I'll point out the 'ten most wanted' so you can stay out of trouble—or dive right in, if you'd prefer."

I was glad that just Randy was coming. Despite all his affectations, Randy was still a good-looking guy, and I had already learned that walking into a bar with another attractive guy could be a big help in scoring.

The rest of them weren't exactly an unattractive lot, but Gerard was always wearing one of his trademark caftans, Bernice could have used an extra-strong set of braces when she was growing up, and everyone knew of Gary's arrest in the Grand Central men's room, which didn't help his social standing.

"Do you want to smoke first?" Randy asked, holding out the joint that was being passed around. I took a hit, kissed everyone hello and good-bye—and off we went.

It was still early in the season, so although Tea Dance was busy, there was still plenty of room to dance inside and walk around outside. There were even chairs at some of the tables overlooking the harbor, so Randy and I sat down at one of those. Another boat pulled in, and we watched the parade of men disembarking. Rick was easy to spot with his shaved head, and next to him was a guy with long blond hair and glasses—kind of bookish-looking—whom I assumed must be Elliot. From the deck of the Blue Whale, people were whistling and calling out to others getting off the boat. I watched Rick and Elliot walk off down the Boulevard to the house.

Tea Dance ended promptly at seven, and Randy and I joined the parade back down Fire Island Boulevard. Back at Randy's front deck, Gerard, Gary, and Bernice were still in nearly identical positions, with cigarettes and drinks like a still-life tableau.

"Come and stay for a cocktail," Randy told me, but I put him off.

"No, I want to get back and see my other housemates," I told him. "One of them I haven't even met yet."

Back at our house, Jim had moved to the picnic table on the outside deck in the back of the house, and Rick and Elliot were there, all drinking beer. It was dusk and they had already lit candles to keep away the mosquitoes. Rick and Elliot got up as they saw me approach.

We introduced ourselves and shook hands before I went in to get a drink. The single black dial phone still sat on the kitchen counter, and the phone guy had already left. I went to the bathroom and then looked around before pouring the scotch. Rick's and Elliot's bags were sitting on the bed in the other bedroom. But on the floor next to one of the two twin beds there now were three more black dial telephones.

My heart started to pound. I really didn't know these guys. All of a sudden, I was sharing a home with four total strangers. I had done nothing to check them out. And Randy and Gerard didn't even know them, although according to Jim, they had been renting out in the Pines for the past three years.

Why would they have had three phones put in? And if it was for John's business, why were they in Rick and Elliot's bedroom? They had to all be dealing drugs, I figured. What else could it be? My mind raced as I tried to think of other explanations. Jim hadn't mentioned *three* extra lines, and he also hadn't mentioned exactly what type of work it was. And it didn't make any sense for John, a bank consultant, to need extra phone lines at a weekend house—banks were closed on weekends, weren't they?

I was trying to figure out what to say as I went to the kitchen and pulled out a glass from the wooden cabinet for my drink, but it didn't look like it had been washed very well. I checked the next one and the one behind that and decided none of them looked very clean. No two glasses matched; they probably were all single remaining remnants of sets of four or six bought in previous summers.

I walked back out on the deck with my glass of scotch. I was hoping the alcohol worked as a disinfectant of sorts. In addition to the citronella candles to ward off the bugs, there were white twinkle lights spread through a big tree with branches that hung over the table. Jim, Rick, and Elliot were sitting there, discussing whether or not to start cooking dinner.

"Josh, can you flip over the cassette before you sit down?" Rick asked.

I put my drink down and walked back into the kitchen. The cassette player was in the boom box on the counter and had been placed up against the window screen. God, I was sick of listening to the Bee Gees.

I decided not to say anything that first night. We smoked a joint, and that, along with the scotch, made me forget about the phone lines. And it was good pot. Even the Bee Gees were starting to sound better.

We had all gone out to the disco, and I hadn't gotten back to the house until nearly three, but I still got up around eight o'clock or so, once the sunlight started to come into the room. There were curtains over the one small window, but they really didn't block out the light very well, and I always had trouble sleeping unless the room was totally dark.

The house was still quiet, but through the kitchen window I saw Elliot sitting on the deck with a cup of coffee, reading the newspaper.

"Good morning," I said. "I thought I'd be the first one up."

"I'm almost always up before 7:00 a.m.," he told me. "That's actually my favorite time here. I like listening to the birds. I made coffee if you want some."

"Where do you get the *New York Times* out here?" I asked.

"They sell them down at the dock; there's a woman there with her lawn chair and umbrella starting at 7:15, as soon as the first ferry gets in," he explained.

I went to get a coffee and then sat down at the table across from Elliot.

"Elliot, can I ask you something?"

He looked up from the paper and pushed his glasses back on his nose. "Yesssss?"

"Why are there three phones in your room?"

Elliot grinned. "They didn't tell you?"

"Tell me what?" I was starting to get annoyed.

"I can already tell you're going to freak out," Elliot said. "So please don't. Do you want to smoke some of a joint? There's still a roach here in the ashtray."

"No, I don't need a joint. I just want to know what's going on in the house if I'm going to be spending the summer here."

"I understand. Makes perfect sense. They really should have told you," Elliot said.

"The phones are in your room, so why is it all 'they'?" I asked. "And told me what?"

"Actually, it's Rick's room; I don't pay for it. I stay with him over the weekends to help with the business."

"If you're dealing drugs, I hope it's just pot."

"No, it's not that. It's like a massage service."

"Pros-ti-tutes?" I stammered.

"You've never seen the ads for Manhattan Men?" Elliot asked.

"No," I told him, and I was pretty sure the look in my eyes made the answer clear without even opening my mouth.

"Well, yeah, it's an escort service. Call boys. Or however you want to say it."

My head was already spinning. It was definitely better than being with a bunch of drug dealers. No one was going to come in and find stockpiles of Quaaludes or coke and get us all arrested. But prostitution was still illegal. That much I knew.

"So these guys are running a prostitution ring out of the house where I'm staying for the next four months?"

"It's not exactly a pros-ti-tu-tion ring," Elliot said, sounding out each syllable. "They provide companionship."

"Naked companionship by the hour?" I asked, my knees shaking from nerves. I was still horrified by the whole thing.

"Well, it's companionship," Elliot said. "That's all we know. What happens after that, we don't know and don't care; they're two consenting adults."

"Don't they ever have trouble with the police?" I asked.

"No, I don't think so. Or they haven't told me. Jim and John started it six years ago, around '72—it's one of the oldest in town. Rick started working with them three years ago, and I know they haven't had any problems since then."

"And Rick is an escort?"

"No, he *was*," Elliot told me. "That's how I first met Jim and John. Jim used to be the main recruiter. He had worked as a model—a professional fashion model—so he was always running into guys from work or at the gym who wanted extra money. He had met Rick at the gym; Rick started escorting and then started to help out with the phones. Now that's all he does. No more fucking for dollars. Just dialing."

"And you?" I asked. "You work for them, too?"

Elliot laughed. "Like I told you last night, I work at the Whitney. But they let me come out for free as long as I help with the phones."

"I haven't heard them ring at all since they were put in yesterday," I said.

"The phone company hasn't actually switched the numbers over to ring here instead of the city," Elliot explained. "They don't know how long that's going to take once the lines are installed, so that's why John's still in the city—he'll come out after they know they've made the transfer."

"Jim had told me that John was on a business trip to Toronto," I said.

"I think he was—he got back yesterday afternoon. That's when Rick met me so we could come out," Elliot told me. "John *really* is a bank consultant. He used to be a big executive for Chase Manhattan, but when he turned fifty-five last year, he told them he didn't want to keep working full time and left to become a consultant—working for himself."

"They seem like nice guys, but it's all pretty weird," I said to Elliot. "And they definitely should have told me."

"You're right. I thought they had," Elliot said. "When Rick told me about meeting you, he said you had some corporate job but that you were cool—you had smoked a joint with them."

"Well, everyone smokes pot," I said. "Not everyone is running a prostitution service. There could be a problem sometime, and then I'd be screwed with my career."

"It's not like you're a surgeon. You work at an ad agency. That's not exactly the pinnacle of high morality," Elliot said

But I could already picture the *Times* headline about the male prostitution ring smashed on Fire Island. *Josh Silver, twenty-three, was one of those arrested and is being held at the Suffolk County Jail.* That would not go over well at all at the Silver household in Westchester.

༄ **6** ༄

As nervous about it as I may have been, I was also curious about Manhattan Men. I certainly hadn't had much exposure to the prostitution business. Back in the city, I had been to 53rd Street between Second and Third, which most gay men seemed to know was the block where the hustlers worked. In March, Randy had taken me up to the Townhouse, a gay bar nearby that also had an after-work happy hour. It was okay but way too much smoke for me, and we both agreed that the crowd and the music were a lot better at Company.

When we came outside the bar around eight o 'clock, we walked south to 53rd and there were at least a dozen guys working that block; about half were probably younger than me. The rest were older, some a lot older. All of them looked pretty scruffy to me. I didn't think any of them were particularly attractive. In front of the post office on Third Avenue, there were more, leaning under the columns, equally unappealing.

Back on the deck at Fire Island, I asked Elliot, "What are they like at Manhattan Men?"

"The boys or the customers?"

"Both."

Elliot laughed. "For someone who doesn't want to get involved at all, you ask a lot of questions."

"I'm really kind of pissed off they didn't tell me they'd be running it from the house," I said. "So I guess I'd at least like to know now what I've gotten myself into for the summer."

"Here's Jim, so he can tell you all about it himself."

Jim opened the screen door and walked out with a cup of coffee in his hand. He had on light blue shorts and no shirt, all the better to display his nice six-pack stomach.

"Josh and I were just talking about Manhattan Men," Elliot said.

"Oh," Jim said. "What made you ask?"

"Well, for starters, the three phones sitting on the floor in the other bedroom," I said. "It's not that I'm opposed on moral grounds," I tried to explain. "You know, I'm just starting my career, and I've got to be careful about what I get involved with."

"I understand," Jim said, putting the cup of coffee down on the table and standing behind Elliot. Jim had a habit of putting one arm behind his neck and rubbing his bicep with the other. It wasn't necessarily a bad habit or anything I particularly minded, just something I couldn't help noticing that he did a lot.

"Involved? You're not going to be involved at all—the only thing that happens here at the house is the phone calls. And we shut them off at midnight and don't turn them on until noon, so it's really not going to bother you," Jim said. "They'll keep the door to the bedroom closed and I guarantee you, you're not going to be spending time inside the house anyway, unless it's raining."

"He wanted to know what they were like," Elliot said. "The boys. And the customers."

Jim sat down at the table. "A lot of the guys have worked for us for years, some of them are friends, some we find, some see the ad and call us.

We have one ad every two weeks in the pink pages of the *Advocate*," Jim said. "That's it. That's all we've ever done since we started six years ago."

Jim explained that most of the customers were regulars. "Most of the boys, too," he said. "You'd be surprised about the people who call. A lot are younger men—attractive guys who wouldn't have any trouble picking up someone or getting picked up if they went out to a bar. But they can't, or they don't want to bother."

"They can't?" I asked.

"Some of them are married with a wife and kids at home," Jim said.

"And the rest are priests," Elliot jumped in and laughed at his own joke.

"No, the priests can't afford it," Jim said. "Anyway, they have their altar boys.

He went on to explain that some were politicians who couldn't be seen in a gay bar. Or people in the entertainment business whose entire careers were built on the belief that they're 100 percent heterosexual.

"And the rest are just lazy," Jim said. "People with more money than time."

"What does it cost?"

"You really want all the details, don't you?"

"I'm curious now," I said. "That's all."

"Usually seventy-five dollars, and the house keeps—well, I shouldn't say *the house*; rather, *we* keep—20 percent so the worker gets sixty bucks. Not bad for an hour's work, right?" Jim said. "And we'll give you a discount." All three of us laughed.

"Yeah, thanks. What about the guys—the guys who work for you?" I asked.

"Well, we know how much Elliot loves to talk—that's why he's so good at working the phones. I'm sure I already told you that Rick and I used to do it," Jim said. "Actually, Rick still sees a few regulars that he's trying to get rid of and pass on to the other guys."

Elliot took off his glasses. "Rick's still working? I didn't know that. He told me he had stopped."

"See how quietly all of this can be done?" Jim said. "Elliot didn't know, and he's Rick's best friend."

"And nothing happens here at the house?"

"No one sees clients here—just the phones, like I told you. Some of the guys may come out for a day to go to the beach, but that's it," Jim said.

I squinted, pondering this. It sounded strange to me every time Jim used the word "clients," as I associated that word with the likes of General Motors.

"They're mostly good-looking guys, trying to pick up extra money. A lot of them have full-time jobs, or else they're still going to college. Most are in their twenties, early thirties," Jim said. "I'm sure you wouldn't throw any of them out of bed if they happened to end up there with you."

Elliot got up to get more coffee. I heard the shower going so that meant Rick was awake.

"I really like all of you guys, and I like the house," I said. "But I really have to think about it. I'll call you Monday or Tuesday after I'm back in the city, okay?"

I went inside to the kitchen to get something to eat. Not much, I decided after staring at Jim's flat stomach for the past fifteen minutes, but I was starving. And I needed to talk with Randy.

"Have you ever heard of Manhattan Men?" I asked him when I finally went over that afternoon.

"The call boy service?" Randy asked.

"Yeah, that's it," I said. "The guys I'm living with at the house are the ones who own it, and over the summer they run it from the house."

"Oh, dear," said Randy with that familiar downward grimace. "Sounds like it will be a busy summer." He flicked the ashes off his cigarette and took another sip of his Bloody Mary. "Starting the day with a Bloody Mary is another Pines tradition," Randy said. "You're sure you don't want one?"

"No, thanks," I said. "And anyway, my day started at long time ago." It was already almost one o 'clock.

"So why are you so glum about it?" Randy asked. "It sounds like a dream come true. Spending your first summer out of the closet at a den of prostitution on Fire Island."

"That doesn't sound like a dream come true," I said. "It sounds like the gay version of a cheap, sleazy dime-store novel—especially the way you say it."

"Sorry, dear," Randy said. "I don't mean to make fun of you. But why all the angst?"

I told him my worries about the police, the headlines, the picture in the paper.

"My, my. You do have a wild imagination, don't you?" Randy said. "No wonder you're so creative there at CBA."

"You think I'm overreacting?"

"Just a tad," he said. "After all, it is the world's oldest profession, so it's been going on for a long time. Anyway, I don't think the police care too much about it. It's like marijuana. They just look the other way. Some of them are probably customers."

"I know, but if something happened, I could lose my job," I said.

"I don't think so," Randy said. "They're hardly ones to pass moral judgments at CBA. Half of them are sleeping with their secretaries. Ask Carole at the front desk—she keeps track."

"I don't know," I said. "I'm just starting out. It's not just a job for me; it's my career."

"Can't you just try to not think of every possible thing to worry about, Josh?" Randy asked. "You've got to have something, right? If nothing's wrong, you'll find something to get the anxiety meter going."

I lounged in one of the chairs on the deck with the familiar back-and-forth motion of my feet while I turned over the various potential outcomes in my head. The sunlight filtering through the leaves created patterns on the deck that shifted each time the wind rustled them that May afternoon. Randy wore shorts and a T-shirt and sat on the edge of the table, resting his feet on one of the opposite chairs. Sometimes when his hair was hanging down over his forehead and the light was just right, I actually found him pretty attractive, but I quickly dismissed that thought.

We went through all the pros and cons of my housemates. Among the former, Randy deemed it nothing short of a miracle that no one in the house smoked cigarettes or seemed to use any drugs harder than marijuana or the occasional Quaalude.

"Believe me, no one out here in this community is going to think any less of you," Randy said. "And if nothing else, you'll have some great stories to share with us at Tea Dance."

Monday morning, waiting for the train on the subway platform at Union Square, I closed my eyes and thought about the weekend. I had really enjoyed it and when the phones started working on Saturday evening, as Jim had predicted, it really didn't bother me. Elliot had made a point of telling me that he had turned down the ringers to the lowest level and anyway, he explained that weekends were actually the slow time of the week for the escort business.

It was steamy again down in the subway already and it was only the end of May. It would definitely be nice to be out of the city every weekend for the summer. I was holding the jacket to my three-piece suit in my hand and had opened the buttons on the vest, but beads of sweat still coated my forehead. I waited for the train to pick up speed in the tunnel so at least the movement of air through the open windows would cool me down.

"Nice tan," Carole told me as I walked in. "Where's that from?"

"I was back at Fire Island for the weekend," I said. "I think I might get a share for the summer."

Besides Randy, Carole was the only other person at CBA who knew I was gay—or at least the only other one that I had told I was gay. Probably being seen going out to lunch with Randy a couple of times a week had already marked me, because Randy's sexual orientation was well known in the office. Carole had also become a good work friend; she was one of the few other people on the floor under thirty.

She put down her coffee and took a puff of her cigarette. "That's great. Leave the rest of us here broiling in the city," she said.

"I'll tell you more about it later," I told her as we went into the office. Sometimes Carole and one of her friends would join me and Randy for lunch. "A double date," as Randy would say. Randy and Carole really hadn't been very close—Randy initially saw her as much beneath his imagined social standing—but I had persisted, and now they had a good time when we all went out together. We had even dragged Carole with us to Company a few times for happy hour, and the other guys loved her color-coordinated red hair, lipstick, and nails. Once, she wore matching red pumps and drove them all wild.

"How's the agonizing over your Fire Island share decision coming along?" Randy asked when he picked up the phone. Although we'd often see one another when the hallway coffee cart arrived around eleven, I usually dialed Randy's extension as soon as I got in with a breathless report on the prior night's adventure.

Often in those calls, Randy poked fun at my overactive mind, but it didn't bother me. It felt good to at least have someone understand why I always seemed so distracted, constantly running through the various possible outcomes that might result from any chosen course of action.

"I guess I'm going to go ahead with it," I told him. "Elliot's great; I could see him becoming a good friend, and Rick's got a nice body to look at while he walks around the house in his tight little shorts."

"I'll have to come over and see that one next weekend," Randy said.

"And Jim is still really handsome—I can't believe you and Gerard don't know any of them."

"Well, once I see their faces I'll probably know them from Tea Dance," Randy said. "And if they take off their pants, maybe I'll recognize them from the meat rack."

"Very funny," I said. "And Carole asked me about the tan, so I told her I had gone to Fire Island."

"That should get all the tongues wagging," Randy said. "And your advertising career will be down the drain, and you won't have the money to pay for your share, so there's no need to spend another moment deciding whether to risk life in prison with your summer housemates."

"I gotta go," I told him. "We've got our 9:30 staff meeting."

❧ 7 ❧

That winter and spring of 1978 had been so full of adventures that my summer housemates' entrepreneurial pursuits seemed a lot less alien to me than they would have a year before. Plus, it seemed like the perfect way to spend the summer, meeting lots of men, any one of whom might be the one I'd fall in love with to live happily ever after.

I quickly got into a regular weekend routine: Friday afternoons I'd shut my door promptly at one o'clock to change clothes, hanging the suit, tie, and white shirt on the hook on the back side of my office door and then emerging minutes later in my sneakers, jeans, and a T-shirt, usually bringing along a sweatshirt in the bag just in case it was cool on the ferry. Then I'd begin the trek by two subway lines, two Long Island Railroad trains, the taxi, the ferry, and finally, the walk down the Fire Island Boulevard boardwalk that would lead me to #10 Seaview.

With time, I mastered all the shortcuts like the all-knowing veterans I had admired on my first trip. I knew exactly which stairway to take at Penn Station to get to the least crowded cars, which door to wait at so I could make a beeline for the taxis at Sayville, and where to sit on the ferry for a quick exit at the Pines harbor.

Most weekends followed the agenda I had learned from Randy that very first visit: Tea Dance on Friday, followed by dinner, and then a nap. I'd set my alarm for 1:00 a.m. so I could walk to the Sandpiper. Sometimes the alarm would sound and I'd just shut it off, too tired to even walk ten minutes to look for the love of my life who might be waiting there for me on the deck under the stars at the Pines harbor. If I was sure that Randy, who would often leave Gerard alone to go out dancing, or Elliot would come along with me, I would usually pull myself together, take a quick shower, and walk back down Fire Island Boulevard.

I never stayed at the Sandpiper much past 2:30; I'd start yawning after an hour unless I happened to connect with someone. Sometimes, connecting might mean kissing there at the disco, sometimes it was a walk to the beach. More often than not, we'd go back to my room to have sex together.

"Just relax," Randy told me. "Enjoy it. It's just a big party." Well, that was easy for him to say since he was already with Gerard. I still needed a boyfriend.

Saturdays I would head to the ocean, as long as the weather was good. People, mostly men—at least in the Pines—spread out their towels in groups, usually with their housemates. I'd head over most of the time with Elliot and Rick, although at noon one of them needed to go back to work the phones unless Jim or John, who rarely went to the beach, offered to take over. Sunny summer afternoons were usually very quiet at Manhattan Men.

When it rained, it was pretty dreary and actually kind of boring in the Pines, as there was no place to go. Although we now had cable television in Manhattan, it hadn't arrived yet on the island, and the reception was spotty at best on the small black-and-white TV with a rabbit-ear antenna at our house. Randy and Elliot had a color set with a big metal antenna on the roof, but the reception there wasn't much better. Usually, we'd occupy ourselves playing cards or Scrabble—there was an old game at the house, and Elliot was a fierce player, usually making two or three words in a single move.

On Saturday nights we had a choice of either staying in the Pines or going to the Ice Palace in Cherry Grove, which was larger and had a better sound system without the claustrophobic low ceilings of the Sandpiper. That involved a twenty-minute walk and, for better or worse, about half of that was through the wilds of the meat rack, the uninhabited stretch between the two communities.

By the end of August, I still had no boyfriend, not even anyone I wanted to date, but I had definitely had a lot of fun and was no longer the innocent, inexperienced kid I had been at the start of the summer. The last week of August, I took my first full week's vacation from CBA to stay out at the house. Elliot planned to be there most of the time, too, since he had arranged to take off part of the week.

"The past five years we've had kind of a tradition of inviting the boys out for a Labor Day barbeque," Jim had told me on Thursday.

By now, I knew that *the boys* euphemistically referred to the workers at Manhattan Men. Over the summer, I had gotten familiar with a few them as they stopped by the house when they were staying—or working— elsewhere on the island for the weekend. Or when Jim or Rick would invite them out to the house for the day. Some of the ones who stopped by weren't even gay—just young guys with nice bodies willing to perform to make sixty bucks in an hour. But the ones invited out for the day were always gay, usually pretty nice, and I was surprised by how much I liked talking with them, once I got over the idea of how we happened to come to be sitting together on the deck in the Pines.

"I hope you won't mind about the party," Jim said, clearly directing the comment to me, although Elliot was sitting right next to me at the table.

"Mind?" Elliot asked. "He'll personally call each of them to be sure they're coming."

I laughed. "It's fine," I said. "I'm a lot more relaxed about it all now."

"Yeah," Jim said. "We noticed."

"How many are coming?" I asked.

"We usually invite just about all of them," Jim said. "So out of forty or fifty or so, probably twenty-five will show up."

Over the weekend, I pitched in and helped get ready for the big event on Monday. I even arranged to take another vacation day on Tuesday—the eighth of my ten that year—so I wouldn't have to worry about taking the last ferry at 8:15 on Monday night. Plus, everyone said that the Labor Day tea dance was one of the best of the season. Randy had warned me that by the next weekend, after Labor Day, things would already be quieting down, and come the end of September, the club would be boarded up until the next May.

Monday morning dawned clear and bright, the humidity of mid-summer giving way to hints of crisp autumn air. I was up early and went out to the beach alone to get a few hours of sun to be extra-tan for the party that afternoon. When I got back to the house at 11:30, the four of them—Jim, John, Elliot, and Rick—were busy with the preparations.

At one o 'clock the first guests arrived. None of the boys was among them; Jim and John had also invited a bunch of their friends who were out on the island. But by three there were close to a hundred people out on the deck. Some of them I knew from earlier visits during the summer; most I met for the first time.

One of them, standing with three other young guys, was stunning—he had totally smooth coppery-brown skin and black hair. The sweat glistened on his cheekbones and reflected the sunlight up so that his eyes appeared to be sparkling. I lifted up my sunglasses to be sure he wasn't just a mirage as I walked over to Rick to find out what I could.

"Who's the guy with the yellow tank top?" I asked.

"The dark one?" Rick responded.

"Yeah, everyone's in love with him, right?" I asked.

"That's Tommy," Rick said. "He's one of our stars."

"How long has he worked for you?" I asked.

"About two years."

"He works somewhere else too?" I asked

"Yeah, but I'm not sure where," Rick said. "He's only available nights, so I know he never calls in until around nine. But we usually have a booking for him almost every night. Plus, he's got a lot of repeats."

"He's hot."

"That's for sure," Rick said as he dried the plastic cups he had just washed out to reuse.

"Is he gay?" I asked

"Yeah, that whole group of them," Rick said. "That's our Latin contingent—Marlon, Rafael, and Eddy, who uses Eduardo for work. He thinks it gets him more customers."

"Probably right," I said. "It sounds sexier."

"They're all nice guys. Tommy and Eddy had a fling a while back—before they started working for us," Rick said. "And Marlon and Rafael are lovers. Rafael just moved in with him a few months back."

"And they're still working?" I asked.

"Yeah," Rick said. "Sometimes they go out together—a package deal."

Elliot walked over. "Come down to the beach with me," I said to him.

It was 3:30, and the party was going strong but a group of the guys, including Tommy and the rest of the "Latin contingent" had gone to the beach about twenty minutes earlier. I couldn't take my eyes off Tommy, but he never left his group of pals, and I was too intimidated to walk up to the four of them. Rick had offered to introduce me, but I had told him no, I'd figure it out myself.

"We should help them clean up first," Elliot said.

"It's their party," I said. "Remember, Jim told us to enjoy ourselves, that we should consider ourselves invited guests."

"Even guests offer to help clean up at a party," Elliot said, his Midwestern manners still perfect to a fault. He went into the kitchen to get a large plastic trash bag and started picking up the empty plastic cups spread along the deck.

"Leave that; we'll take care of it later," Jim told him. "Why don't you guys go to the beach and relax."

When we arrived, the beach was full of people. In terms of the weather, it was one of the best days of the entire summer. Standing at the end of the wooden walkway as we took off our sandals to walk out on the sand, I looked at the parade of bronzed bodies walking by in their tight Speedo bathing suits. Maybe it was the relaxed atmosphere at summer's end in comparison to the frenzy of the spring, or maybe it was just the summer tans, but everything and everyone seemed so peaceful in that late golden afternoon sunlight.

The party guests had spread out in a couple of groups with towels placed side by side to define the territorial limits. Tommy was still in his group of four with Marlon, Rafael, and Eddy. "Let's go sit over there at the end, next to Patrick and those other guys," I said to Elliot as I planned out the approach strategy.

There were five people there, and Elliot and I knew Patrick pretty well. He had been a regular visitor over the summer.

"Let me put my towel at the end," I said, "so I'll have an unobstructed view of Tommy."

"Or whatever his real name is," Elliot said.

"Rick told me it was Tommy."

"That doesn't mean anything," Elliot told me. "Half the time we *never* know their real names. This is a cash business—it's not like they send out W-2s at the end of the year."

"Well, fine," I said. "To me it doesn't matter. All I'm going to do is soak up his beauty so I can dream about him tonight."

"And then talk about him incessantly," Elliot teased.

The towels were placed, the sunscreen applied, and Tommy never even seemed to glance in our direction. It didn't matter. I was happy just to lie there looking at Tommy's body. He was about five-foot-nine but with his oversized chest and biceps, looked like he weighed as much as I did—180—or more. The bright sun reflected off his smooth, bronzed skin sending flashes of light that singed me. Tommy lay on his stomach with his chin propped up on his fists, so his head was raised to the perfect height for conversation.

Staring at that pose—his arms flayed out to the side—I closed my eyes and started to dream, romanticizing being wrapped in Tommy's arms, and more, his living with me, the boyfriend I had been seeking to be the salve for my loneliness and desire.

I came back to reality as Elliot nudged me and asked me if I wanted to go in the water. We waded in together, and I started talking about Tommy.

"See, you're already infatuated," Elliot said. "At least wait until you say hello. So far, he doesn't even know you exist."

Elliot was never one to remain in the water long; he liked to get in, cool off, and get out. I stayed in, paddling around the lazy waves. It was rare for the ocean to be that calm, and this was it—there was only one more weekend left at the house.

I looked back at the beach and saw Tommy get up to come to the water. I prayed that none of the others in that seemingly inseparable group would get up. Fortunately, it looked like the rest were asleep, passed out from a combination of pot and beer—and probably working late the night before.

As he walked down to the water, I could see the muscles tighten in his legs with each step. His chest was amazing—it seemed to reflect the glare of the light just at the point it curved around back to his flat stomach. Behind Tommy, I saw Elliot sit up on his towel. He smiled and gave me a thumbs-up.

Tommy walked into the water as I floated around, bending down when I stopped and touched bottom so the water was up to my neck. I smiled as Tommy started to come toward me.

"Hi," he said as he smiled at me, a wide grin with perfect teeth, which against his dark skin appeared incredibly bright white.

"Hi." I wondered how many relationships started out with that same two-letter word. "I'm Josh."

"Tommy."

"Good to meet you."

"Same here," Tommy said. "So you're the innocent housemate."

"I was innocent until I spent the summer here with these guys."

Tommy laughed. "Yeah, they destroyed my innocence too."

"You're working for them?" I asked, feigning ignorance.

"Yeah, sometimes," Tommy said. "Not much. I saw you staring at me."

My face turned red. "Sorry. I didn't mean to make you feel uncomfortable," I said. "You must be used to it. Especially out here."

"I usually don't pay any attention to it," Tommy said.

I could feel the pressure rising inside my head. I wondered if the fact that Tommy noticed I was staring meant something.

"You should have come over to say hello before," Tommy said.

"Well, you were with your friends."

"My posse."

"Yeah, your posse," I said. "And I didn't want to interrupt."

"What do you do?"

That was a standard question whenever I met someone in New York, so I had a pretty standard answer. In thirty seconds or less, I could describe my advertising job, the task made easier by the fact that nearly everyone knew Pontiac, and most New Yorkers—even people not in the industry—had heard of CBA.

"I would have loved to work at CBA," Tommy said. Tommy told me how he was supposed to go to college on a wrestling scholarship but lost it after an elbow injury and didn't have the money to go. "I was going to work for a year and try to save up, but then my parents caught me in bed with Eddy, the tall guy up there," he said, nodding toward the shore. "They threw me out of the house the next day."

"So that's why you started working for these guys?"

"Eddy was doing it first," Tommy told me.

"And you two are still together?" I asked.

"No." Tommy smiled. "That lasted about three months after my father threw me out. It probably wouldn't have even gone on that long, except after all the drama I felt like I had to stick with it. Now we're all just buddies. Eddy had answered an ad and started working for Jim and John; then I saw the money he was making, and I went to talk to them too," he told me. "Eddy got Marlon into it, and then he got Rafael working, although they're going to quit as soon as they saved up some money to move out of Marlon's place and get a bigger apartment."

"Is Tommy your real name?" I asked.

"Tommy Hawk."

"No, really," I said. "You expect me to believe that?"

"It's from my mother. Her father was a Cherokee Indian, and she was living in Arizona was she met my father. 'Hawk' was their family name. My father's 100 percent Puerto Rican," Tommy added. "Like the rest of the posse. Officially, my last name is Perez."

"I grew up in Westchester," I told him.

"Suburban boy."

"Yeah, the station wagon, the white fence, the 2.3 kids, the swimming pool."

"Wait," Tommy interrupted me. "The swimming pool?"

"Yeah, we had a pool."

"Oh, *rich* suburban boy."

"Don't blame me, okay?" I said, and we both laughed.

We probably would have kept on talking but the conversation ended as Marlon, Rafael, and Eddy all came in the water and started splashing around. He introduced me, but right afterwards I excused myself and headed back to the shore. Our moment in the sun together had ended.

❧ 8 ❧

I loved waking up on Fire Island; it was nice not to have to set the alarm for 7:30 to rush to the subway and get to the office. On those Sunday nights during the summer when I had managed to stay over, I had felt an incredible feeling of peacefulness descend as the last ferry pulled away from the dock Sunday night. At that point, short of chartering a boat to come from the mainland, there was no way off the island for the next ten hours.

Elliot had stayed over Monday night of Labor Day with me, and it felt especially tranquil that Tuesday morning after the party. Looking at the deck, I noticed that the angle of light had already changed; the picnic table that had been in the shade all summer was now mostly in the sun. I sat there and basked in its warmth; it felt good since the temperature had dropped below sixty the night before for the first time that season. Elliot came out with a cup of coffee and sat there reading the *Times*.

"So you're in love, right?" he asked. Over the summer I had gotten used to Elliot's giving me a hard time about my falling in love quickly and often. "I don't think Tommy's a good idea—for you or for anyone," he added without skipping a beat.

"He's a lot different than he seems," I said.

"They all are," Elliot said. "It's like you always read in the newspaper after someone is killed: once they find out the murderer was their neighbor, everyone always talks about how gentle he was, how he helped old ladies, no one ever thought he could hurt a fly, and all that."

"I don't think he's a murderer," I said. "He's had a lot of rough breaks in his life. He didn't have parents to pay for him to go to Notre Dame for four years."

"I worked," Elliot protested.

"You know what I mean."

"Tommy's got a lot of problems," Elliot said. "I've heard Rick talk about them. I don't even really know all the details, but he was arrested for dealing coke, I think. He didn't tell you about that as part of his sob story, did he?"

"I think he's a genuinely nice guy who's gotten dealt a lot of shitty cards in life and has tried to get by the best he can," I said.

"Yeah, he got dealt a rough deck. A lot of people would like to suffer by going through life looking like Tommy," Elliot said. "He's wasted all of it. He'll turn tricks for these guys for a couple years and then once people don't want to pay for him anymore, he'll go back to selling drugs."

"He lost a college scholarship because he got hurt," I said.

"I don't think that's why he lost the scholarship," Elliot said, rolling his eyes. "But go ahead. Do what you want. I don't see a happy ending in the crystal ball."

"I don't know," I said. "Maybe you're right." And in my gut I knew that Elliot was doing a good job playing the role of the former, sensible me.

"I just don't want to see you get hurt," Elliot said. "Maybe you should volunteer at the Gay Switchboard or someplace like that if you want to help poor lost souls."

Wednesday morning back at CBA, Randy was even more horrified when I told him the tale.

"A hustler? A rent boy? Oh, dear," he said, tapping the ashes from his cigarette and making that now-familiar scowl. "Think what your mother would say the first time you brought him up to Scarsdale." It was, of course, something I had already spent time thinking about.

"Don't tell Carole or anyone else about it, okay?" I asked. I was sorry I'd even mentioned it, as I knew that Randy would certainly tell Gerard, and the tale of my attraction would be in wide circulation before the end of the day.

Back in my office, I closed the door and turned off the lights. The only illumination came from the clear, round, plastic line-selection buttons on the phone that showed my colleagues hard at work. I put a sheet of paper in the typewriter and began writing out everything I could recall from Monday with Tommy, closing my eyes as I sat there in my suit and tie, beginning with that first moment when I saw him walk out on the deck in that tight yellow shirt, trying to recall and capture every minute of our conversation together. I wrote like I was in a trance—the words spilled out from my memory and onto the paper. In less than twenty minutes, I had typed two double-spaced pages.

The ringing phone brought me back to reality.

"They're waiting for you in the conference room," Rita said.

I folded the papers in half and stuck them in my briefcase before I straightened my tie and turned on the lights. When I opened the door to the hallway, the fluorescent light startled me like an unexpected bolt of lightning on a summer evening.

It was hard for me to concentrate the rest of that week. Every day, I was physically present at CBA but spent a good part of every hour thinking about Tommy. We hadn't even exchanged phone numbers; really, we hadn't even spoken about any future plans, other than to say "see you around" as Tommy and his friends changed clothes after the beach to head back to the city.

I thought about having Randy call Manhattan Men to hire Tommy, only when Tommy showed up, I would be there in Randy's bedroom. In my fantasy version, Tommy would grab me as soon as he saw me, tell me to forget about the seventy-five dollars, adding, "You'll never have to pay to be with me," just before we made mad passionate love and lived happily ever after. Then Rita called again on the intercom, and I was back to figuring out how to sell more Pontiacs.

Finally, Friday afternoon arrived and although CBA had returned to regular Friday hours after Labor Day, I arranged to leave right after lunch so I could go out early to help close up the house for the season. The ferry was half-empty, and it was chilly even at four o 'clock. For the first time, I sat downstairs in the enclosed part of the boat instead of on the open upper deck. I called the house from the pay phone at the dock. Jim was already there, and I bought food. This was it, the weekend after Labor Day, the last one of the season.

When I arrived at the house, I saw Jim drinking a beer through the sliding glass doors and reading the latest issue of *GQ* at the round wooden kitchen table, the painted surface now a little more scratched than at the start of the summer. He was pretty much in exactly the same position where I had found him that first Friday night in May. I said hi, threw the backpack in my room, and grabbed a beer for myself.

"Wow, we've got a lot of beer left to drink in forty-eight hours," I said, surveying the remaining inventory in the refrigerator. "The Labor Day party was great."

"You looked like you were having a good time," Jim said. "But I hadn't been too worried about that."

"Y'know," I said, "now I'm kind of embarrassed about making such a big deal about everything at the beginning of the summer."

"Don't worry about it," Jim told me. "I think it was pretty natural. Even John and Rick didn't think you were totally neurotic, at the time."

"But they thought I was a little neurotic?"

"Yeah," Jim smiled. "A little."

"I wanted to ask you about one of the guys," I said.

"Yesssss," Jim said, drawing it out and grinning while he waited for me to continue.

"You already know, right?"

"I've heard rumblings," Jim said.

"Figures," I said. I had learned pretty quickly that summer that secrets didn't last very long on Fire Island. "It's Tommy."

Jim smiled. "You should get in touch with him," he said, finishing off the last of that bottle of beer. "Who knows? But I don't even have a home number for him. And even if I did, it wouldn't be right for me to give it out."

"I understand," I said, although I was amused at the level of ethics that apparently went into running a prostitution service.

"But listen, next time I talk to Tommy, I'll tell him you were asking about him and give him your number, okay?"

"That would be great," I said, already fantasizing about the call and especially what would come next.

Gerard had stayed in the city to finish up next year's spring collection, which was to be shown the following week, so Randy was alone at their house. The Manhattan Men house already looked deserted. By Sunday afternoon, the shelves in the kitchen, which had been full of liquor bottles and cereal boxes, were empty. I finished packing up my room and went over to Randy's, as we were planning to take the ferry back together.

"I feel sad the summer's ending," I told him. "All that anxiety for nothing."

"And now you've got not a care in the world," Randy joked, still making fun of the way I was constantly worried about one thing or another. "You know the worrying is a control thing," Randy told me. "You worry about the negative consequences so much so that when things turn out okay, you feel like somehow you're successfully in control of your life."

I nodded.

"Which of course you're not. So what are you agonizing about these days?" Randy asked as we walked along the mostly deserted beach.

"Tommy, I guess, mostly."

"The hustler?" Randy asked. "That Tommy?"

"That's the one."

"Honestly, Josh," Randy said, "unless you want to torture yourself for months with unrequited love, just forget about him. Have you even talked to him since the party?"

"I don't have his number," I said. "Jim told me he doesn't have his own phone; he uses a service."

"That's just great," Randy said. "I rest my case. Do yourself a favor and forget about him."

"I don't know," I said. "What if there really is something there? He could be the great love of my life."

"He could," Randy said. "But really, I would like to feel you've learned something in the past year. For all you know, you're just another route to money for him. His whole life is playing a role people want him to play for cash."

"He was different than that," I insisted. "I'm not giving up so fast."

"Josh, don't be ridiculous," Randy said. "Even if he remembers you still exist, you can't pluck him from the real world and insert him into that fantasy life you manufacture in your head. Real life is not like a Pontiac commercial."

❧ 9 ❧

Although schooldays were long in my past, I marveled at how everyone in New York City still seemed to keep on the same schedule, where little happened during the sultry months of July and August and then in September, the entire population seemed to come alive, like bears emerging from hibernation.

I got back into my nightly cruising habits at the bars, but I came to realize I wasn't even interested in trying to pick up anyone until I had a chance to see Tommy again. By Friday, I couldn't understand why Tommy hadn't at least phoned if Jim had given him the message. I hated not to be able to do anything; to just sit there waiting and hoping and praying for the phone to ring. As soon as I got home, I'd race up the stairs to see if the red light was flashing on the answering machine.

That first Saturday back in the city was drizzly and gloomy—it was the kind of day I'd always planned I'd go to one of the museums, but instead, I just went out to get the *Times* and a bagel and crawled back into bed.

Still, I couldn't stop thinking about Tommy. The feet were in active running mode, still under the sheets, as usual.

By three in the afternoon, I decided to call Jim and after some chat, I finally got up the courage to ask. "Did you ever get a chance to give

Tommy my number?" I said as though it were a random thought that just happened to pop into my head while we were speaking, not something I had been rehearsing while lying in the bed for the past three hours.

"Yeah, I did," Jim said. "Either Tuesday or Wednesday. He never called?"

"Not yet."

"Hmm. I'm kind of surprised," Jim said. "He definitely seemed like he remembered you from the barbeque when I told him. I would have sworn he was going to call you."

"Well, when you hear from him again, you can tell him we talked and I said I've been waiting by the phone," I said with a little laugh so Jim would know I wasn't *really* serious about sitting home waiting for Tommy to call.

I wanted to go out that night but was already tired of making the trek back and forth to Third Avenue. There were bars closer to me—much closer—in the West Village. I just never went, mostly because it seemed like a different crowd than the preppie boys I was used to at Company and Uncle Charlie's. But maybe that was just my overactive mind.

I loved living in Greenwich Village. The tree-lined streets south of 14th Street were filled with brownstones and smaller buildings. It was mostly residential and small stores, with almost no office buildings. And the rectangular grid of Manhattan streets didn't exist, since west of Sixth Avenue—the West Village—the straight lines disappeared, so when I got back from the office in Midtown, it felt like home was in a different place. The geographic disarray was not only in the layout; the unruliness here extended to the nomenclature as well, where the chronological organization of the rest of the city gave way to a jumble of names commemorating people, places, and things long forgotten: Jane, Charles, Perry, and Christopher. Who were they?

I had often walked around the Village on Saturday or Sunday afternoons and sometimes I stopped in Bagel And, the coffee shop on Christopher Street with its bright-white round globe lights which now occupied the storefront where the original Stonewall Tavern had been located.

That was the mafia-run gay bar, where one hot summer night on the last Saturday night in June 1969, the patrons famously fought back against the police in a routine raid, marking a turning point in the movement for gay rights. The quickly organized rally the next day is still memorialized on the last Sunday in June with a parade in New York and celebrations around the world. I had been in junior high school in 1969, and if I'd read anything about Stonewall, it was buried along with most of my feelings from that time.

Between Stonewall and the annual parade, Christopher Street had now become the epicenter of gay New York. But the first times I ventured out to the bars there, I decided they were too smoky and had an older, rougher-looking crowd. But I was getting bored with same old places. I was no longer a new face, and probably the other patrons were as tired of seeing me as I was of seeing them. So I decided it was time to give the West Village another try.

Crossing Fifth Avenue at Ninth Street and looking downtown to the left, I could see the blazing lights in the offices of the twin towers of the World Trade Center. A glance uptown showed the illuminated crown of the Empire State Building. I felt like I was in the middle of the most exciting place in the world.

After Sixth Avenue, where Ninth Street morphed into Christopher, I walked past the Oscar Wilde Bookshop and, across the street, Uncle Paul's, presumably no relation to Uncle Charlie.

There was the Ninth Circle, one of the bars that Randy had originally written on my list that first evening but then crossed out. "You won't find anything there except gonorrhea," he had told me.

But I had been intrigued enough by the huge hanging sign over the street, with nine white round circles and the words "Steak House" underneath, that I had walked up the steps once and gone in. Maybe Randy's comments had just prejudiced me, or maybe the crowd really was that frightening, but I stayed less than five minutes before I walked out.

West of Seventh Avenue, the sidewalk traffic became more exclusively male. The overall look was plaid flannel shirt, mustache, long sideburns, and leather jacket. I was getting into it slowly; the mustache had grown in but like most of the guys under thirty, I hadn't adopted the full uniform yet.

I was on a mission—to get past Tommy, distracted by someone else who could more readily sign on to make my romantic dreams come true. Or, as Randy would say, I just needed a good fuck. I passed by Boots and Saddle, with the ersatz cowboys posed on the stoop and leaning against the railings lining the steps outside, and then, after crossing Bleecker Street, went into Ty's. Ty's was a lot smaller than Uncle Charlie's, but the décor, with smoke-stained wood walls, was similar.

I was surprised how crowded it was at 10:30. There were stools lined up in front of the bar and along the back wall. The ones in front were occupied mostly by what appeared to be long-time regulars. Most of them looked as though they'd been sitting there since happy hour—and not necessarily that particular day's happy hour.

I could see over most of the men and had a pretty clear view of the bar. I walked to the counter, ordered a Dewar's—I had switched brands for some variety now as well—and then headed back to find a place along the wall. For a so-called "leather bar," it seemed like the only relevant attire many of the men were wearing was perhaps, at most, a Gucci belt. There were two other tall guys talking in the corner. *Probably lovers*, I thought.

But why in the world, if you had actually been lucky enough to find love, would you come back to spend the evening in a place like this?

I studied them from the opposite corner. They seemed to be about my age, although both were a little taller. Each of them looked over as I tried to effect as nonchalant a pose as possible. One, his straight brown hair lightened by the summer sun, smiled before joining his partner back in conversation. Both were smoking. Actually, I was probably one of only a handful of men in the place who wasn't.

Warmed by the scotch, I went to the bar to get a napkin so I'd have an excuse to reposition myself closer. I strained to listen to what they were saying and heard them talking about apartments. Definitely New Yorkers. Because I was looking for love, not just sex, I usually tried to avoid tourists—that robbed the encounter of any romantic possibility that somehow this one night, this one trick, could be the one.

I would have taken either one of them. The taller one had dark wavy hair and a mustache, really nice-looking, I thought. The other, with the light brown hair, was my second choice.

I stood there watching both, refining the choreography I had been practicing since Thanksgiving, looking over to see if I caught their attention and then looking away as though I couldn't have cared less. The shorter of the two smiled again before I could turn away. He motioned for me to come over.

"You're not just going to stand there watching us all night without coming over to say hello, are you?" he said with a Southern drawl.

I laughed. "I'm shy," I said.

"Well, hello, Shy. I'm David and this is Russell."

"It's Josh, actually."

"Okay, Shy Josh," David said, sticking out his hand.

Both of them had just graduated from the University of North

Carolina the year before and had moved together to New York, where they shared an apartment on Charles Street, two blocks north of Christopher.

Russell was the taller of the two at six-foot-three, and David was an inch shorter. Conversation flowed easily between me and David; Russell was standing next to us, giving some indication of listening every few minutes but mostly scanning the crowd to see who was looking at him that might be worthy of a return glance. David told me that he had grown up nearby the campus in Greensboro, but that Russell was from Great Neck, which I knew was another of the New York suburbs in the same demographic sphere as Scarsdale.

At one o 'clock the three of us left together and walked down Christopher Street to "Once Upon a Cookie," a bright new store that somehow planned to pay the rent by selling cookies at a dollar a piece to passersby and which, to no one's surprise, closed months later.

Munching cookies on the sidewalk, the three of us decided to call it a night. My mind went into overdrive, trying to figure out how I might ask David upstairs. Russell was busy checking out other men we passed on the sidewalk and by now, David had grown on me; now I was more interested in him than in Russell.

We walked back up Christopher Street. Even in the cold weather there were always a lot of people outside the bars, as groups of men gathered on the sidewalk to get away from all the smokers inside.

As we paused at the corner by my place, I asked, "Do you want to come up for one last drink?"

Now Russell was the one who spoke. "No, thanks, *we* have to be getting home. *We* need our beauty rest for a big party tomorrow."

David laughed and put his hand on my shoulder. "I'm not sure there's enough time between now and the party for us to get sufficient 'beauty sleep,' but we may as well try." His soft Southern accent made whatever he said come in out in this soothing tone that made it all seem so relaxed.

Under the streetlamp on the corner, we exchanged numbers. I always tried to remember to take a pen in my pocket for just such an eventuality. David wrote down both his and Russell's names, along with the number. David included his last name as well, a marker of sorts that I had learned greatly increased the odds of ever seeing the person again. Maybe David was destined to be the love of my life instead of Tommy. He was a real person with a real phone number and a real job.

The next morning was gray and before even opening the shade that darkened the bedroom, I could hear the sound of light rain hitting the top of the air conditioner.

At noon I decided to go to the gym. By then it would be already humming with the sounds of exercise bikes and unfulfilled sexual energy from the night before. Tommy said he never went to the gym, but I wasn't so sure. Maybe one of his customers would invite him to come along. I always fantasized about how he might walk in, and I'd watch him work out in a tank top and tight pair of shorts.

I packed my bag, switched on the answering machine, and went down the stairs to the street. I had brought my umbrella but now the drizzle had turned to such a light mist that I didn't even need to open it for the four-block walk.

I went up the third floor to use the new Stairmaster machines, mini-escalators that recreated the childhood entertainment of trying to walk up the down-escalator at the department store, only now it was possible to adjust the speed with the specific intent of not making any progress climbing. As I went upstairs I smiled to myself, watching a group of women waiting for the elevator to take them up to the third floor so they could then use the Stairmaster to simulate the exercise they would have gotten just by climbing the stairs. Not that I didn't have my own shortcuts; I usually stopped after twenty-nine minutes, rationalizing that the stairs back up my apartment would count for the final sixty seconds.

The big change in my gym routine since coming out was that now I spent more time fixing my hair before the workout than after. I had heard about encounters in the steam room and the sauna, including one in which the female manager had reportedly stormed in to personally break up the offending twosome, but I had never seen one myself, much less participated.

The red light was flashing on the answering machine when I got back home. Even now, two months since we'd met, each time I saw that light my heart skipped a beat, wondering if Tommy might have called. I still couldn't accept the possibility that he wouldn't.

I turned the dial to play back the tape with the messages. It was David from the night before. I called him back, told him about the gym, and asked about his plans for the evening. The big party that Russell had mentioned was actually a dinner party at Alan Nesoir's Park Avenue apartment. David worked as one of three salespeople for Alan, who had been a well-known fashion designer for more than twenty years. He had never made it big, like Halston or Bill Blass, but was a favorite with wealthy Manhattan socialites and the women around the country who wanted to dress like them.

David told me the whole story of how Alan had been born to a Jewish family in Brooklyn as Alan Rosen, but he reversed the letters to Nesor and added the extra "i" and *voilà*, he was now Alan Nesoir, whose press biography described his father as a Paris furrier rather than the New York butcher he had actually been.

David had worked there for nearly a year, but this was the first time he had been invited to one of Alan's famous dinner parties, and he was excited about it despite the fact that Alan had proffered the invitation with the comment that he and Russell would be "eye candy" for the other guests.

"Call me tomorrow with a full report," I told David. I didn't have any special plans of my own for Saturday evening, but it didn't matter. Saturday night was always a good night to be out on the prowl, and although it was definitely more fun to go out tagging along with someone, the complex cruising process of receiving attention and transmitting attentive stares in return was best accomplished alone.

Just before noon on Sunday, David phoned with the rundown on the previous evening's goings-on at the home of Alan Nesoir, or Mr. Rosen, as David and the other employees usually referred to him out of his hearing. David and Russell had been suitably adored as the handsome young men at the table, but they had to share the eye-candy limelight with Alan's houseboy, Lance, who was actually from Paris, although he looked more Mediterranean, according to David.

"Lance sounds like the name of a porno star," I said.

"Believe me," David said, "this one probably was or easily could have been."

David reported that the other guests were all fashionistas, and the conversation was entirely focused on the blood sport of the New York fashion industry. Here the discussion went well beyond the gossip-column speculation of whether or not particular designers were gay, because everyone in the room knew they were. David breathlessly reported the stories of designers strung out on drugs, their work being done mostly by their hot young assistants, and the one caught having sex on a cutting room table by investor partners being shown the studio on a visit from Tokyo.

We had a good time talking on the phone, and I was getting more and more interested in David. He seemed like good boyfriend material: tall, handsome, college-degree, and a lot of fun. And I was sure I could convince him to stop smoking. More and more, he was edging Tommy to the margins of my fantasies.

"Do you want to get together later for dinner?" I asked.

"I would, but I promised Russell I'd go with him for the new tea dance at Ice Palace 57," David said. "Why don't you come with us?"

I was disappointed. David and Russell sure acted like boyfriends—even more inseparable than most couples, I thought. I was wondering if I'd ever manage to be alone with David.

Ice Palace 57 was one of a series of new discos that had opened in the wake of the success of Studio 54 the year before. I had been to Studio 54 only once since it had opened, back at the beginning of September, when I had gone to a private party sponsored by one of the magazines that CBA did a lot of business with. Studio 54, or just "Studio," was already a phenomenon, and the crowd battles to be chosen to enter the front doors of what had been a former theater and CBS-TV studio were legendary.

But many nights there were private parties that used a separate entrance on 53rd Street. No screaming and no waiting to be selected. There was still a velvet rope but no crowds of people screaming for attention, just an orderly line walking past a couple of people with clipboards and walkie-talkies. That first night, I hadn't seen any of the famed celebrities that supposedly filled the place, but what had surprised me, because it was never reported in the *New York Times* or *People* magazine, was how gay Studio 54 seemed. The bartenders and waiters were all great-looking guys with silver lamé shorts, big chests, and no shirts. The crowd, while predominantly straight, was filled with lots of gay men dancing together or making out in the rows of seats in the balconies, leftover from the venue's theatrical past.

"Come back Thursday or Sunday," one of the bartenders told me. "Those are the big gay nights. Use this card, and you won't have to wait in line." But when I tried, it didn't seem to do any good; I couldn't even get close enough to the doorman to show him the card. So Ice Palace 57 seemed like it might be a good alternative. Plus, maybe I could finally manage to get some time alone with David.

"Definitely, you should come with us," David said. "And we're going to go for a late lunch before."

"What time?" I asked.

"We're going to need to discuss that after we get set with our outfits," David said. "One thing at a time."

"I'm just going to wear jeans and a sweater, I guess," I said, never giving my clothes the attention that someone who worked in the fashion business would.

"Come over to our apartment at three o'clock, and we'll go from here," he said, giving me the address to write down. "We'd love to have a gentleman caller."

David was ironing a shirt when I walked in. "I'm just the washerwoman here," he joked.

"I should have brought over my laundry," I said.

"Seriously, I love ironing."

"That's why you're the ultimate garmento," Russell said as he came in from the bedroom. "You're only happy with fabric in your hands."

Russell made us screwdrivers, and I looked at the flyer for the tea dance, which started at four. We sat there discussing the proper time to arrive. We knew it was critical to not get there too early as to seem desperate or unknowledgeable about such things, but then certainly not so late as to have to stand in line with what Randy always referred to as the "unwashed masses" that came from Brooklyn and Queens, or worse, New Jersey.

We decided 5:30 would be just about right. No one other than the employees would dare arrive before five o 'clock, and by six there was a risk it might actually be too crowded.

I was excited as we went down into the massive underground complex of the West 4th Street IND station; for someone like me, always worried about being in control, for some reason the prospect of setting out for another evening of adventure without having any idea where or how it might end seemed uncharacteristically enticing.

The three of us paid the fifty-cent fare, and we each got the paper coupon that would cover our return trip the same day. The subways were half-price on Sunday, a remnant of measures taken during the city's fiscal crisis in the mid-'70s to stimulate business and tourism. I tucked the return voucher carefully in my billfold for easy retrieval later. Even on this newer line, the subway cars were covered with graffiti, inside and out, most of it elaborately drawn multicolored names. The glass windows were etched with similar art, minus only the colors but filled with scratched lines creating patterns inside each of the letters.

As we came upstairs at 57th and Sixth, we realized we had seriously miscalculated the arrival time. A long line of men and a few women stretched from the door about two hundred feet down the block, around Sixth Avenue, and then curved eastward again onto 58th Street. It was amazing to see hundreds of gay men lined up in Midtown like that.

Just past six o 'clock the three of us descended the staircase to the movie cashier-like window and paid the entrance fee of four dollars, which included two free drinks. Between that and the half-price subway, the night out cost us five dollars—even my father, Herb, would say that was a good deal.

Ice Palace 57 was located in the basement of a nondescript office building. Like the warehouses being turned into discos and clubs along the waterfront, it was a space that previously had probably housed cardboard boxes of corporate files and records—a vast, open floor plan that, with the addition of neon lights and mirrored balls and cigarette smoke, was quickly transformed into an atmosphere conducive to drinking, dancing, and the pursuit of happiness.

That pursuit was foremost on my mind as I maneuvered to try to talk with David alone, but Russell seemed to be intentionally making sure that didn't happen. Even when I asked David to dance, Russell somehow assumed that the "you" in "Do you want to dance?" was plural and included both of them. The three of us sat down on the couches by the entrance, where we had a good view of those still coming into the club. Now it was filled to capacity, and people were only allowed in as others left.

I couldn't believe it: Russell excused himself to go to the men's room. It was the first time since we had first met on Friday night that I was actually alone with David. I reached out and touched his forearm. "Your skin is really smooth," I said. "It feels good."

"Thanks," David said, looking directly at me.

"Sometimes it really seems like you guys are boyfriends," I said.

"I know," David sighed. "He works really hard to be sure everyone thinks I'm taken."

"But you're not?"

"No," David said. "And we've never slept together."

I nodded and held David's hand. Wow. The warmth flowed through my body.

"Russell just wants to make sure that I don't find a boyfriend before he does," David said, just as Russell came back from the men's room. He looked at David holding hands with me but didn't say a word about it.

David pulled his hand free. "Let's dance again," he said.

Around 10:30 we took the subway back downtown. At West 4th Street we walked out of the north end of the station by Waverly Place. "Time for bed," Russell announced. "*We* have to work tomorrow." Russell was as an editorial assistant at Andy Warhol's *Interview* magazine. Although he made it sound like he was at Warhol's side all day, he was so far down the pecking order that David had told me on the phone that Russell actually had only met Warhol once and seen him only a handful of times.

"I'm kind of hungry," I said. "I might go to Sandolino and just get something light." Sandolino, nearby on Barrow Street, was one of my favorite places, cheap and always open late.

"Me, too," David said.

"David, it's late," Russell said. "And it's a school night. *We* have to get up early tomorrow."

"Please, Mother," David said. I laughed. Russell didn't.

"I'm going home," Russell said. "Are you coming with me or not?"

"I'm going to go with Josh," David said. "I'll be there in an hour. Promise."

Russell turned and walked away.

"Aren't you even going to say good night?" David asked as I stood watching.

Russell turned around. "Good night." And then he walked up Sixth Avenue.

"He's going to be furious," David told me. "This is the first time since we moved to the city that I've gone off alone like this."

"Go ahead home if you want," I said. "I don't want to cause any problems."

"No, he'll get over it," David said. "I'm tired of being his little pet, tagging along at his side all the time."

"Well if you're just roommates, it shouldn't be such a big deal," I said.

"But it is, Blanche, it is." David said. He liked his classic movie lines. "I don't know what's going on with him."

Sandolino was a comfortable diner, Greenwich Village-style, with lots of real wood instead of Formica and candles instead of fluorescents. We ate dessert and sat and talked. I brushed my legs against David's under the table. He smiled over at me.

"Do you want to come over to see my apartment?" I asked. "We can have a nightcap."

"Sure," David said. "But not for long. If I'm not home by midnight, Russell will have the police out looking for me."

It took less than ten minutes to walk over to my building and was nearly 11:30 when we finally got to the top of the stairs. I poured two small glasses of scotch in tumblers with ice. I put on a George Benson jazz album and as we sat on the couch, I rested my hand on David's leg. And the excitement that flowed wasn't from the feelings of that moment but from imagining what might come from it. David was someone I could live together with; someone who could sit around the Silver family dining table in Scarsdale.

We kissed. I unbuttoned David's shirt and felt his chest. Then I took off my own. "Do you want to go in the bedroom?" I asked.

I lit a candle. I wanted it to be perfect.

We lay down on the bed and embraced, our bodies wrapped together. He wrapped his long arms around me and held me tight, with my head buried in his chest. The silence ended in less than a minute, though, and we started talking again; talking as though we'd known one another for many years not just the forty-eight hours since we first met. And then we talked more.

At midnight, David told me he really should get going. It had seemed so perfect but nothing happened. I wondered if maybe I should have been more aggressive.

I still went to Company with Randy at least once each week, usually on Friday, when there was the biggest crowd and I was sure to see a bunch of people I knew. That was a great place to meet other people because it was more relaxed than going out at night with the pressure to hook up and with one eye on the clicking clock, like the countdown on a TV game show to make a choice before the buzzer sounded.

David and I spoke almost every day by phone, but he and Russell and their friends were separate from Randy's crowd. On the weekends we would often go out together, but that meant a threesome and putting up with Russell.

But about two months later, Russell found a boyfriend, which meant that David could usually pal around with me alone at night. We would take up our usual positions at Uncle Charlie's or the Barefoot Boy and analyze the crowd passing by. After a year, I already knew a lot of the people that frequented these bars—some through one-night stands, some through short romances, and others just from checking one another out night after night.

By the beginning of November, David and I were going out to the bars together at least three or four nights of the week. We had developed our own shorthand, our personal Morse code, where one could quickly say "CBS" and the other knew immediately the rating was "Cute But Short."

The New York gay world seemed smaller to me each month, as I'd run into the same people over and over again, including many of "the boys," which made it even more puzzling that Tommy and I never seemed to cross paths.

I had gotten together with Elliot and Rick a couple of times, but it had been kind of surprising to me how little we had to talk about once the summer was over. At the Pines we had spent hours at that table under the tree, talking, and now it seemed we had so little to say to one another.

At CBA, my boss, "Scoot"—Virgil Scootman—sat with me for my first-year performance review at the beginning of October, and he told me I was one of the rising young stars at the agency. "Some people think you're a little too full of yourself," he said, "but this is a business where confident people succeed."

"Thanks, I appreciate that," I said.

"The truth of the matter is that if you're going to be successful, you're probably going to end up ruffling a few feathers," Scoot told me. "So remember that. You just have to know whose feathers you can get away with ruffling and whose asses need to be kissed."

After a year, I had already heard enough around the hallways of CBA to know that it wasn't necessarily the most talented or the smartest that made it to the top.

"Really, at this point, 90 percent of what I do all day is deal with the politics—either internally here or with the clients—and then about 10 percent is actual work," Scoot told me.

I had always appreciated Scoot's honesty during the year I had worked for him. At the end, Scoot told me how happy he was to have me on his team and told me I was getting a $3,000 raise to $24,000 a year.

I was thrilled. That meant nearly $1,500 a month in take-home pay which gave me an extra couple of hundred in spending money each month. With the monthly rent at $325, my total housing costs, including the phone, cable TV, and electric, came to less than five hundred dollars. The gym was another fifty dollars, but that was worth it. Although it was a very mixed crowd, there were plenty of gay men there, and I probably had as many dates that fall from people I met at the gym as I did at the bars. Plus, it was better hanging out at the gym, exercising, instead of drinking. And there was no cigarette smoke at the gym.

I took David out that night to celebrate my raise. It was Wednesday night—two for one at Uncle Charlie's—and the place was packed. That was the night I saw Robert, "Bachelor #1," as I called him, for the first time since our night together last November. As soon as he saw me, he walked over to say hello, and I introduced him to David.

"I never heard from you last fall," I said.

"I know," Robert said. "Sorry. I ended up meeting someone the weekend right after I saw you, and we were kind of boyfriends for a while, but that's over now."

I nodded.

"I've got my own place and a phone now," Robert said as the two of us walked over to the bar. He wrote down the number on one of the yellow cards sitting by the register. "Call me sometime," he said.

"I will," I said as Robert headed off to the back, but I was pretty sure the card would just end up in my kitchen counter cookie-jar repository of numbers for guys I would never call.

In mid-November I decided to host a party at my place to celebrate my first year of gay life. David helped me with the guest list, which was augmented by some of David and Russell's own friends and a bunch of the people I'd met through Randy and Gerard.

I had gotten friendly with one of the art directors at the office, Gabriel, a big bear of a guy who, unfortunately, had a high squeaky voice that killed any fantasy one might have from eyeing his burly body. I had run into him in the West Village one night, and we had a drink together.

We never became good friends, but we were both acknowledged "Friends of Dorothy," as Randy would say, so the bond had been forged.

Now that everyone just said gay, I would laugh whenever Randy used "Friends of Dorothy," although at times I even used it in mixed company as a secret code to describe someone gay, as in, "Isn't that one by the window a friend of Dorothy?" Randy had told me it came into use after Stonewall, because the funeral for the singer Judy Garland, famous for portraying Dorothy in *The Wizard of Oz*, had been the same night as the famous rebellion.

Gabriel helped me put together the invitation. It showed a bunch of intersecting staircases, sort of like an Escher drawing, New York brownstone-style. And on the top, it read *Move On Up*, the title of one of my favorite dance tunes.

There were more than forty people there over the course of the evening. It had been an exciting year. Not every trick had been satisfying, and there was that guy with the twenty cats in his apartment that I'd had to walk out on, but no one had threatened me, no one had called me names, and even at work, I was pretty sure Scoot and the others knew but hadn't said anything. I still hadn't told my parents, but I had decided to follow Randy's advice and was going to wait 'til they asked me. "By then, it means they know and they're psychologically prepared—or at least think they are—to hear you tell them."

As the last guests left, I stared down the stairway and couldn't help closing my and eyes and imagining—just for a moment—Tommy coming up the stairs. But the party was over. And there were no rent boys there that evening. At least, not as far as I knew then.

❧ 10 ❧

At noon on Thanksgiving Day, Grand Central Station was jammed as I stood waiting for David by the circular information booth in the center of the main hall. Last year, taking the train up to Scarsdale, I was alone, daydreaming about Robert, with a smile on my face the entire day. Even my sister had asked me what I was so happy about.

This year, David was coming along with me. We had become good friends, and he didn't have the money to fly home to North Carolina. Randy and Gerard had invited me to come to their house. "We bring in all the orphans to have a nice holiday dinner together," Randy said, but I told him I'd be going up to be with my family for the afternoon.

When I had spoken to my parents the week before, I had asked if I could bring my friend David along for Thanksgiving dinner, and neither had missed a beat in saying, "Yes, of course."

I liked being with David. From spending so much time together, one of us would often know what the other was thinking and if not, usually even just a glance at the other with a roll of the eyes in a certain direction communicated instantly what the other was thinking. The train was packed with families coming back from the Thanksgiving Day parade, but it had emptied out by the time it pulled into the Scarsdale station just after one o 'clock. I saw my father in the family station wagon, parked off to the side, as soon as we walked off the train.

He got out of the car as we approached. I held a large paper-wrapped bouquet of flowers I had bought, and David had a bottle of wine.

I shook my father's hand. We were never much for hugging. As a matter of fact, I had no recollections of hugging my father or my mother, although I could see in the old black-and-white family photographs boxed in the attic that they had held me close that way when I was a child. I went to introduce David, but my father beat me to it. "You must be David," my father said, extending his hand.

'That's me. Nice to meet you, Mr. Silver."

"You can call me Herb."

My father was about the same height as me, six feet even, but at six foot two, David seemed much taller, especially because his shoulders were broader. The ride back to the house was quick. I sat in front with my father; David, alone in the back. We talked about the train ride, and as we drove through downtown Scarsdale, I pointed out the high school I graduated from, the same one as both of my parents, who had met in those same hallways.

At the house, the door from the garage led directly into the kitchen and as we walked in, my mother came over, wiping her hands on the terrycloth apron after she turned down the burner on the stove.

"Hi, Mrs. Silver," David said.

"It's wonderful that you can be here with us," she told him and seemed genuinely happy to have a new guest in the home. Although my mother complained about it, I knew that she loved entertaining. Every holiday— and with the Jewish holidays added to the traditional American ones, plus birthdays and anniversaries, there were a lot to celebrate—meant days of preparation. Lillian would write out a 5x8 index card with the menu on top and then a schedule of preparation and cooking times, leading to the all-important line on the bottom: "Serve Food." I knew where I had gotten the organizational skills that helped me put together the promotional activity calendar for Pontiac each month.

We went upstairs to look for my little brother, Toby. My sister hadn't arrived yet from Boston, where she was just finishing her last year of med school at Tufts. Toby, now in his sophomore year of high school and not so little any more, was in his room playing with his Atari game console connected to an old black-and-white TV. I introduced him to David.

"Can I try?" I asked, and we put in a one of his newer cartridges to play PAC-MAN while David watched.

"I should get one of these. It would be fun to have," I said.

"Yeah, you could have a lot of excitement in your bedroom for a change," David said, and Toby laughed. I figured he must have thought David was making a joke about my luck with women in bed, but then again, I wasn't quite sure.

Annie finally arrived from Boston, driving the old family Plymouth. My father took pride in the fact that he managed to keep ten-year-old cars still operating. Fortunately for CBA and my career, most people wanted to buy new cars more frequently than that. We sat down at the dinner table, which looked as artfully arranged as the one on the cover of *Women's Day* magazine that Lillian had sitting on the kitchen counter.

David's WASP-ish good looks, smooth skin, and straight golden-brown hair looked out of place at the Silver family table but my parents, especially my father, were amused whenever David said *schlmiel* or *schlep* or any of the other Yiddish words he'd picked up working in the garment district. Coming from David, especially mixed with his Southern accent, which he amped up when he was trying to turn on the charm, was entertaining.

Still, I noticed my father kept staring at David after he stopped talking. Maybe it was because David sounded so effeminate when he laughed—I had never noticed that before, but I guess from Randy's friends and being around so many fashion people, I had grown accepting of what most people outside of New York City wouldn't consider a particularly masculine tone.

My brother went to watch a football game on TV in the den, while the rest of the family gathered in the living room. Lillian believed a TV didn't belong in the living room, so we would all crowd into the much-smaller den, with its old, worn sofa, when there was something the whole family wanted to watch.

After dinner, my father pulled me into his office. It was on the other side of the kitchen from the den—it probably used to be the maid's room at the time the house was first built.

"Sit down," he said, though it was spoken very much as an invitation, not an order, as he closed the door. "Let's talk for a minute."

My father sat down in the chair and swiveled around so he was looking at me on the sofa. Was this the moment Randy warned me about?

"What's up?" I asked, worried that maybe it was something serious about his health or my mother's.

"Mom and I are concerned that you are living a homosexual lifestyle," he said.

Thank God, I thought. Now I didn't have to worry any longer about when the moment would come. And after the raise and great review the week before last, I felt more self-confident than ever. As usual, I was prepared. In addition to Randy's counsel, I had gotten a pamphlet, "How to Tell Your Family," from an organization called Parents of Gays, which was housed in a church on 13th and Fifth, right up the street from where I lived.

"Yes, I'm gay," I said. "It's not a lifestyle; it's the way I am."

"When did you decide this?" my father asked. He didn't sound angry. It sounded a lot like the business discussions we might have at CBA.

"It's not something I decided," I explained. "It's something I felt as long as I can remember. Since I was a kid in first grade. It's just that now I'm being honest with myself."

"What about Karen?" my father asked. Karen had been my best friend in high school. We had been inseparable, and most people thought we were dating, including my mother and father. I did nothing to dispel the notion with either my parents or my friends, but in fact, we had never even kissed. This didn't seem to bother Karen; she never pressed me for anything more.

"Karen was a friend, a good friend," I said, thinking it would be nice to see her again sometime. "Believe me; I wanted nothing more than to be straight—that's what the whole world expects of me—but I'm not, and trying to be something I'm not was making me really unhappy. You want me to be happy, right?" I asked.

"Have you thought about changing, about going to a doctor?" my father asked.

"It's not something I can change; it's who I am," I said. "Do you think you could go to a doctor, and he'd do something or say something to make you homosexual instead of heterosexual?" I asked, quoting one of the lines from the Parents of Gays pamphlet I'd read months ago. And at that point I wasn't going to mention anything about my earlier ignorant attempts to be electroshocked into heterosexuality.

My mother opened the door and came in. It was the first time I'd seen her all night without the apron. Her eyes looked red from crying, and I realized that probably she and my father had discussed this numerous times over the past year, trying to decide when was the right moment to broach the subject. Probably having David come with me today was the last straw.

I took control. "Yes, I was just telling Dad that yes, I'm gay," I said.

Tears began to form in her eyes. "Why did you decide to do this?" she asked.

"It's nothing I decided," I said. "And it's not something I'm doing. It's what I am. The only thing I decided was to stop living a lie, trying to be someone that I wasn't."

"And when did you decide that? After you met David?" she asked.

"No, David—and no one else—had anything to do with it," I said firmly. "It's something I felt inside of me since I was a kid, attracted to other kids at Riverfield Elementary. I've been living this way—as an openly gay man—for a year, and it's been the best year of my life. I've never felt better, been happier, or felt more alive," I told them, remembering back to those miserable weeks with Radofsky trying to change me.

"And what about your job? What's going to happen when they find out?" my father asked, back to his business-like tone.

"They already know," I said. Actually, I wasn't exactly sure about that, but I really didn't think it was a secret any longer. Everyone seemed to know the details of everyone else's personal lives. And not once did anyone ever ask me if I had a girlfriend or try to fix me up. "They don't care. There are a lot of gay people at CBA."

"And what about when you get older?" my mother asked. "Then what? Aren't you going to want to have a family? Who's going to take care of you when you're sick? What about when you get old?"

"Hopefully, I'm going to find someone and fall in love," I said. "And that person's going to love me back. I don't plan to get married and have children just as an insurance policy that someone will be around to take care of me when I'm old."

There was a knock on the door. It was Annie. "Everything okay in here?" she asked.

"Fine," my father replied and thankfully Annie took his word for it. He was still calm and collected, although my mother was sniffling into a Kleenex, one of several she had brought in with her for the occasion.

"I think you should tell your brother and sister," my father said.

"Really?" I responded. "We don't know much about Toby's sex life, do we? And we certainly don't know who Annie's been sleeping with the past six years she's been up in Boston."

"They should know about your decision," he said.

"I told you, it's not a decision," I said. "The decision was to stop lying. And the only change is that now I'm actually having sex I enjoy. With men. So unless you want to have a family meeting where we all sit down at the table and discuss who each of us is having sex with, I don't think I should be under the spotlight."

"And what about us?" my mother asked, dabbing her eyes. "How are we going to feel when everyone finds out? When all our friends are talking about their children?"

"They don't talk about their children's sex lives, right?" I asked.

"Our friends' children are getting married. They're having kids of their own," my mother said. "We want to have grandchildren too."

So that's what the tears were about. "Well, you're lucky that you two had sex more than once, and I'm not an only child," I said. "Hopefully, Annie and Toby will both get busy in bed."

"So this is our fault?" she asked.

"Where in the world did you get that from?" I asked. "I don't think that for a moment. My earliest thoughts, my earliest sexual feelings, going back to five or six years old, were about other boys."

The Kleenex was about to fall apart in her lap.

"Do you think there's something Grandma or Grandpa could have done to make you attracted to women instead of men?" I asked her.

"So no one did anything to you?" she asked.

"No one's ever done anything to me that I didn't want them to do," I said. "No one ever grabbed me in a public toilet." I was remembering her fears about letting me go into the men's room alone at the train station.

"There are doctors who can change you," she said, surprising me that apparently she had been reading up for this day as well.

"I don't want to change," I said. "I don't want to be anyone other than who I really am."

"It's selfish," my mother said. "Thinking only of yourself." She got up to leave the room as the last Kleenex disintegrated.

"Not one thing has changed about me since last Thanksgiving or the Thanksgiving before or the ten of them before that one," I said. "I'm still the same Josh."

After she left, my father asked, "Is David your boyfriend?"

"No, we're just friends," I said. "There's no one special."

"We love you, Josh. Just take care of yourself," my father said. "I'll talk to Mom; she'll come around. We just want you to be happy and to be okay."

That seemed a good note to end it on but it was hard watching my mother cry. And as we left, with her eyes still red, I couldn't help thinking that all those years before, when I had been closeted and miserable, my mother was delighted, content, and proud. And now that I was finally feeling good about myself and able to be happy about who I was, she was in tears.

❧ 11 ❧

On the train back to Grand Central, I recounted the entire episode to David, line by line. He listened, wide-eyed, and my knees were still shaking as I told him the story. It was probably the most dramatic encounter between me and my mother since my birth, and that one I didn't remember.

"I hope it goes as well with my parents," he said.

"I don't know that it went that well," I said, remembering Lillian's red eyes as she stood at the door when we left. "It's not like they could have thrown me out. I'm already living on my own."

"You know what I mean," David said. "Look at Russell. He has to keep it a big secret—his parents still have never spoken with his older brother since he told them."

"Randy was right with what he said about it," I told him. "To wait until they ask. It would have been much worse if I had told them a year ago. I wouldn't have known how to answer their questions."

"They must have figured out what was going on," David said.

"I'm sure they had their suspicions," I said. "And then when they met you, they knew for sure."

David punched me in the shoulder. It was only playful, but I was thinking it felt pretty good to have David touch me and that calmed me down and made me feel better for the rest of the ride.

The end of that first week in December, Jim left a message on the answering machine about a holiday party he and John were having at their apartment the Sunday before Christmas. This would be the first time we'd all be together since the summer.

"Don't worry; it will be early, so unless there's a police raid, you'll be home in plenty of time to get a good night's rest, and it won't interfere with your professional career," Jim said when I called him back, still teasing me about my anxiety last May.

"Is Tommy going to be there?" I asked. I hadn't talked about Tommy in months. If David or Randy happened to ask, I feigned disinterest, pretending I was trying to remember who Tommy even was. But oh, I knew.

"Did you guys ever connect?" Jim asked.

"No, he never called me."

"Hmm, I'm surprised. I thought he would," Jim said. "Well, he might be here. We invited him. With Tommy, you never know."

"Is it okay if I bring my friend David?" I asked. "He's taller than me and better looking too."

"You can bring all the tall good-looking guys you want along with you."

That Sunday brought one of those miserable winter storms in New York, when the forecast had promised the possibility of snow or just rain, but instead it was a sloppy mix of the two—the inconvenience of a winter storm without the beauty of the coating of white. David and I walked over to the 14th Street station. It was rare that the warmth of the subway platform was something to look forward to, but this was one of those nights.

By the time we emerged uptown, the miserable mix was gone, and light snow flurries were falling, already sticking to the roofs of the cars parked along Lexington Avenue. It was just before ten, which David and

I had decided would be the perfect time to arrive for a 9:00 p.m. party on Sunday evening—a school night.

The door wasn't closed completely, and I could hear "Native New Yorker," one of my favorite songs, playing as we walked down the hallway:

Music plays, everyone's dancing closer and closer
Making friends and finding lovers
There you are, lost in the shadows
Searching for someone (searchin' for someone)
To set you free from New York City
You should know the score
You should know the score by now
You're a native New Yorker ...

The apartment was packed, and it seemed much larger than I remembered it the last time I had been there for my pre-share interview, although I had been so nervous that night I didn't recall much.

I spotted Rick in the kitchen, and he waved as we walked in. The party was a mix of Jim's and John's friends, mostly in their forties or fifties, along with some of their regular clients in the same age range or even older, and then at least a dozen or so of "the boys."

Elliot came along with his friend Franklin. There was a buffet table covered with a red tablecloth and candles and filled with platters of food. Lillian Silver would have definitely approved. In front of the fireplace, a bar had been set up, and one of the workers I knew, Adam, poured drinks, wearing no shirt and only a black bow tie around his neck. He remembered me from the summer.

"Hey, Josh, looking good," Adam said with a smile.

David was impressed. The crowd was spread throughout the living room and both of the bedrooms, one of which served as the office for Manhattan Men, as well as John's financial consulting business.

I scanned the room, but didn't see Tommy. I didn't dare say a word to David. I had promised months ago, after talking about him incessantly all through the fall, never to mention Tommy's name again.

David recognized a couple of the guests from "Seventh Avenue," as he referred to anyone else in the fashion business, whether or not they actually worked on Seventh Avenue, which was where most of the big designers were headquartered. Besides Elliot and Franklin, I knew a lot of the people at the party from the summer, including a couple of the boys, in addition to Adam, with whom I'd had quick afternoon trysts in my bedroom before they had to rush back to the city for the evening's appointments. All of them looked great dressed up for the party. Most were very preppie, even the ones who before I had only observed parading around Fire Island in their tiny G-string bathing suits—or less.

It was nearly midnight when Tommy came through the door, alone. I hadn't seen Marlon or any of the rest of "the posse" and had given up any thought that Tommy might show up. He was wearing a beige camel-stitch sweater and jeans. Even through the loose sweater I could see his chest and broad shoulders. David was over on the other side of the living room, but like the others, his head turned toward the door as Tommy walked in. He looked even better than I remembered, though not as dark with the summer tan faded, and his black hair was trimmed more neatly and held in place with shiny gel. Tommy was quickly surrounded, by some of the older men as well as the other boys. Within sixty seconds, he was already the center of attention.

I decided to wait until the excitement of Tommy's arrival died down, so I made my way over to where David was standing.

"That's Tommy," I said. "Tommy Perez. The one I told you about."

David turned back around to look over at him without being noticed; it was a move he and I had both perfected after many nights examining prospective pick-ups for one another while out on the town.

"He's hot, Josh," David said. "You definitely have good taste."

"Thanks."

"You and half the people in the room," David said. "Since that's how many of them here have probably already slept with him. Or have appointments for later this week."

"I knew I could count on you for support."

"Josh, honestly, you've been at this for a while," David said. "If anything, just have a quick roll in the hay with him, and then be done with it. That'll be something you can think about to warm you up when you're alone on cold winter nights."

"I don't want to just be another one on his list," I said. "I want candles, romance—"

"Josh," David cut me off, "you really think this guy is into candlelight dinners and walks in the moonlight?"

"I talked to him that day at the beach," I said. "There's a lot more to him than you think. And anyway, he's going to stop hustling."

"I guarantee you that every one of the call boys in the room would tell you he's going to stop hustling soon."

"Tommy's a smart guy. He would have gone to college if things had worked out differently," I said.

"Yeah, and I could have been the Pope if I didn't like sucking dick," David said. "Do what you want. Just don't tell me about it. Especially after he breaks your heart."

"Nothing ventured, nothing gained," I said. "I'm at least going to go say hello."

Elliot came over. "I thought I'd bring over a napkin to wipe up the drool," he told me.

"David's just finished verbally abusing me, so try to be nice," I said. "Anyway, I'm not drooling, but he does look good. I haven't seen him since Labor Day."

"Once your hard-on goes down, you can walk over and give him a kiss hello," Elliot said. "Hopefully, he'll have some recollection of having met you, although I doubt he'll remember whether or not you were a paying customer."

"Fine," I said. "Thanks to both of you for all of the helpful advice."

"You're really a masochist," David said as I walked away. "Enjoy your suffering."

By midnight, there were probably still at least forty people in the apartment. Rick, serving as DJ for the evening, had turned down the volume on the cassette player. Tommy was standing with a group of three older men. I looked over, and he nodded at me and shook hands with one of the men like he was saying good-bye.

Then he came over and gave me a kiss on the cheek like we were old friends.

"Hi."

I could still remember that first "hi," delivered with the same smile in the water at the Pines more than three months earlier.

"Hi, thanks for making that easy," I told him. "I was afraid I was going to have to try to cut in on your audience."

"How are you, Josh?"

"You remembered my name?" My eyes widened.

"Of course. Do you remember mine?"

"Both of them," I said. "Tommy Hawk and Tommy Perez."

Tommy smiled. "What have you been up to?" he asked.

Telling him that I'd thought about him every day for the past four months didn't seem like a good idea.

"Mostly working. I asked Jim to give you my number," I added, trying to sound as off-hand about it as possible. "It had been nice talking with you that day at the beach. I thought maybe we could get together in the city."

"Yeah, I got the message. I was going to call you, and then I was always busy or never seemed to have a dime for the phone," Tommy said. "And then I lost the number."

"I'll write it down for you tonight," I said. "And you can give me yours."

I wasn't sure if Tommy heard me because he didn't answer, but I picked up the conversation that had been left incomplete on the beach at Fire Island that Labor Day afternoon,

"You had been telling me that story, about how your parents got all upset when they found out you were gay," I said.

"Yeah, big help that faggot priest was when my parents went to talk with him," Tommy said. "He told them they should put me out and treat me as though I was dead."

"And they did?"

"They tossed me out, and I went to live with my aunt, my mother's sister, sleeping on the couch," Tommy said. "My mother—she didn't want to do it. She was crying when I left, but my father's a mean son of a bitch, even to her. He ignores her except when he's ordering her around."

"So what have you been doing the past three years?"

"Now I live with my cousins, work in construction, and I'm trying to save enough money to get my own place. And go back to school."

I was trying to pay attention, but all I was thinking about was how much I wanted to feel Tommy's body next to mine. I reached out and touched his forearm while we chatted. A few people came over to say good-bye to Tommy, but mostly I had him all to myself for the next fifteen minutes. David wanted to go, and when I decided to stay—something

David was very understanding about, because we frequently started the evenings together but finished separately—he walked out with Elliot and Franklin. There were fewer than a dozen people left. In the background, Billy Joel sang "I Love You Just the Way You Are."

"Let's go have a drink somewhere else," I suggested.

"Okay, sure, where?" Tommy asked.

"We can go to Harry's Back East over on Third," I said.

"Let's not go to a gay bar," Tommy said. "I might see people I know and don't want to talk to."

"We'll walk and find some place," I told him, as I could understand that he didn't want to run into any clients.

We said good night, and Jim winked at me as he handed me my coat.

"Don't you have a jacket?" I asked Tommy.

"No, I'm always too hot."

We walked down Third Avenue about one o 'clock on Monday morning. So much for getting to bed early. The snow had stopped, and it was clear. I needed to be at work at CBA in eight hours, but I wasn't thinking about that.

Despite the popular song lyrics about New York being a town that never slept, we walked four blocks and didn't pass one open bar, other than a seedy pub with a flashing neon sign in the window. There wasn't a restaurant open; hardly anyone on the streets.

"Harry's is in the next block," I said. "Let's just go there. There's not going to be anyone there at this hour. And anyway, it's so dark, you can hardly see anything there."

Tommy didn't say anything but the nod seemed to indicate he was okay with that, and I wasn't interested in clarifying it further.

Harry's was deserted. A few people sat at the bar, talking to the bartender. The DJ had finished, and a tape was playing, with the lighting effects on the small dance floor set to automatic. We went to the back, where there were some sofas, to sit down.

"The waiters are already gone for the night," I said, taking charge. "I'll get us drinks; what do you want?"

I got Tommy a Bud Light and ordered the same.

"Cheers," Tommy said as we tapped the bottle necks together.

"I'm glad to get out of the party," I said. "I'd been there a long time. I'm really surprised you remembered me. I've been thinking about you a lot."

"I'm sorry I didn't call you," he said. "I'm bad about stuff like that. Making plans and everything."

I pushed up the sleeves of his sweater, which, if he even noticed, he didn't seem to mind. "I have to admit, though, I feel really self-conscious with you. I just remember Fire Island and everyone looking at you, everyone talking about you," I said, resting my hand on his now-bare forearm.

"They don't know me. They like the way I look. They stare like I'm on a billboard or a magazine cover," he said. "When I talked to you at the beach that day of the party, that was probably the first time anyone had an entire conversation with me all summer out there that didn't include 'fuck' or 'suck.'"

"Okay, you want to fuck?"

"Josh, you're funny," Tommy said. "I like that. And I like that you joke with me. All these guys don't even know me. And they don't care about knowing me."

"Okay, well, I do want to know you," I said. And I started to say more but Tommy grabbed the back of my neck with his hand.

"Don't talk," he said as he pulled his lips against mine.

I rested one hand on the sofa and put the other on Tommy's sweater as we kissed. His lips felt soft, smoother than I imagined, but the chest was just as I dreamed about. It was hard and the more I pushed on it, the more

Tommy flexed it. I could feel his nipples through the sweater. I moved my hand over to feel his bicep, which brought on more flexing. After years of fantasizing about all the guys on the swim team and watching jocks on TV, here he was in flesh and blood, Tommy.

"You feel great."

"Don't talk," Tommy told me again as he thrust his tongue into my mouth. He reached down to rub my cock, and it was completely hard. Tommy touched the tip where a wet spot had already started to ooze through my jeans.

"You're coming?" he asked.

"No, don't worry. It's just pre-cum," I said. "I probably could though. Right here."

Tommy pressed his chest against me so he was nearly on top of me on the sofa, its old frame sagging from the weight of the two of us. Thanks to Radofsky's treatment, a little pain now only made it more erotic for me. I reached up with my other hand so both were rubbing against Tommy's arms as our lips and tongues intertwined.

"This is really different for me," Tommy said. "No one ever really talks to me like you did. And it's kinda exciting that you are getting so turned on by me—like, me, the person, not just the body."

I was doubtful myself whether I'd be there if Tommy didn't have the body that he had, but I certainly didn't intend to mention that. "Let's go back to my place," I told him, trying to catch my breath.

"Where is it?" he asked to my surprise, now seriously getting me even more turned on.

"In the Village. Down on Ninth Street and Fifth."

"Don't you have to work in the morning?" Tommy asked.

"I can be a little late. I'll call in sick."

"That's too far down," Tommy said.

"We can take a cab. We'll be there in less than fifteen minutes."

"I can't call in sick. I've got to be at my regular job at eight o 'clock," Tommy said.

"What's your regular job?" I asked.

"It's construction, same as before," Tommy said. "Don't talk." And I was pumping with excitement as Tommy put his left palm over my mouth and pushed me back against the sofa and began kissing my neck.

"C'mon, let's get out of here," I pleaded. I was ready to pay for a hotel room in the neighborhood if I thought we could find one.

"It's already two o 'clock. I've got to get up at six," Tommy said. "I'll call you. We'll get together this week, I promise."

"Let's just make plans now," I said. "What about tomorrow night?"

"I can't on Monday or Tuesday," Tommy replied. He sounded impatient, like he wanted to leave.

I assumed he had Manhattan Men appointments but didn't ask. I didn't want to know the answer.

"What are you doing Wednesday, for Christmas Eve?" I asked. There was nothing on my calendar. The Silver family had never celebrated the holiday and usually went away to visit my grandparents who spent the entire winter in Miami Beach. And I already knew from what he had told me that there was little chance Tommy would be spending a quiet Christmas at home with his parents.

"Yeah, okay, Wednesday," Tommy said. "Wednesday could be okay."

"Well, can we plan on that?" I asked. "I'll cook, since most everything will be closed."

"I don't know, Josh. It's hard for me to make plans," he said. And that made me start to wonder if Randy and David and everyone else was right. But then, maybe noticing how the expression on my face had changed, he said, "That would be great. I don't think I've had a home-cooked

Christmas Eve dinner in four years—not since my folks tossed me out."

I wrote out the address for him on scrap of paper I got from the bartender.

I put "8:30 Wednesday," underlining the 8:30 and drawing a little heart next to the "y" in Wednesday. Then I crossed it out so he couldn't see it because I thought that probably wasn't Tommy's style.

"Can you write down your number for me?" I asked him.

"I don't have a phone where I live," Tommy said. "I'm sharing a place with three of my cousins. We don't have a phone there."

"So how do I ever get in touch with you?" I asked.

"The service. You just leave me a message, and then I'll call you back," Tommy said.

We walked out to Third Avenue, and Tommy wrapped his arms around me and squeezed tight. "Here's a hug to remember me by," Tommy said. I put my hand around his back, and we kissed again.

"I'm just going to take a cab down," I said. "You're sure you don't want to come with me?"

"Wednesday, my friend," Tommy said. "I'll see you Wednesday."

I walked him over to the subway entrance on Lex. An empty cab was across 77th. We kissed on the lips as I flagged it down. "Call me if anything changes; otherwise, I'll see you Wednesday," I said. From the cab I watched as Tommy headed down the stairs into the subway, wondering if I'd really see him again.

❧ *12* ❧

CBA closed at 1:00 p.m. on Christmas Eve, but even that morning the place was deserted, as few of the executives had bothered to take the train in from the suburbs where most of them lived. Almost nothing happened that entire week at the office; everyone seemed in a state of suspended animation, waiting for January to roll around and the new year to begin.

Carole and Randy were both there, so we went out for a Christmas Eve lunch together. I already had plans to go over to Randy and Gerard's for dinner on Christmas Day. "You're welcome to come over tonight, too, if you don't have anything else on the calendar," Randy told me.

"Or you could come to Queens with the Rubinos," Carole said. "We take in strays too."

I told them I had a date, although I didn't want to bring up Tommy's name again.

"Which one is it?" Randy asked.

"It's someone new," I said. "I don't want to jinx it."

"Oh, you think that's why you're not in love," Randy said. "Because Carole and I cast a spell on you when you tell us about your dates so it doesn't work out?"

"I'll fill you in afterwards, okay?" I told them.

In the mailbox at home was a letter from my mother, written on a monogrammed note card, with the Scarsdale return address engraved in matching blue on the back of the envelope, wishing me a happy new year. She included the name of a psychiatrist she had read about nearby in Connecticut who had great success in "curing" homosexuality. At the word homosexual, there was a blot of ink after the second "o," as though she had paused, unable to write out the word. I put it down on the desk, shaking my head. I had more important things to think about, like getting ready for Tommy Perez.

I had told Tommy I'd make dinner, but really, it was more a matter of selecting prepared dishes at Balducci's, the gourmet food store down the street, and then heating them up.

In the apartment, the kitchen was actually just the back wall of the living room, opposite the French windows overlooking the street. When I rented the place, Irving Feinberg, the landlord, told me he had just renovated, but in a glance I could see that kitchen renovation to Irving was a process that involved considerably less time and money than one would normally expend on such an undertaking. A new range and refrigerator had been stuck into the existing spaces between the old wooden cabinets, and a stainless steel sink had been mounted in a hole that was just a little too big, so large mounds of caulking had been used as filler, caked around the sides and now cracked and discolored.

Irving lived on the parlor floor of the brownstone—the second—with a terrace and high ceilings. He was in his late sixties, a retired stockbroker who had bought the entire brownstone a few years before for $85,000, according to one of my neighbors.

I spent extra time in front of the mirror when I got out of the shower. I had stopped by the gym before picking up the food—not that I was going to have a body like Tommy's no matter how much time I spent working out, but I was in decent shape and, as David used to joke, at least my chest was bigger than my stomach, which put me in the upper half of the pecking order.

I wore my tightest jeans and a flannel shirt. Sometimes when David and I went out, we would roll up the sleeves on our flannel shirts to make our arms look bigger. This time I rolled them just them a few inches toward my elbows. There was no use trying to impress Tommy with the size of my biceps. I'd have to settle for my wit; he had told me he liked that I talked to him and thought I was funny.

At 8:30 I was ready for what I was sure would be the most romantic night of my life. I had gotten a bottle of wine and set two glasses on the counter. I lit the candles on the holiday centerpiece, which had never been used since I bought it at the beginning of the month. The candles glowed in the mirror behind the table. I adjusted the floor lamp with its dimmer and put on my George Benson jazz album.

At 8:45 I was pacing around the apartment, which wasn't easy because there wasn't a lot of floor space to cover. I hadn't talked to Tommy since I'd left him on Sunday night—rather, early Monday morning. But surely he would have called if something had come up. Maybe I could call Jim and find out if Tommy was working. I remembered Jim's telling me that the only days they closed were December 24 and 25. I'd wait until 9:00 p.m. and try the service. Was the answering service even open on Christmas Eve, I wondered.

I looked out the window. The street was empty; as I looked over toward Fifth Avenue, there were hardly any cars. By 9:15 I thought maybe I should call Jim to at least be sure nothing had happened to Tommy. There could have been a construction accident. Or maybe one of the customers had killed him. I called the service. Someone answered right away, but the guy sounded like he was asleep. "Silver, right? Like sterling silver?"

"Yeah, that's right, Josh Silver. Merry Christmas."

"Merry Christmas to you. I don't know if he'll call in tonight, but I'll definitely be sure he gets the message."

I opened the bottle of wine. I figured I might as well enjoy the dinner. I turned on the oven to heat it up and stood by the window with the glass of wine. Maybe Tommy had lost the paper where I had written down the address and was wandering around out on Ninth Street, looking for the building. I could go downstairs to the sidewalk. The fresh air would feel good, but then if Tommy did call, I'd miss him. I could record a special message on the machine, saying the time and that I'd just gone downstairs for a minute. No, that would be a pain. I could just take the phone off the hook. That way, if Tommy called he'd figure I was just talking to someone and know that I was home.

I walked down the stairs, opened the front door, and stepped out on to the sidewalk. The street looked as deserted at ground level as it appeared from four flights up. I hadn't taken a jacket and even with the flannel shirt, I was cold just walking to the corner of Fifth. I circled back to the building and went upstairs. Irving opened his door as I passed the third landing.

"I didn't know you were here," Irving said. "I thought you had gone away."

"No, I'm staying in town," I said. "Merry Christmas, Irving."

"Happy Chanukah," he replied, closing the door.

Back upstairs, the phone was emitting an annoying screeching sound. *There appears to be a receiver off the hook.* I put the handset back in its cradle and poured myself another glass of wine. The bottle was nearly half empty. It was after ten, and I heated up one of the stuffed chicken breasts I had bought for dinner. I blew out the candles and took the food into the bedroom to eat while I watched TV. Or at least, sat in the same room with the TV on, as I had no idea what I was watching.

I didn't eat more than a few bites of the chicken before I put it aside. I wasn't really hungry anyway. I fell asleep in the middle of *It's a Wonderful Life*.

At 11:30 the buzzer rang and woke me up. I stood and my head hurt from all the wine, so much that I put my hand on one of those old childhood cabinets that lined both side walls of the bedroom to steady myself. We didn't have an intercom at the building—just the buzzers. I opened the window and looked down to the steps leading to the entrance. It was starting to flurry outside. "Tommy?" I called out. It did seem like a scene from a movie, but this was not the one I had been dreaming about.

It was him. I pushed the button to unlock the front door and heard the downstairs door slam shut. I hoped Irving was asleep and wouldn't be opening his own door to survey who was climbing the stairs at this hour on Christmas Eve.

Tommy came into view on the stairway.

"I'm sorry, Josh. I really can't explain," he said.

"I bought wine," I said. "Made dinner."

"I know," Tommy said, looking at me with those brown eyes so breathtaking that I couldn't say a word. "I'm really sorry."

"Are you hungry?" I asked. "The food's still in the oven. I can heat it up."

"No, not really," Tommy said. "But is there any wine left?"

I poured him a glass and took what was left in the bottle for myself. I lit the candles in the centerpiece for a second time that night.

"I wish you had at least called me," I said.

Tommy wrapped his arms around me and kissed my lips. I rested on the back of the sofa, putting my hands on Tommy's thighs, which were stretching his jeans to the breaking point.

"I'll make it up to you," Tommy said.

Before I'd dozed off earlier, I had been filled with a mix of worry and anger. But now, with his arms around me, I just wanted to enjoy that feeling of being wanted and protected.

"I'm glad you're here."

"Josh, I'm glad I'm here, too," he said. "I don't want to tell you where I spent the last three Christmas Eves. It didn't involve candles or glasses of wine, though."

Still, I couldn't help but wonder what had happened during the three hours I had been miserably pacing around waiting for him, although I managed to put it out of my mind a few minutes later when he led me to the bedroom, and we both fell to the bed, rolling around together in a tangle of arms, legs, and bodies as our mouths devoured one another. So much for romance. I felt his body pushing me down, his chest pressing against my back, and his muscular thighs wrapped around my legs, and the bed shook with each thrust. I could never remember such ecstasy. I lay there without falling asleep, thinking about what a life together with Tommy might be like. I didn't want to sleep; I wanted to savor every moment that he was lying next to me.

I did finally fall asleep, though I didn't get more than a couple of hours all night. I woke up with Tommy's arm across my chest and lay there just looking at him. I never would have imagined that watching someone sleep could hold my interest this long.

Finally, he started to stir and kissed me on the neck. I went to look through the window. Outside, the flurries had turned into a major snowstorm, totally unpredicted. I got back into bed with Tommy and turned on the TV. As we started kissing again, I heard the newscaster say it was the first white Christmas in New York in more than twenty-five years.

❧ 13 ❧

Tommy didn't have much to say the next morning, other than something about going to some undefined relative's house for Christmas lunch. When I pressed him about it, he held his finger in front of those gorgeous lips to silence me.

"When are we going to see each other again?" I asked.

"Josh, I told you; it's hard for me to make plans."

"But I can't call you, so what I am supposed to do?"

"I'll call you."

I should have left it there, but I pressed him more. "What about next Wednesday, New Year's Eve?" I had been thinking for months how I was hoping not to spend another New Year's Eve alone, without a boyfriend.

Tommy looked up like there was some imaginary calendar there on ceiling. "Okay. Next Wednesday. I'll be here by nine. I promise."

Shortly after he left that morning, I went out to get the *Times*. Like most snowstorms in New York City, the beauty of the initial blanket of whiteness quickly faded and was replaced with a filthy, slushy mess that was nearly impossible to navigate on foot without getting wet.

New Year's Eve afternoon, I turned on the big floor lamp and the holiday twinkle lights in the living room, lit the candles, and put on an album of disco versions of classic Christmas songs. I had gotten a Duraflame log and lit that in the fireplace. By 8:45 I was already dreading a repeat of getting stood up like the week before, but Tommy arrived five minutes before nine and out of breath. He told me he'd run from the subway station, afraid he'd be late.

He wore a big parka, a military-olive color on the outside, bright orange on the inside, with fake fur trim around the edge of the hood. I pulled it off as we kissed, and underneath he wore a gray T-shirt, probably a size too small, so that his biceps seemed like they were bursting through the sleeves. We sat together on the brown sofa, facing the two big windows looking out on Ninth Street.

"Wow. A real fire in the fireplace," he said. "Just like in the movies."

I couldn't picture Tommy watching some romantic old movie, and just the thought was starting to destroy my tough-guy fantasies about him, so I put it out of mind.

As we kissed I felt electrified, touching the smooth skin of Tommy's cheeks. I closed my eyes and lost myself again in what was now becoming a familiar daydream of what our lives together might be like.

The winter was the worst since I'd moved to New York. Other than the big snowfall at Christmas, there had just been annoying mixes of sleet and freezing rain, mixed with clear, sunny days, accompanied by biting-cold temperatures. And indoors, things hadn't been much better for me. At work my routine had been turned upside down because I had a new contact person to deal with at Pontiac, Edna—or "Miss Edna," as we called her when she wasn't around. She was an overweight, unattractive, middle-aged woman who had never married and seemed to fill up the lonely void of her weekends by demanding emergency meetings and conference calls with the agency nearly every Saturday. She especially seemed to enjoy bossing around the men at CBA as a salve for all the pain she had suffered from the male species in her personal life.

My personal life had become even more agonizing; I was totally at Tommy's mercy. I called the service occasionally to leave a message, but I didn't know why I bothered. Each of the operators at the answering service knew me by name, and they never even had to ask for my number. "We'll tell him when he calls," they'd sigh, sounding as though they were sharing my pain, even though they'd never met Tommy in person. If they had, I was sure they would understand my obsession.

Then again, Randy, who of course had met Tommy in person, had gotten to the point where he refused to let me mention Tommy's name.

"You may as well be sharing your angst over some fictional character you read about in a novel," he said. "That's how real your Tommy is to everyone else."

I'd become a slave to my own answering machine, racing up the stairs at the end of the day to see if the red light was flashing. Although I had given Tommy my office number at CBA so he could call me there during the day, he never did.

The nights he did call, it would usually be sometime between eleven and twelve; he'd come over, we'd talk first for a while, sometimes—but not always—have sex, and then sleep before Tommy would leave at 6:30 to go to work. When we did have sex, which was almost always initiated by me, I really enjoyed it, but I guess for Tommy that wasn't the big attraction for his coming over to see me. I wasn't really sure what he was getting out of it since we spent little time together when we weren't either sleeping or fucking.

I knew Randy would just say that Tommy needed a place to sleep that night, but it wasn't like Tommy was homeless. He didn't carry much with him when he came over and was always wearing different clothes, usually pretty nice ones. And even the nights when we didn't have sex, we still would sit and talk—no matter how late he arrived—for at least an hour or so over a glass or two of wine.

Sometimes when he left, if I was lucky, he'd predict when we might see one another again. "I'll probably come by on Thursday," he'd say, and I would get home from work, shave, get dressed, and wait for the phone to ring all night.

David was losing patience with me. "You're not going to go out tonight so you can be home in case he decides to grace you with his presence?"

Randy and Carole at the office were even less tolerant. When the three of us went out to lunch the day before Washington's Birthday weekend, Randy said, "Let's have a Tommy moratorium. Not only are you not allowed to mention his name for the entire lunch, but you're also not allowed to think of him."

"Or of Edna," Carole added, as the oppressive client contact at Pontiac was the other one making my life miserable.

"Here's the deal," Randy said. "If you don't talk about Tommy or Edna for the entire lunch, Carole and I pay for it. If you do, you take both of us out."

"Okay," I said. "Fine. I get the message."

"And if you never talk about Tommy the rest of the year, if I never have to hear his name, I'll give you five hundred dollars."

Carole laughed. "I wouldn't worry about saving up for that," she told Randy.

Tommy came by the next evening, and while no one else believed me, I was sure there was something special with him that just needed more time to blossom for both of us. I wanted to love, and Tommy wanted to be loved. It seemed so perfect, or at least that was the way I hoped I could make it. But by March, the reality of the situation with Tommy, helped along by the constant badgering of Randy and David, led me to start losing interest.

It was still easy to close my eyes and think of him, but not one shred of the fabric of the life I had fantasized when Tommy was lying in bed that Christmas morning had come true. We had never spent time together with any of my friends. In fact, we had never even been outside of the apartment together since our drink at the bar that first evening after Jim's party.

But every time that winter that I said to myself this was it, that I wasn't going to put up with it anymore, Tommy must have sensed it, and he would call that night or the next and come over, often bringing me a single rose. I wondered where he got them at that hour.

"It's simple," Randy told me. "The client he sees right before he comes over to meet you plucks it out of some gorgeous arrangement in his Park Avenue apartment and hands it to Tommy with the seventy-five dollars as he holds the door open for him to leave."

The force that Tommy seemed to have over me was startling. I wasn't used to being in a situation so out of my control. I felt powerless and I hated that. Tommy promised me he was going to stop hustling, always setting deadlines that seemed to come and go. Once, he brought over a City College catalog to show me he was serious about going to school in September.

But I had to admit that Randy and David were right—not only that waiting for Tommy to phone me all the time was torturous for me, but also that my obsession with Tommy was keeping me from meeting anyone who might actually turn out to be the real-life partner I was seeking.

"And on top of that, you're also not going to have any friends left," David had told me. "We're all sick about hearing how Tommy's going to change and go back to school. You can bring me his first report card, and I'll then believe it."

Randy would just hum the tune "I'm Gonna Wash That Man Right Outta My Hair."

"Just be obnoxious and self-confident," he told me, "the way you are at work."

But the truth, apparent to me and maybe me alone, was that in matters of the heart, I didn't have that same self-confidence I had at the office.

"Throw away his phone number," Randy said. "The service will probably send over a gold wristwatch or some other gift to thank you for never calling again. And for God's sake, change your own number so he can't call you."

"I don't want to change my number—I've had that since I moved to New York," I told him.

"Oh, please," Randy said. "You should get over that; it's done all the time when one wants to start all over again."

❧ 14 ❧

I didn't change my phone number, deciding it would be too hard to explain at CBA and especially to my parents. Anyway, I had accepted the fact that Tommy was not going to be my lover, that I was lucky just to be able to have this gorgeous guy in my life a few times a month. Sexually, I was still excited just by looking at him and if I didn't do the same for him, he got off from my being so turned on and kept telling me how much he liked talking in bed with me afterwards. I didn't speak about Tommy to Randy or David, as I knew they were both tired of hearing about him. Sometimes I'd mention to David, very casually, "Tommy came over last night." To Randy, not a word.

Tommy called maybe once a week, even less frequently than before. I had started going out with other men, including one, Daniel, who was a lawyer and Jewish. Lillian would be thrilled, as he met all of the requirements for a perfect mate for me, except for the one big gender problem, of course. But he was definitely presentable at the dinner table in Scarsdale or at Temple Shalom. Moving up to the "going out" category only meant that he was someone I saw more than once. One night, when Tommy called, Daniel was there, so I told Tommy I couldn't see him.

When I mentioned it to David the next evening at Uncle Charlie's, he slapped me on the back. "Whoa!" he said. "I didn't know you had it in you. Drinks are on me the whole night."

"He sounded kind of hurt," I said.

"Yeah, well, I'm sure not too many people tell Tommy Perez not to come over when he calls, offering to show up at their door," David said. "And he was probably shocked you finally had the guts to say it to him."

We surveyed the bar. Despite the fact that Daniel had stayed over the night before and just left that morning, I was on the prowl for more. I usually got bored once someone was actually interested in me; it was the hunt and the pursuit that I liked the best, just as Randy had predicted.

"And I definitely wouldn't sit around waiting for him to call," David said. "Once Tommy knows you won't drop everything to see him, he's going to lose interest real fast."

But Tommy did call, although the relationship, or whatever it was we had together, changed. I had pretty much stopped thinking about our future life together. I was starting to realize it probably wasn't going to be much different from the present.

There was no more discussion about Tommy's going back to school or quitting Manhattan Men. He still loved to talk and continued to laugh at my jokes and, for me, there was nothing better than lying next to Tommy with my head resting on his arm wrapped around the back of my neck, and his body pushed up against mine in the bed. But I no longer looked at what we had as the prelude to something else—something bigger, something better. This was it.

Jim called at the beginning of April to see if I wanted to share the house with them again. "We got the same place, and it's only going up a little, so it would be eighteen hundred dollars for the bedroom all summer."

"Sounds pretty good," I told him. I told Jim I'd get back to him by the end of the week—I had wanted to see if I might arrange something else. I had been thinking about trying to organize a summer rental on my own, wondering if I could share a place with Elliot, maybe Franklin or someone else, David, and a couple of other people yet to be determined.

In the end, no one was willing to make a commitment, and I called Jim and told him I'd like the room again for the summer. Franklin had thought he might be going to LA a lot for his job, Elliot was still helping out on the phones at Manhattan Men and decided it would just be easier to be there sharing with Rick, and David had told me he just didn't have the extra money to spend.

"Well, there's always Manhattan Men," I told him. "That could solve all your financial problems."

David laughed.

Elliot joined me on the trip from the city that first weekend. Although it was nearly 7:45 when we got on the ferry, it was still light outside and warm enough to be up on the top deck of the boat. Talking together on the train ride out, I realized how much I had missed Elliot during the winter. He read a lot and was always talking about the latest book or a story in that week's *New Yorker* magazine. Last year he had given me all the old copies, but I couldn't get into reading the stories. I'd flip through them, look at the cartoons, and then throw them on a huge pile of magazines, read and unread, that accumulated all summer next to the couch.

Although we hadn't gotten together very often in the city, we spoke by phone occasionally, and Elliot knew bits and pieces of the affair with Tommy. It was actually faster to get home to my parents in Scarsdale than it was to get to Elliot's apartment on 106th and Broadway, up by Columbia University, where he had gone to grad school. And if I did make it up to Elliot's, there was no place for us to go out, as the nearest gay bar was the Wildwood on Columbus and 74th.

Occasionally, Elliot would come to the Village, sometimes bringing along Franklin, who also lived uptown, and we'd meet for a drink. Sometimes it seemed to me that Elliot and Franklin were a lot more than friends, but Elliot said they had never slept together. "It's the same as with you and David," Elliot told me. "The way you are when you're together with one another, anyone who doesn't know better would swear you two are lovers."

The lights of the Pines harbor came into view, and I stood by the railing, remembering the anticipation of last summer, like a little kid going to summer camp for the first time, worried about whether the other boys would be nice to me. I was an old pro at the game now, feeling a little embarrassed when I thought back to how naïve I had been the year before.

Walking down Fire Island Boulevard, I told Elliot how I couldn't believe I had made such a big deal about Manhattan Men. "Don't worry about it," Elliot told me. "I'm surprised you're still thinking about that."

"I was just thinking about it now, walking back to the house," I said.

"I can understand; it was something you had never been exposed to before," Elliot said. "I was pretty shocked when Rick first told me about it. And then after a while, you realize they're all pretty decent guys, both the boys and the customers."

"Yeah, that's true," I said.

"If you're old and alone in your fifties, it's probably pretty nice to be able to call Manhattan Men and have a hot little gym bunny show up at your doorstep," Elliot said. "And for the boys, most of them are making more money than they could doing anything else."

I nodded in agreement, but I wondered whether I was losing my good judgment, if my moral compass had gone astray after a year of Manhattan

Men and the infatuation with Tommy.

When we got to the house, it was as if someone had played back an old movie of the previous year. Jim was sitting at the round table behind the sliding glass doors, drinking a beer and reading a magazine, which turned out to be *GQ*, just like the first weekend the year before. I teased him about it. "It's not still the same issue, is it?" I asked.

"No," Jim laughed as he stood up to hug both of us.

Elliot and I had picked up a pizza at the dock, and we went outside on the deck to eat on the table under the tree where I had spent so many mornings last summer recounting the previous night's escapades.

"And the phones?" I asked.

"Tomorrow," Jim said. "Supposedly. And then we'll switch over the lines."

After dinner, I took a joint out of the plastic case I had brought from the city, and Elliot joined me as we walked over to Randy and Gerard's. As expected, in addition to the four housemates, there were a dozen other people on the deck. It wasn't even Memorial Day and already their house was the center of the Pines summer social scene.

I went out to the island every weekend in June, usually making the trip by myself, as CBA had started summer hours but Elliot didn't get off work until five o'clock, and Randy would usually take the bus later in the afternoon with Gerard.

I got back into the scene, following the rituals of the tea dance and then back to the Sandpiper at midnight or 1:00 a.m., except on Saturdays, when I'd try to find someone to make the trek with me over to the Ice Palace in Cherry Grove. I still never had sex outdoors in the meat rack, anonymous or otherwise. I was willing to give up romance for a quickie with a hot guy but not enough to just do it in the dark amid the prickly bushes, the mosquitoes, and the wandering wildlife.

On days when the weather wasn't good enough to go to the beach, Elliot liked to roam about the island with me. One day we walked east to Water Island, another community with some gays but zero social life; the place you might go to rent when you were tired of the constant preening required in the Pines. Another time we walked through Cherry Grove, west to the Sailor's Haven ranger station, where uniformed Park Service employees gave tours of the flora and fauna to visiting families, and then on to Point O'Woods, a notoriously old-money heterosexual community. Randy loved that even the Pines, filled with lust and sex and drugs, was part of the Fire Island National Seashore, administered by the Interior Department.

"When you see how much they take out of your paycheck in taxes every two weeks," Randy had told me, "you can at least take comfort in knowing that a few pennies go to maintain that gorgeous stretch of white sand at the Pines beach. It'll make you feel better."

The last weekend in June was the tenth anniversary of the '69 Stonewall riots, and I decided I wouldn't go out to Fire Island. The Christopher Street Liberation Day parade had been getting bigger and bigger each year and had now been moved off Christopher Street and over to Fifth Avenue, just like the big St. Patrick's Day parade in March and the Columbus Day parade in October. It had been renamed the Gay Pride parade, and I got goose bumps the Thursday night before when I had watched from my apartment window while city workers painted a purple stripe down the length of Fifth Avenue.

Actually, it felt relaxing on Friday afternoon, not to be rushing to Penn Station when CBA closed at one o'clock. I took the subway downtown, went to the gym, and afterwards, since it was still only 5:00 p.m. and sunny outside, I went for a walk down Christopher Street. A lot of people had already come in to the city for the weekend festivities, and the sidewalk was crowded. Pink and purple flags were hung on the storefronts and from the fire escapes on many of the buildings.

In front of the bar at the end of the street, Badlands, there was a large crowd of men standing on the sidewalk, most of them drinking beer. The elevated West Side Highway had just been taken down, so now the sun shone brightly on the crowd from over the Jersey City skyline across the river. The empty trucks from all the meatpackers in the neighborhood could no longer park under the rusting structure. I'd heard how the trucks had been the scene of late-night trysts and supposedly, most of the businesses had taken to leaving the backs of the trucks unlocked so they wouldn't be damaged by people trying to get inside. No longer would guys leaving the bar say they were going "to the trucks."

Out on the sidewalk at Badlands, I saw Elliot's friend Franklin, and we talked for a while. Elliot had gone out to the house to help Rick with the phones on what was expected to be one of the busiest weekends of the year. I had been learning the intricacies of the prostitution business and generally, Monday to Thursday nights were the busy ones. Many of the customers were either married men trying to sneak in an evening of pleasure before heading home to their wives and kids in the suburbs, or they were businessmen, often in New York on a business trip, where no excuses would be necessary about having to stay late at the office that particular evening.

At seven, I left to walk back up Christopher Street and then cut over to Waverly to the old Julius bar, where I had made plans to meet up with David after he got off work. Inside, the walls at Julius were covered with newspaper articles and photos from decades before, and the most of the crowd hailed from the same era. It was supposedly the oldest gay bar in the city. Julius was unusual in that they served burgers, and it started to

fill up earlier than any of the other nearby bars, so even afternoons—
especially on weekends—were usually quite busy.

I was standing in the back, listening to Cher sing "Take Me Home,"
when David walked in the side door. He had on a black tank top and
had gotten serious about working out over the winter. With rounded
shoulders now on his tall frame, he turned heads as he walked over and
gave me a kiss.

"You're starting early today," David said, glancing at the beer in my hand.

"Well, it's Gay Pride," I said. "We have to celebrate." Actually, for me
it wasn't unusual to have my first drink around now, the only difference
being that instead of a beer, generally it was a Black Label on the rocks at
Company.

"Get a drink here to have with me while I finish this one," I told David.
"And then we'll walk down to Badlands. It was packed when I went by—
everyone was out on the sidewalk."

"That sounds good."

"And we can see the sunset down there. It'll be very romantic," I teased.

The crowd outside Badlands had grown and spilled out into the street.
Around the corner, the other bars on West Street were also crowded early:
Keller's, Sneakers, and the Ramrod all had groups of men in T-shirts and
jeans standing outside. It was warm enough to wear shorts, but no one
ever did that in the city. At least, not the men.

Around ten David tried to convince me to go over to the Anvil, down
at the west end of 14th Street, with him to dance. I was exhausted, so I
told him I was going to go home to take a shower and then maybe meet
up with him later. But we both knew that once I got home and climbed
those stairs, a return trip the same evening was unlikely.

Saturday night, we went to Flamingo together, and I picked up a
cute young guy from Los Angeles. I met David on Sunday morning at

Bagel And for breakfast, thinking it was only appropriate to do so in the spot where gay liberation all began. Hardly anyone else knew that, and I wouldn't have either, if Randy hadn't told me. There was no plaque to indicate that it had been the site of the Stonewall Bar. David had gone home with someone else from out of town, too—a guy from Denver, staying at the Plaza Hotel—and we compared notes from the night before over our coffee.

The rest of the weekend, I enjoyed walking around with David, and the weather on Sunday for the parade was magnificent—clear blue skies. Randy had told me that for the past ten years, it had never rained on the Sunday of the Stonewall anniversary celebrations. "See?" Randy had said. "God loves us after all."

The parade started with a group of lesbians on motorcycles, "Dykes on Bikes," followed by the mayor and some city officials. The sidewalks along Fifth Avenue were filled with onlookers, a lot of straight couples and families. People waved the new rainbow flags, which had just begun to be used as a symbol for gay pride, and you could see variations of the multicolored striped banner hanging from windows and balconies overlooking the parade route.

The crowd erupted into cheers as Mayor Koch walked past, taller than anyone else around, and with his large bald head and dark suit he stood above the rest of the crowd as he waved. He and his entourage were followed by thousands of marchers behind banners, identifying groups from different states and countries. Koch was a single man, rumored to be homosexual, but Randy had his doubts.

"Unless he's never had sex in his life, there'd be no way that's not gotten past the rumor stage by now," he told me.

There was a gay marching band and clubs ranging from gay chess players to runners. Rollarena, a drag queen on roller skates and a familiar sight in the West Village, went by, twirling a baton.

A flatbed truck passed, with five guys dancing in Speedos and large speakers blasting out the music from Donna Summer's "Hot Stuff." The crowd blew whistles and cheered. There were policemen on every corner, and they were smiling, too.

A big cheer went up when the contingent from the Parents of Gays group went by. I was relieved to see Lillian and Herb weren't there marching.

The next Friday was already Fourth of July weekend, and back at the Pines, at Tea Dance, I saw Daniel, the lawyer I had gone out with a few times in the spring, and we reconnected. He was around the entire weekend and ended up spending a good deal of it in my bedroom, although when Sunday came and he left to go back to the city, I was glad to see him go.

I had learned to enjoy sex without the expectation that it was ever going to lead to anything more, although that hadn't diminished the burning desire to find the love of my life and settle down. I was trying to follow Randy's advice. "Stop looking for it," he had told me. "And that's when you'll find it."

The ones who wanted to get serious, like Daniel, were never the ones who really interested me. "You just have to accept that we're eights, always pursued by fives or less and chasing after the nines and tens," David said, using the numerical rating system we now used to rank other men's sexual attractiveness when we went out together.

Certainly over the summer on Fire Island, no one was too serious. The Pines was a big gay sexual playground. Even Gerard, who rarely said much to me when I was over there, told me, "For heaven's sake, stop thinking so much and just enjoy it—you're not going to have another summer at twenty-six again in the Pines for the rest of your life."

So I did. Helped along by marijuana, alcohol, and the occasional Quaalude, I learned to relax and enjoy sex with lots of anonymous partners. I still didn't go to the meat rack in the middle of the night, as I at least wanted to see what they looked like and anyway, it wasn't hard to meet people at parties, Tea Dance, or even on the ferry ride over.

The boys from Manhattan Men were around that year too, but not Tommy or any of that group. I didn't see Marlon, Rafael, or Eddy the entire summer. I was no longer embarrassed about being at the Manhattan Men house; instead, I wore it like a badge of pride among those who knew. And Randy and Gerard's houseguests always stared wide-eyed when I would tell them stories, egged on by Randy's revelation of the Manhattan Men connection. I couldn't resist embellishing them a little for the audience. No one seemed to believe anyway that the house wasn't full of prostitutes and non-stop fucking all weekend, and I didn't want to disappoint them.

Still, I couldn't help thinking about Tommy. Each time I walked by the Manhattan Men house, I remembered that first afternoon I saw him, and I'll admit, there wasn't a day spent lying on the sand, looking at the ocean there, that thoughts of him didn't enter my mind at least once.

At the end of August was Beach, an elaborate outdoor event promoted as the most extravagant party of the decade, being held to raise money for the Pines Volunteer Fire Department. Preparations had begun the weekend before, with construction of a huge dance floor on top of the sand by the ocean. The weather on Saturday evening was perfect; the humidity from the day before had cleared, and I could pick out the constellations overhead that I remembered from Boy Scouts as the whole group of us from the house walked over to the party at a little past eleven.

The dance floor was surrounded by a dozen forty-foot posts with triangular pink banners that waved in the breeze. White netting was strung from each of the posts to a taller one in the center so it looked like an imaginary circus tent, bathed in red spotlights that projected from each of the four towers, which held the speakers facing the dance floor from each corner.

The party was sold out and by midnight, it was filled with two thousand people, nearly all men. Many had taken off their shirts and danced just in their jeans—the temperature was still about seventy at that hour. Champagne and beer were passed around in plastic cups.

The advertising posters promised surprise entertainers. That was the night I heard "Come to Me" for the first time, performed live by France Joli. And just as the party was coming to a close at 2:00 a.m., a helicopter touched down on the beach. Bonnie Pointer went on stage and the crowd cheered as she closed the set with "Heaven Must Have Sent You."

I walked home alone that night, and the next morning after the beach party, as I was sitting outside on the back deck reading the *Times*, Elliot came out with his cup of coffee.

"Have you heard from Tommy?" he asked me.

"No. Why?"

"It's strange," Elliot said. "Rick's saying they haven't heard from him in weeks."

"I haven't heard from him in nearly three months," I told him, but just the thought of people talking about Tommy sent an electric jolt through my body.

"I guess Jim had one number for an aunt who lived somewhere in the Bronx, but it's disconnected," Elliot told me.

"You know," I said. "I never even knew his address or the name of the company he worked for. Some construction business up there."

"I didn't even know anything about his having another job," Elliot said.

"What about the other guys he was friends with? Rafael or Marlon or

Eddy?" I asked.

"Eddy is the only one still working for them," Elliot said. "Marlon and Rafael are still going strong; they moved together to Boston when Marlon got a full scholarship for this graduate architecture program at MIT."

"And what about Eddy? Did he know anything about Tommy?" I asked.

"Rick called him, but he hadn't heard from him either," Elliot said. "I guess that wasn't unusual, according to Eddy. It's not like Tommy is big on regular communications with anyone."

"That's for sure," I said. "Although did he manage to call the service every night to pick up his jobs."

"That's what Rick thought was strange. He'd been one of the more dependable ones in a group that's not exactly known for being conscientious," Elliot said.

Jim and John would always tease Elliot when he used a big word. "Let's see, how many syllables was that?" Jim would say, counting off each one on his fingers as he sounded out the word.

"I'll call you guys if I hear anything, but he's pretty much crossed off my list, and it seems like I'm off his—unless I want to hire him sometime," I said.

"And now you might even be too late for that," Elliot said. "He's not even working."

Again that summer I arranged again to take the week before Labor Day off from CBA and spend it out at the house. By the time the annual Labor Day barbeque rolled around, Tommy still hadn't been heard from, and Eddy didn't show up but had told Rick he'd heard in the neighborhood that Tommy had gone to stay with a sister in Pittsburgh.

Pittsburgh? I didn't know anything about a sister in Pittsburgh. Actually, what did I care? The summer had been great, especially free of being tormented about Tommy. Thinking back on the spring, I was embarrassed I had put up with the way he treated me all those months. It was clearly a hopeless situation, and yet I refused to just close the door and move on. I seemed to be able to make all the right decisions, except when it came to love.

Once I heard Tommy's name, it was just like someone flipped a switch in my brain so that normal functioning ceased and some magic fluid began to circulate in my skull that blocked all rational thought—or nearly all thoughts unrelated to Tommy.

By the end of the vacation, as I helped pack up the house on the weekend after Labor Day, I was thinking this might be my last summer with Jim, John, and the boys. We put on the Bonnie Pointer cassette we had bought after her performance at Beach. If I came back to Fire Island next summer, it would be my own house. And not alone, I hoped. I was getting tired of the single life.

I've cried through many endless nights
Just holding my pillow tight
Then you came into my lonely days
With your tender love and sweet ways
Now I don't know where you come from, baby
Don't know where you been now, baby
Heaven must have sent you into my arms

❧ 15 ❦

The city came alive again in the fall and just as I had been excited in May about getting out of the city and going away for the weekends, now I was looking forward to that first Friday in September when I didn't have to dash off to Penn Station. My boss, Scoot, had given me theater tickets for *The Best Little Whorehouse in Texas* on Broadway, and I invited David to go with me Saturday night.

Autumn was my favorite season in the city, especially October. The weather was cool but still comfortable most days. It got dark earlier, but I liked that better than getting out of work when it was still light outside. New York was a city best enjoyed after nightfall; I hated it during the summer months when I would get home from work, and it would stay light until 9:30 or later. It was one thing when I was growing up and the extra hours of daylight meant time to play tennis or go swimming. But now, playtime for me no longer required sunlight.

It also seemed like the most romantic time of year in New York. It wasn't like the forced romanticism of Valentine's Day with its red hearts and teddy bears, but the cooler nights, changing leaves, and the smell of wood burning in the many fireplaces all seemed to promise that love was just around the corner. While looking for romance I had managed to enjoy fleeting sexual escapades; it had been two years now since that first night at Company and I had probably slept with more than fifty men; at least, that was what I thought until David corrected me.

"Let's say you went out an average of four nights a week, right?" David said.

"Okay, so that's about two hundred nights in the year," I calculated.

"Right, and then you went home with someone at least one of four," David said. "Around one a week."

"Yeah."

"So then that's at least a hundred men."

"Yeah, but there were repeats, like Daniel; plus, during my infatuation period with Tommy, I didn't go out."

"But some weeks you slept with more than one person, so it evens out," David said. "Anyway, I'm sure you've been with more than a hundred guys. Make a list."

I decided I'd definitely do that on my yellow notepad the next time I was bored during a meeting at CBA. In some ways, it was depressing; all those men and not one potential lover. And Tommy was nothing more than a fantasy. Hell, I didn't even know where he lived.

No, I was never going to find the love of my life one smoky night at Uncle Charlie's. I had seen the classified ads in the back of the *Village Voice* each week; now I was thinking I should give one of those a try. There were also classifieds in the pink pages of the pull-out section of the *Advocate*, but I figured the *Voice* made more sense, as it circulated mostly just here in the city.

Randy wasn't too keen on the idea. "I told you that it's when you're not looking that you're going to find love," he said. "Totally unexpected, he'll walk into your life." Still, he helped me compose the ad. I looked through some of the others to get some idea of how they were written and came up with a draft, being sure to include my status as a nonsmoker in the hope of attracting the same.

GWM, 26, seeks same under 30, to enjoy NYC and live happily ever after together. 6', 180, NS, work out regularly and in good shape; you should be too. Your photo gets mine.

As usual, Randy had suggestions. "What's with the cut-off at thirty?" he asked. Then holding up his chin in a pose, he said, "There are attractive men over thirty out there, you know. At the very least, I'd make it thirty-five. And why limit it to gay white males? Tommy wasn't exactly the whitest guy in the room, and you didn't have any trouble falling in love with him."

"I wasn't in love," I corrected him, although I guess I probably had been. "Anyway, we're not allowed to talk about Tommy, remember?" It was nice to be able to joke about it without feeling anxious and tense.

"Yeah, you're right," he said. "I just think your tastes aren't as narrow as you make them out to be. There's a dark side to Josh Silver."

In the end, I kept the "seeks same" for GWM but did increase the age to thirty-five and took out the NS. "Look, almost everyone smokes," Randy told me. "It's going to be hard enough to find the right person. Then you can always send him to Smokenders—or maybe he'll just stop for love." Randy chuckled to himself, tapping his cigarette on the side of the ashtray.

I walked over to the office and paid the $15 in cash to run it for two weeks. The woman taking the ad suggested I include my first name. "That way, they can write you a more personal note, like 'Dear Josh,' instead of just 'Hi' or 'Dear GWM,'" she said. "It's just a suggestion."

I decided against it. Having my name in there, even just my first name, seemed to work against the anonymity of the whole thing. I had begged Randy not to tell Carole. "I don't want anyone to know about it," I said. But of course, I told David.

"I think it's a mah-vah-lous idea, dah-ling," David said, imitating some movie diva, only making it sound even more exaggerated with his accent. It was a Saturday morning, and we were sitting at the ZZZ coffee shop on the corner of 11th Street and University Place. David and I called it "the three Z's," although when I heard the cashier answering the phone for takeout orders, she would always say "Zee-Zee-Zee," sounding out each letter. It was one of dozens of Greek coffee shops around the city that all seemed to have revolving, illuminated display cases of pies covered with mountains of meringue and whipped cream, plus stacks of blue-and-white paper coffee cups with pictures of the Acropolis.

Lots of times David and I would meet there for a late breakfast on Saturday or Sunday if we didn't feel like going to Christopher Street, to the Bagel And, or the Potbelly Café. There was a $1.99 special during the week for eggs, bacon, toast, and coffee that increased to $2.99 on weekends. "Such a deal," David would say, imitating the Jewish accents of his bosses and making me laugh.

The other attraction at ZZZ was the waiter, probably a son of the owner, definitely Greek, tall and hunky with curly black hair. He would roll up the sleeves on his white uniform to show off his arms and always had a big smile for me and David. David used to refer to him as "diner boy," and he was one other standard for comparison that we would use when out surveying the bar crowd: "Not as cute as diner boy."

It was after a breakfast like that on a drizzly Saturday three weeks later that we went back to my apartment to look through the responses to my classified ad. I had been stopping by the *Village Voice* office every few days to pick them up, and although there had been more than a hundred in total, there was only a single one the afternoon before, and I was pretty sure I was at the end of the reply cycle.

The letters were all spread out on the table. I had sorted them into five piles: definite, maybe, and no—by far the largest of the stacks. The definites and maybes had then been filtered into the ones with photos and those without.

"I like this one," David said, reaching for one of the photos I had paper-clipped together with the original envelope and the letter. It was one of the longer letters, and it was typed, nearly a full page.

"That's one of the rejects," I said. "He's all yours."

"What's wrong with him?" David asked.

"I don't know," I said. "We almost never like the same guys when we're out. I guess he's too German, too Aryan-looking."

"You're worried he'll have swastika flags hanging over his bed?"

"No, you know I like that Mediterranean look or the Latin guys."

"Yes, dear," David said. "We know. But what's Lillian going to say when you bring him home to Scarsdale?" David read the letter. "His name is Hendrik, and he lives in Brooklyn." "Well, see?" I said. "That's another minus-ten right there."

I hadn't actually used a point system, but I had read all the letters unless the photograph provided grounds for an immediate disqualification. Even the ones without photos I read through, and a few of them sounded like they had real potential. I figured they were reluctant to send a photo to a total stranger, as I probably would have been too. Like a teacher correcting students' papers, I went through them with my red pen, underlining high points and lows, marking them with either a check for positive or an X for negative. If they included a phone number, I circled that.

People who lived in Manhattan got a check. South of 14th Street, two checks. A college graduate, check. Professional job, double check.

Just coming out, X. Married, XX. Mentioned something romantic like candlelight dinners or walks on the beach, double check.

I showed David my system.

"Honestly, Josh," he said. "You're too much."

"I had to have a way to sort through them and keep track."

"No wonder they love you at CBA," David told me. "You're Mister Organization. Was there anyone we know?"

"One," I said. "That guy Daniel, the lawyer I went out with last year."

As we sat at the table looking through them, David commented on my evaluation of each. When we were done I had reconsidered at least a dozen, shifting them among the definite, maybe, and no stacks, so that when we finished, nearly an hour and a half later, there were twelve in the definites pile, eight of them with photos. David left to go do some errands, and I decided I might as well get started and try calling some of the ones with photos and phone numbers. I had sent him off with Hendrik's letter and photo.

"You might as well take it," I said. "I'm definitely not going to call him." David folded the letter up and stuck it in the back pocket of his jeans. They were tight around his ass and looked particularly good on him that afternoon.

The ones who had sent work numbers, I couldn't call until Monday, and I guessed they were probably married or lived at home with their parents, so I wasn't too optimistic about them anyway. The first one I called, Barry in Queens, seemed like a good candidate. Barry was Jewish (check, check) and was an accountant who worked at one of the big accounting firms in Lower Manhattan. We spoke for about fifteen minutes—about coming out, about whether our parents knew (Barry's didn't), and whether we went out a lot to bars (I lied). We made plans to meet after work on Tuesday. I got him to agree to come to my neighborhood and meet at the Cedar Tavern, which was a straight bar and a pretty old one at that, around the corner on University Place next to ZZZ. Barry really sounded great on the phone, and I was looking forward to Tuesday.

But when the time came, Barry was the first one to reveal to me that it's possible for exceedingly unattractive people to take a very appealing photo, if the lighting and angles are just right and God happens to be extremely kind to them for a moment. Barry was nice enough, with the same self-deprecating humor that I had found so appealing over the phone. Herb and Lillian would have loved him, looking like he could have just walked out of Leonard's of Great Neck following a bar mitzvah.

But there was zero physical attraction, and once I realized that, within five seconds of our meeting, the conversation, which had come so easy over the phone, was difficult to keep going. My original plan had been to get Barry to meet me near the apartment, so if things had clicked, we could have gone home right then and gotten right to work on starting our relationship together. But nothing was going to happen with Barry, and after about a half hour, I looked at my watch and excused myself, telling him I had to meet my friend David for dinner.

"Am I going to see you again?" Barry asked.

"Sure," I said. "I'll give you a call." But I guess we both knew that I wouldn't.

Most of the others followed the same formula. I would talk to them over the phone, picture them as the perfect lover, and then have reality come along and quickly destroy my fantasies once we met. Generally, they actually did look like the photos they had sent; I realized that I was the one who was really building up their potential appeal— I had expectations that were probably unlikely any mortal could fulfill.

Still, I felt guilty enough that, having lured them to the Cedar Tavern or some other rendezvous point that usually I selected, I thought I had to stay, at the least, for twenty minutes or so. I'd feign interest, even though, like with Barry, I knew in an instant that this one was not the one I would want to kiss, date, or even touch.

By Thanksgiving I had pretty much given up. There was one guy, Jeremy, who was very cute, and we actually had great sex, not just that first night but a few other times during October. That ended when Jeremy revealed he actually had a lover and that was why he could never get together on weekends. I decided that just going out for the nightly hunt with David was a lot more fun. Even if I didn't meet anyone, at least I had a good time talking with David and discussing all the past and future sex partners that circled around. Plus, it was certainly true that everyone looked more attractive after a couple of drinks.

David had called Hendrik, who was pissed off at first after hearing about his letter and photo being passed around among friends. But David had apparently turned on the charm, and they had gotten together for a hot Sunday afternoon tryst.

"Are you going to see him again?" I asked.

"No, I guess not," David said, surprising me by answering after a long pause, as though he had never thought about it before.

ᴥ 16 ᴥ

Thanksgiving 1979, I went to Scarsdale alone. My parents seemed to have made great progress over the past year since the visit with David led to our conversation. We still spoke most Sundays by phone and, like before, the talk had gone back to being more routine, revolving around the health of various relatives, my job, and the news.

"We saw the pictures on TV of the memorial services for Harvey Milk," Herb told me. I had been out gallivanting around town and hadn't even realized a year had passed since the gay councilman had been assassinated in San Francisco.

Herb would often mention something he'd seen in the media recently about gay issues and was careful to tell me that "Mom and I both watched it." I was glad that they were more accepting in an intellectual sense, but they didn't seem to want to know any details— and that was okay with me, too.

Christmas seemed to creep up before I was ready. Thanksgiving had fallen late in the month and when I went back to work the Monday after, it was already December. Jim called to invite me again for the Christmas cocktail party, and as much as I tried, I couldn't resist asking whether he'd heard from Tommy.

"Not a word," Jim said. "I thought you might be in touch with him."

"No," I told him, and actually, I felt relieved, knowing Tommy wasn't around. It was a lot easier to be free of him, knowing he was God-knows-where, instead of a subway ride away.

There were a lot of parties those three weeks between Thanksgiving and Christmas, and I ended up spending a lot of time with David. I went alone to the CBA Christmas party, which was at the Cloud Club, a private club on the top floor of the Chrysler building, where the ceiling was painted light blue with puffy white clouds. Randy came but left early, and I ended up spending much of the night with Carole, looking out through the little triangular windows at the sparkling city, seventy-seven floors below. And, yes, even though I didn't know where in the universe he might be, it was hard not to think about waking up last Christmas morning with Tommy's arms around me in bed.

Alan Nesoir invited David and Russell to sit at his table at the annual Costume Institute dinner, a *Who's Who* of the fashion world held at the Metropolitan Museum of Art as a fund-raiser for the museum's Costume Institute on the first Monday night in December. But Russell had to be away for work, and David had asked Alan if I could come along in his place. We rented tuxedos for the occasion, and it was a memorable night, starting with cocktails in the glassed-in atrium housing the Temple of Dendur, recently transported from the banks of the Nile to the Upper East Side of Manhattan.

That was followed by dinner in the Met cafeteria, which was upgraded considerably for the evening, decorated in the style of a Parisian bistro. David pointed out Ralph Lauren, Bill Blass, Halston, Yves St. Laurent, and the other stars of the fashion world. The next week there was a photo of me and David in our tuxedos in a spread of pictures from the party in *WWD—Women's Wear Daily*, the fashion industry newspaper. We looked like a very handsome couple together.

Christmas Eve was warm and gray; it didn't even feel like December. CBA closed early again, but it didn't really matter—there were even fewer people around than last year, and I don't think I heard a phone ring once all morning. Carole was rushing out to buy gifts before she headed back to Queens; Randy needed to go shopping for tonight's dinner. I was glad to be able to go to Randy and Gerard's for the evening; otherwise, it would have been depressing to spend the holiday alone. And of course, it was hard not to remember the Christmas with Tommy.

David was back in North Carolina with his family; Elliot was with his parents in Indiana. I decided that next year, if I was still single, I would try to talk one of them into going away somewhere together. The Silvers were in Puerto Rico this year. They had invited me to join them although I wasn't sure they really wanted me to come and in any case, I thought it would feel too uncomfortable for everyone if I were to go on vacation with my parents at this point in my life.

It was still so warm at eight o'clock that I decided to walk up to Randy and Gerard's place. Maybe it was just the weather, but the city didn't seem as deserted as last Christmas Eve, and there were more people on the street. Still, I felt lonely, and when I got to Randy and Gerard's, the table was set for thirteen—six couples and me. I should have just gone to Miami Beach and visited my grandparents. If nothing else, I'd at least be getting a tan.

But after a few glasses of wine, I started to feel a lot better. Most of the people at the table had been friends for years, and it really did seem like a family dinner—everyone knew about one another's marriages and divorces, successes and failures. People started to leave around 11:30, and Randy urged me to walk over to Uncle Charlie's.

"They're open," Randy told me. "The only reason they'd close would be if it caught on fire. And even then, they'd set up kegs out on the sidewalk to sell you beer while you watched it go up in flames."

"I don't know," I said. "It's going to be a weird crowd."

"Go over, dear," Randy said. "It'll cheer you up. All it takes is one."

It was less than a five-minute walk over to 38th and Third. I was surprised to find the place so crowded, but as I stood there, posing with one leg against the wall, I started to feel depressed again. I decided to leave, and as soon as I got outside, a Checker cab was just pulling up to drop someone off. I hopped in.

It had been a long night, and by the time I reached the top of the stairs, I was exhausted. I opened the door, and on my desk, the red light was flashing on the answering machine.

❧ 17 ❧

Tommy had left the message on the machine about thirty minutes earlier, just before midnight. It had been more than seven months since I'd heard from him, before the summer. "Hey, Josh, merry Christmas ... or happy Chanukah," he said, laughing to himself. Hearing the laugh, I could close my eyes and imagine Tommy's face, his black hair hanging down over the dark brown eyes, and that great smile.

"Well, you know, I just wanted to say hello, because I was remembering last Christmas with you. You probably forgot all about it but anyway, well, here I am, and I just wanted to let you know I was thinking about you, and maybe we could get together again sometime, if you want. Well, *adios*, my friend."

I played the message back four times. There were people talking in the background, but I couldn't make out any of the voices. One sounded like a woman. Of course, there was no number to return the call. Same old Tommy. Maybe he just enjoyed playing games with me. Was I really ready to go back to being trapped in the same old role?

I didn't think about it too long. I still knew the number of Tommy's service by heart—I figured I'd probably never forget it as long as I lived—and I dialed it. Why or what I hoped to accomplish, I wasn't sure. It wasn't like Tommy would answer the phone and ease the pain of my loneliness. All I could do was leave a message and then wait. At least I'd know if Tommy was still using the same service.

The phone rang about twenty times before I hung up. Maybe now they'd decided to close for Christmas too. I poured a half glass of Black Label and threw in three ice cubes, lit one of the red candles in my holiday centerpiece, and sat there in the silence, watching it burn in its glass holder, before I drifted off to sleep.

The ringing phone jolted me from sleep. Still on the couch, I had been dreaming about being on a jet, but instead of flying through the air, this one was trying to navigate along the streets, its wings hitting the sides of the buildings.

I picked up the phone. "Tommy?"

But there was no response. This time, in the background I could hear people speaking Spanish. I said "Hello? Hello?" in English but no one answered, and then the line went dead. I looked at the clock. It was 2:30. *It could have been one of Tommy's relatives calling to say something had happened to Tommy*, I thought, my mind racing. But no, that wouldn't make any sense. How would they even know my number? Unless maybe they found it in his wallet.

I stood up and looked out the window at the deserted street. The gingko tree outside was still full of leaves in mid-winter, its life cycle totally disrupted by the constant light every evening from the mercury-vapor lamp less than ten feet away. The streetlight was beneath my vantage point, so the entire street scene was illuminated as a stage set, appearing like the backdrop for an Edward Hopper painting.

I went into the bathroom and took two Tylenol PM, got into bed, and fell quickly back to sleep before the pills could have even worked. I was still fast asleep when the phone rang again at 8:00 a.m.

"I'm right around the corner," he said, casual as ever, as though we had last spoken a day or two before instead seven months ago. "Can I come by?"

"I'm still in bed," I told him, groggy from the drinking and the pills.

"Great," Tommy said. "I'll join you."

The buzzer sounded less than five minutes later. I pushed the button to unlock the front door, put on some sweats, and walked down to the fourth floor landing where I could watch Tommy coming up the stairs. The building was empty, probably just me and Irving alone in our apartments for Christmas. Tommy looked up, as though he already knew I'd be standing there watching him. He had on a denim jacket and jeans, and I as soon as I set eyes on him, I could feel any remaining willpower draining out of my body.

I started to say something, but Tommy put his finger up to my lips. "Don't talk," he said as wrapped his arms around me and we started to kiss there in the stairway. Upstairs, Tommy pulled off his jacket, and it slid from the sofa arm on to the floor. We sat on the couch and barely came up for air as the passion I had craved through the summer was suddenly reawakened. I rubbed my hand along Tommy's forearms and touched his legs through the jeans. The fabric was worn thin where Tommy's thighs brushed against one another when he walked, and I loved rubbing my hands against the smooth cotton and feeling Tommy's muscles underneath.

"I missed you," I said.

"Me, too," Tommy told me. "Let's go to the bedroom. I'm tired; I need to sleep."

We undressed and cuddled up together in the bed, with me resting my head on Tommy's chest. "That's your pillow, baby," Tommy told me right before I drifted off. I had a headache from the drinking. Or maybe it was just all the tension and excitement. I lay there trying to calculate how many hours it had been since I took the first two Tylenol PM but fell back asleep before I could get up to go to the medicine cabinet for more, so it didn't make any difference.

I woke up first, around 11:30. I left Tommy a note on the desk in case he happened to wake up while I was gone. *Went to get coffee. Back in a min. xoxo*

The deli around the corner was open and crowded, one of the only businesses in the neighborhood not shut down for the holiday. I had been gone less than ten minutes, and when I opened the door to the bedroom, Tommy hadn't moved.

I got back into the bed and pressed my body next to Tommy, wrapped my arms around his chest, and put my mouth next to his ear, whispering, "Merry Christmas." Tommy rolled over on his back and brought his finger up to his lips, blowing softly.

I started to say that I just wanted to let him know I had gotten breakfast, but Tommy rolled over on top of me and started to stick his tongue down my mouth before I could get any words out. Once it started, the lovemaking was fast and furious.

His body pressed against mine made me feel alive in a way I never did before, and the way he held me—so tight, so ferociously—satisfied something I couldn't define but clearly needed and desperately wanted. Despite the muscular body, there was something incredibly tender about the way Tommy held me, with his arm pressing my head against his chest, so I felt his strength but not hurting me—just controlling me in a way that I couldn't move away from him.

We were both drenched with sweat when it was over. I turned on the air conditioner, and it was so warm outside that the condenser actually clicked on. It was the hottest Christmas Day I could ever remember in New York.

The coffee from the deli was cold by the time we got to it. I put it into a saucepan and heated it up on stove, and we sat down at the table to have breakfast together. It was first time we'd done that; before, Tommy always had to go to work or had some other reason for having to run out of the apartment, either right after sex at night or as soon as the alarm sounded in the morning.

"Why did you call me after all this time?" I asked him.

Tommy looked down. "I'm going to stop hustling," he said. "And go back to school. This time it's for real."

"You said that a year ago—actually, more than a year ago, when I first met you," I said. "And I don't trust this. I don't understand it. Why does hot, sexy Tommy Hawk want to be here cuddling up with me?"

"You always have to analyze everything, right?" Tommy said. "Can you just enjoy the moment?"

I was trying not to get excited, trying to see it from his point of view, but the words just sputtered out. "That's not my life, living by the moment," I said. "I have a career, a lease with rent due on the first, a phone bill to pay each month."

Tommy looked right at me with those big brown eyes. "Maybe that's why I'm here, Josh. Did you ever think about that?" he said. "Maybe a real job and some stability seem pretty appealing when you've never had it."

"Yeah, okay, I get that. But you're beyond good-looking—you're one of the hottest guys I've ever met," I said. "And you know it, Tommy; you're a star. And I'm just one of your admirers who puts up with this stuff because of it."

"You can say 'puts up with this shit,'" he told me. "I deserve it. I know I haven't treated you well. But Josh, I think you can be good for me. I want to be like you."

"Well, that's funny since I'd love to look like you."

"Josh, we're not talking about looks. I mean you. Your life. With your job. Your friends."

"Oh, Tommy, okay, I get it, but I don't want to know you like this," I said. "Just getting a random phone call every once in a while when you feel like settling down—we both know that doesn't last."

"No, I've had it. Last night just made it obvious that it's time to stop," Tommy said. "I'm sick of this shit."

"What happened?"

"It was a bad scene," Tommy said. "This guy from out of town had hired me for the whole night for two hundred. It wasn't from Manhattan Men; this guy called and said he had just gotten my number from someone, although he never told me who."

"I thought you only did it through Jim and John so they screened everyone first," I said.

"Usually, but two hundred bucks is a lot of cash, and those guys aren't even open for business on Christmas Eve. So I called the guy back at the number he left, and it's not a hotel but he's staying at a friend's apartment a few blocks from here," Tommy said. "He was a big guy—not worked out, just huge and really strong."

I nodded, eager to hear the rest.

"He takes me into the bedroom right away, which is strange," Tommy told me. "Especially on an overnight. Usually they'll offer me a drink first and sit and talk for a while."

There was a time when I would have been shocked to even have a conversation like this, but after the past two summers I was now used to hearing details of sex for pay.

"In the bedroom, he throws me down on the bed and starts wrestling with me. Not like the way you and I play around, but really trying to hurt me. So I'm fighting back. Not really punching him, just kind of slamming my fist into the pillow. I figure we're still just into this sex play. But then he's on top of me with one arm around my neck and the other holding my forehead. I told him, 'You're choking me,' but he just squeezes harder. 'Shut up, you faggot,' he says. And I'm thinking this is really fucked up, that I've got to get out of there."

"You're so strong. I can't believe he could hold you down," I said, and now I was wide awake, although I had only had a little of the coffee.

"The guy was big, Josh. He outweighed me by at least sixty pounds," Tommy said. "I'm squirming, trying to get out from under him, but he's just grinding on top of me with this massive hard-on. 'Suffer, you little faggot,' he says, right before I managed to get out from under him.

Now I was beginning to think it sounded kind of hot but was trying not get aroused.

"I was fuckin' scared, Josh," Tommy continued. "We never even took off our shorts. I just grabbed my jeans, the shirt, the jacket, and my shoes and headed for the door. He ran into the kitchen and grabbed a knife from one of those wooden blocks and shouts, 'Get back here, fucker, if you don't want to see that pretty face destroyed.'"

It wasn't sounding very erotic anymore. I reached out and held Tommy's hand. "Shit," I said. "Tommy, you've got to call the police."

"Yeah, what do you suggest I tell them I was doing there in the first place?" he said to me, raising his voice for the first time all morning. "They couldn't care less about faggots beating each other up."

"This wasn't just fighting. The guy tried to kill you."

"Let me just finish, okay, Josh?" Tommy told me how he had kicked the guy in the balls, and the guy fell down against the wall in the kitchen. His clothes were still on a chair by the front door, so he opened the door, threw the clothes out on the hallway floor, and dashed out before the other guy could stand up.

"You wouldn't believe how fast I got dressed, and then I'm outside there, right by Sheridan Square. I'm thinking the guy could even come after me with a gun," Tommy said. "So, I went into the Monster on Seventh and Grove. It was nearly two o'clock, and there was no one there. It was strange, sitting there with the Christmas decorations after what I'd just been through. I've never been scared—never at all—out on a job."

"And that's when you called me?" I asked.

"No, the first time I called you was when I was on my way over there," he said. "When I thought it was just going to be another normal trick—in, out, count the cash. I was walking by your apartment and thought about you and about last Christmas. You probably don't believe me, but I've thought a lot of times this year about our Christmas morning together."

"I was at Uncle Charlie's," I told him. "I had stopped by after dinner at Randy's."

"Well, I knew you weren't at church," Tommy said. "Then, when I called the second time, it was from the Monster."

"But you didn't say anything."

"I was embarrassed," Tommy told me. "First I was sure you wouldn't be home, and then right after you picked up, I thought, why am I bothering the poor guy? He doesn't want to hear my story—especially not in the middle of the night."

"And then?"

"I stayed at the Monster until they closed at four and then walked over to the Mineshaft—they don't close until eight."

"So you were drinking all night?" I asked.

"No, not really, two beers at the Monster and then another one at the Mineshaft," Tommy said. "Anyway, sitting there at the Mineshaft, all alone on Christmas morning, I decided that was my last trick."

I leaned closer and squeezed Tommy's hand.

"I don't need the money," Tommy said. "I'm getting more shifts at the construction job now, working almost full time. And I'll do something else at night if I have to—wait tables or something."

"I don't know, Tommy," I said. "We've been here before. No more hustling. Going back to college."

"I'm starting in January," Tommy said. "You'll see, Josh; this is it. You know that saying, 'Today is the first day of the rest of your life'? This is mine."

We spent that Friday, Christmas Day, together, never leaving the apartment. In the afternoon it started to rain, and as we cuddled up under the covers, it felt really peaceful having Tommy asleep next to me. I listened to the raindrops hitting the top of the air conditioner outside the window and started to dream again about a life of going to sleep every night and waking up every morning next to this gorgeous guy. When Tommy finally opened his eyes, we talked more about what our lives had been like growing up.

Tommy was so different from me—all my years through high school, college, and even grad school trying to be straight and secretly in love with a whole series of guys. Always unrequited, always anguished. Tommy had been the golden boy in school, the one all the guys and girls loved, the jock that every closet case like me fantasized about at night, the one to whom everything seemed to come so easily—at least back then.

Now his looks were his meal ticket to being a hustler, and I had the college degree and the good job. My life was filled with possibilities in a way that Tommy's wasn't, and he certainly knew there wasn't a lucrative career awaiting middle-aged call boys.

As we talked that morning in bed, I began to understand that for Tommy, his childhood experience wasn't quite as simple as I imagined it. Growing up had been tough. There was no swimming pool in the backyard or summer camp. And one reason he was so tough was from constantly fighting with his father.

I listened to his stories and rubbed Tommy's shoulders and back as he talked.

"Don't stop," Tommy said. "That feels great."

"For me, too," I said. His shoulders were round and hard. I could have easily massaged Tommy's smooth brown skin for hours.

"Is it okay if I stay over tonight?" Tommy asked as I wrapped my arm around his shoulder, and he pressed up closer against me. Despite the body, Tommy looked so vulnerable all of a sudden. Now he seemed like the weak one.

"Tommy, I don't want to get back into this whole game again. I know you like me and okay, I believe you want to settle down, but I don't think it's going to happen, and I'm just going to end up feeling like shit again."

"Josh, can you give me a chance? Okay?" he said, those dark brown eyes locked on mine.

"Okay, fine," I said. "I don't have any place I need to be until Monday morning.

"Me, either," Tommy said and as he went to hug me, we started to kiss again.

Later, we smoked a joint and watched *Chinatown* together on TV. As Tommy fell asleep next to me, I was already in fantasyland, beginning to plan out our lives together—how I'd help him get a résumé together so he could find a job in an office, and how I'd help get information about the adult programs at City College so *we* could figure out how to pay for it.

Saturday morning, it was still raining, and we spent the rest of the day together, mostly in bed. When we went out that night for dinner, Tommy wore the same jeans and denim jacket he had worn over on Friday morning. I loaned him one of my shirts, a large, which Tommy filled out with his broad shoulders, although the sleeves were long on his shorter, more compact body.

When we made love together that Saturday afternoon, we reversed roles for the first time, with me on top. Depending on whatever fantasy was being played in my head, I had always been more versatile than most guys, but with Tommy, he had always taken the lead.

And that wasn't the only first that same day. Afterwards, when I told Tommy how I wanted to help him find a better job and start night school, Tommy got tears in his eyes, the first time I had seen that.

"That makes you sad?" I asked him.

"Yeah, I guess," Tommy said. "I'm not used to talking much about being sad or happy—no one has much cared how I felt. Maybe way back my mom did, but for the past three years no one would even notice if I was dead or alive."

I started to get tears in my eyes, too, as I held Tommy close, kissing the side of his neck.

The alarm went off at 6:30 that Monday morning. We had set it to give Tommy enough time to get back to the Bronx and start the construction shift at eight o'clock.

"When are we going to see each other next?" I asked as he pulled the white T-shirt over his chest. It had gotten a lot colder after the rain, and I loaned Tommy one of my sweaters to wear home under the denim jacket.

"Around seven," Tommy said.

"Tonight?" I asked. "You're going to come back down here tonight?"

"I'm not going to be working," Tommy smiled. "So unless you don't want me to see me, I'll be here."

"You'll call me if something comes up?" I asked.

"Don't worry," Tommy said. "I'll be here."

At CBA, I surprised Carole with a good morning kiss.

"What was that for?" she asked me.

"Just leftover Christmas spirit," I said.

"So that's why you have the big smile on your face?" Carole asked. "Santa was good to you?"

"Yeah, it was a great Christmas."

As expected, Randy had nothing encouraging to say. "Just bring me a knife and let me put you out of your misery before it starts again," he told me. "You're not seriously going to get back on the *Titanic* are you?"

"He's not turning tricks anymore, and he's going back to school."

"Yeah," Randy said, rolling his eyes back to make the point, "and I'm going to find a cure for cancer and win the Nobel Prize next year."

"I think I'm falling in love with him," I said.

"Oh, my," said Randy between cigarette puffs. "You don't give up easily, do you?"

❧ 18 ❦

The buzzer rang at two minutes to seven that night. I barely had time to take a shower and change from my suit after getting back from CBA. I shaved again to get ready, although no matter how many times a day I pulled that blade over my skin, I knew my face wouldn't feel as smooth as Tommy's. "Don't worry about it," he had told me when I first said something about it. "It's what's behind your face that I like; that's what I care about."

This time we ate the food together that I had picked up at Balducci's. I had gotten a bottle of wine and lit tall white candles on the table. It was the candlelight dinner with Tommy that I had fantasized about since that first day I saw him more than a year before. Tommy had told me over the weekend about the place where he was living in the Bronx, sharing a two-bedroom apartment with three other guys, all straight. One of them was his cousin who worked with him at the construction job. None of them, including the cousin, knew he was gay. And none of them knew any of the details of his old evening job.

"Don't you at least have a phone there? I hate not being able to ever call you," I told him.

"No," Tommy said. "But I was thinking of getting one if I can save up the money for the deposit."

That first Saturday we were together after Christmas, I had gotten a toothbrush for Tommy at the drugstore. After he left, it stayed there in the toothbrush holder mounted on the wall with its cup holder filled with a stack of paper cups. It made me smile to see another of the four holes occupied, Tommy's brush there next to mine. When we had been out walking around that afternoon, Tommy had bought a tube of hair gel and that had been the first thing of his to make it into my medicine cabinet.

On New Year's Eve we went together to Randy and Gerard's party. It was the first time in two years I had ever gone to dinner at Randy and Gerard's with another guy. I had showed Randy pictures of Tommy, but they had never met before, and Randy was impressed with how smart he seemed.

Tommy was talking very animatedly, probably speaking more that night than he had in all our previous dates combined.

"A step up from your average call boy, I have to admit," Randy said when we were alone in the kitchen.

"He's not a call boy," I told him. "Not anymore."

Randy's eyes rolled skyward as he tilted back his head to exhale a plume of cigarette smoke. "Since when?" he asked. "Last Saturday, right?"

"We'll see, okay?" I said. "People can change."

"Ah, the innocence of youth," Randy sighed.

"I've got to try it," I said. "Otherwise, I'm going to always wonder what would have happened. It's like your story about moving here from New Orleans. If you hadn't come you'd have spent the rest of your life in Louisiana, wondering what your life would have been like if you had gone to New York."

As the new face at the party—and a pretty handsome one at that—Tommy was the center of attention. Although usually dinner at Randy and Gerard's was a sit-down affair, the New Year's party had nearly forty guests, and they had pushed the table back along the wall and set up a buffet. Tommy and I went out on the small terrace to get away from the smoke. It wasn't as warm as it had been over Christmas, but it was still unusually mild, and we stood there kissing and looking at the lights of the Empire State Building just a few blocks away, with only a water tower on the next building blocking the view.

"It would be perfect if it wasn't for that water tower," I said.

Tommy put his finger to my lips. "Don't talk, Josh. Don't think," he said. "Just kiss."

We spent every weekend together in January. I took Tommy with me to the gym for what he claimed was the first time he'd been since school. It didn't matter much, because with the big chest and shoulders he had inherited from a benevolent gene pool, combined with the years of construction work, he still had one of the best bodies at the place.

Tommy left his gym clothes in one of my drawers, in those same wooden cabinets from my childhood bedroom that my father had helped me carry up the stairs four years before. Later, I cleared out one drawer completely for him to use and, the same weekend, one shelf in the medicine cabinet was assigned to Tommy. On January 25, I took Tommy out for a nice dinner at One If By Land, a romantic spot in the Village where, supposedly, Jackie Onassis loved to dine.

"We should celebrate our one-month anniversary," I said. Tommy had worn a freshly ironed button-down shirt and black slacks for the occasion; it was the first time I had seen him in anything other than jeans. If he were taller, he probably could have been a professional model. When Tommy went back uptown, he changed back into jeans and left the shirt and slacks hanging at one end of the closet.

I had gone over to City College from the CBA offices one day at lunchtime and had picked up a catalog and application for the evening part-time program. Tommy wouldn't have been able to go over during the day anyway, and it was easy enough for me to walk over there. The next night, I showed them to Tommy, pointing out the courses he could take between 6:15 and 7:30, so we could still get together for dinner afterwards. And I showed him how he could apply for financial aid.

"I couldn't start until the fall then. Without the night work," he said, using the new euphemism we applied to his previous career, "I don't have the money to pay two hundred dollars a class."

"I'll loan it to you," I told him, "and you can pay me back."

Tommy's construction job wasn't a union job. It was just pick-up work, doing a shift whenever there was something available and getting paid in cash, five dollars an hour.

"It doesn't make sense," I told him. "Where would they get the cash?"

"I don't know," Tommy told me. "But that's the way it's done in my neighborhood."

"And what about taxes?" I asked.

"Taxes?" Tommy just laughed.

By the first week in February, I had managed to get Tommy's new life as well organized as the Pontiac spring advertising schedule. I helped him get a job, manning the front desk at one of the vendors we worked with, Atlantic Productions, which did a lot of the editing and post-production on the CBA television commercials. It was a salaried job at $12,000 a year, so in the end, the take-home pay wasn't that much different than the construction gig, but it was steady work, and for the first time, Tommy had insurance.

I helped him complete all the paperwork for City College, typing out the forms as Tommy answered the questions, standing behind me and massaging my shoulders as he spoke. Tommy signed up for two classes. They were on alternate days, Monday/Wednesday and Tuesday/Thursday in the time slots after work when I had already calculated Tommy could easily attend.

I kept Randy posted at work and told him I was worried that maybe things were moving along too fast.

"You've been anxious for the past two years, trying to find a boyfriend," Randy said. "And now you have one, and you're worried about that."

"I like to worry, I guess."

"Yes, dear." Randy said. "I would say you do."

In April, as Passover approached, I lay awake in bed, thinking about whether to bring Tommy up to Scarsdale for the family Seder dinner. It was on a Saturday night and would be the first Saturday since Christmas weekend that he and I didn't spend together. I didn't want to leave Tommy alone, but I wasn't sure Herb and Lillian were ready to meet Tommy. Or that Tommy was ready to meet the Silvers.

"I'll be here waiting for you," Tommy told me. "Just go. It's your holiday."

And so I went alone. But unlike other recent trips up to Scarsdale, this time I felt tense and anxious on the train. When I got to my parents' house, I called the apartment, and there was no answer. I hung up without leaving a message—Tommy wouldn't have listened to it anyway—and tried to think of all the possible explanations. Maybe Tommy was in the shower. Maybe he had gone to get something to eat. I felt anxious and distracted, the way I had last year when I could do nothing to get in touch with Tommy except wait for him to call.

Twice in that first hour, I went into my parents' bedroom and dialed the number on Ninth Street. We sat down for the dinner, but I couldn't focus at all. "It's a good thing you know the story of Passover so you don't need to pay attention," my sister, Annie, remarked.

When we finished with the ceremony, I excused myself from the dinner table and went to try Tommy again. "Is everything okay?" Annie asked. Lillian was oblivious, as always, busy orchestrating the serving of the meal, and my father would have never noticed.

"I'm fine," I said, thinking quickly. "I left my credit card at a restaurant last night, and I'm trying to see if they found it." No one at the Silvers knew Tommy Perez even existed.

This time, Tommy answered when I called.

"Where were you?" I asked. "I was trying to call you."

"Why?" Tommy said. "What's wrong?"

"Nothing," I said. "I just missed you. I wanted to be sure everything was okay."

"It's only been two hours," Tommy said. "I'm fine. Relax, Josh. Enjoy the evening with your family, okay?"

"Okay, I will," I told him. "I'll take the ten o 'clock train, and I'll be back by eleven."

"That's fine. I'm here waiting for you," Tommy said. "Just watching TV now. I went out to McDonald's."

"McDonald's?" I asked.

"Hey, I like McDonald's," Tommy said. "You miss me; I miss McDonald's."

I laughed. I felt relieved after I talked to Tommy, like a drug addict receiving my shot of methadone. When I went back to the table, I felt relaxed for the first time all evening. "They found it?" Annie asked, probably noticing the smile on my face as I walked out of the bedroom.

"Found what?"

"The card?"

"Oh, yeah, they found it," I said, but I was pretty sure Annie doubted that was the reason for my happiness at that moment.

By the time I got back to Ninth Street, Tommy had fallen asleep in the bedroom with the TV on. Half a joint lay in an ashtray by the bed.

"I asked you not to smoke pot in the bed," I told him. Tommy's response was the familiar finger in front of my mouth. "Don't talk," he said, pulling me down on top of him in the bed. As Tommy kissed me, pulling off my shirt and wrapping his thighs around my body, I decided it didn't really matter. Tommy could do what he wanted as long as I could come home to this every night.

That year it seemed like the winter had just turned into summer with no spring. February and March had been bitterly cold, April was cooler than normal, and then by May, when Tommy's first semester at City College ended successfully, it was already hot and steamy in the city. We had never discussed moving in together. "It just happened" was the way I later explained it to friends. I couldn't even calculate a date when we started living together, when the assumption became that we would spend the nights and weekends together unless we planned otherwise, rather than the reverse.

One drawer had become two, then three. Then our clothes, which had been hanging on opposite ends of the closet, began to mix together. Tommy had taken to wearing my dress shirts anyway, which fit him fine as long as they were tucked in, disguising the additional length. Tommy's hair gel sat along the sink, as well as his box of ear-cleaning Q-tips.

So that was how it came to be. There was no getting down on one knee. No diamond ring. No family and friends clapping as I broke the glass. At some point, Tommy just started spending more time at my place than he did in the Bronx. And Josh Silver finally had a lover.

❧ 19 ❧

By spring of 1982, it had been two years since Tommy had given up his room in the Bronx and been living full time with me on East Ninth Street. I was surprised that Irving, the landlord, hadn't given me a hard time about that sooner. The rent stabilization laws were strict about only immediate family living in the apartment, and Tommy was definitely not immediate family, and there were no provisions for gay relationships.

Probably Irving wouldn't have even cared, except that if Tommy was officially living there, that meant a new lease and he'd be able to raise the rent 15 percent, much closer to the $650 or so the apartment could fetch on the open market than the $343.08 I was paying. Irving insisted on increasing the rent to the full maximum allowed by the Rent Stabilization Board, and every tenant in the building had the rent calculated each year down to the exact penny of the permitted increase.

As with my parents, I had figured it was best with Irving to wait until asked. Irving obliged, cornering me one evening on the way home from work as he stood out on the sidewalk, snow shovel in hand. It wasn't an unusual pose. The entire winter of '82 had been mild, and today's accumulation had been next to nothing. There was certainly nothing to shovel at that point, even for the most diligent snow-shoveler. But it gave Irving something to do, a reason to stand in front of the building and talk to the tenants and neighbors as they walked by.

"Is he living here now?" he asked me.

"Who?"

"Your friend," Irving said. "Tommy."

"He's staying with me for a while," I said.

"A while?" Irving asked. "The mailman told me he's been getting mail here for at least a year. To me, that means he's living here—not visiting."

"Irving, what do you want?" I asked. With Irving usually eager for conversation and companionship, I knew this could easily go on for an hour.

"Well, the regulations say I should be entitled to a vacancy allowance and a 6 percent rent increase for a new tenant."

"But I'm not a new tenant," I said. "I've been here for nearly ten years already." It was actually only eight, but I was so used to exaggerating at work, both in internal comments and in the advertising, that it came out naturally. Eight *was* nearly ten, just like three weeks was *almost* a month and ninety-five, a hundred.

"*He's* new," Irving said, referring to Tommy again by the impersonal pronoun. "And it costs me more to have him here—more hot water, more gas for the stove, more wear and tear on the steps."

At that, I looked at him and laughed, because the stairway, probably last renovated in the early 1900s, couldn't possibly show much more in terms of wear and tear. "Irving, come on," I said.

"He can't get mail here unless his name is on the box," Irving said. "Those are the rules. Not my rules, but those are the rules."

We could have easily gone on, but I was eager to get upstairs and end it. "How about I'll give you five hundred to cover putting his name on the mailbox and buzzer, the extra hot water, and"—I rolled my eyes, the way Randy might have done—"the wear and tear on the stairs."

"A thousand," Irving said. "You give me a thousand now, or else we do a new lease for both of you, and the new rent is $514.62."

I smiled, realizing that Irving had already figured it all out down to the penny. "Fine," I said. "I'll give you a check for a thousand."

I never told Tommy about the extra payment; he already couldn't stand Irving and that would have just made him angrier. About two weeks later, the shiny black plastic tabs with the hyphenated Silver-Perez name arrived and were inserted on top of the buzzer by the entrance and the mailbox cover. I saw them for the first time that night when I came home from work. Since the others were years or, in some cases, decades old, ours stood out, proclaiming our relationship to all who saw them. I smiled and stared at it for a minute before opening the mailbox. Every time I saw it I beamed with pride.

At work, I had been promoted again and at twenty-nine was the youngest account manager at CBA, with more than a dozen people reporting to me. I got to sit in at the monthly agency management meetings, where Scoot told me I was the first person under thirty to ever participate. The conference table had four huge, round glass ashtrays, and I was the only one who didn't smoke constantly. When it was over, I'd go out for a walk, unless it was freezing outside, just to get some of the smell from the smoke out of my suit and my hair.

I was still on the Pontiac business but miserable Edna had moved on to some other job at GM, where she could torture someone else to keep her company with her emergency Saturday meetings and conference calls. Her replacement was Gordon, a mild-mannered guy from California, middle-aged, and handsome, I thought, with his neatly combed gray hair.

"I hope I look that good when I get gray hair," I told Tommy, along with my suspicions that Gordon was probably gay. Gordon didn't wear a ring, and neither of us had said a word about our personal lives to one another, which was unusual to me, as the start of any business relationship would usually begin with the inevitable discussion of whether or not I had a family.

"I'm not married," I would say, "but I live with someone." That seemed to be the best response, as it usually brought a quick end to the discussion and left open the question of just whom I might be living with. And it also avoided any friendly suggestions of possible blind dates or fix-ups from those determined to help along my love life.

Atlantic Productions was a small office, and Tommy would frequently get up from his seat at the front desk to watch the editors cut and edit the 16mm film into 30- and 60-second commercials. His athletic coordination made him adept with the razor blades and tape, and soon he was helping out with the editing. Within six months someone else had been brought in to replace him at the front desk, and he was made an apprentice film editor.

I was really proud of him. He still went to City College in the evenings and was now about a third of the way done toward his degree. Tommy was so good at the film editing that he decided to change his major from sociology to communications arts, specializing in film. That seemed like a good idea to me. I never thought a degree in sociology would lead to anything very lucrative, but Tommy and I had an argument when I first brought it up, so hadn't mentioned the choice of major again.

I was spending less time with Randy and Gerard. Their dinner parties had started to seem monotonous, each one a virtual repeat of the one before, with the talk only about different people—the same stories and only the names were changed. Plus, Tommy really didn't like going there. Randy and I got along fine, but Tommy never felt comfortable with that whole fashion crowd. "I just want to be with you," he would tell me.

And David and I had grown apart. We still spoke by phone but hadn't been out much together in the past couple of years. I had made an effort to keep the friendship alive, but it was difficult with David still single and Tommy and me as a couple. We didn't have any disagreement; our paths had just diverged. Occasionally, Tommy and I would meet David for dinner, but he would get upset with what he called our public displays of affection—"PDAs"—because Tommy always had his arm around me, which I thoroughly enjoyed. "Enough already with the PDAs," David would say.

David had come with us a few times on Saturday night to the Saint that first season it opened in 1980, two years before. Tommy knew one of the guys who worked the front door, a former Manhattan Men colleague, and he would always let us in without standing in line, so then David would put up with our PDAs without any complaint.

I had already become bored with most of the gay clubs, but that first night I walked into the Saint in the fall of 1980, it was breathtaking. Like Studio 54, it was in an old theater—the Fillmore East on Second Avenue and Fifth Street. The upper balconies had been left intact with seats, but the lower floors had been gutted, and there was a steel structure in the middle of the auditorium that held the dance floor, one flight up a set of metal industrial stairs.

The dance area was covered with a huge fabric dome, said to be larger than the dome at the Hayden Planetarium. Throughout the evening, the entire room would darken and in the center of the dance floor, a planetarium projector would rise up and display a pattern of stars on the dome, which would then rotate, giving the impression that the entire room was spinning. Other times, colored lights bathed the dome, and green laser beams created designs and words against the white background.

Tommy and I went up to the balcony to smoke a joint and stood at the railing, watching pulsating lights and the crowd. I would have stood there longer, but he was the one who usually pulled me down the stairs, and then we'd dance until—both of us covered in sweat, with our T-shirts tucked into our jeans—we would embrace and kiss and go downstairs to get a drink. There was no liquor license and no alcohol was served, but there were long tables full of bottled water and juice, bowls of fruit, and plates of cookies. Like us, everyone brought their own mood-altering substances.

My parents had finally met Tommy the year before. My engineering of the carefully planned day was marred only by an unexpected strike by private trash haulers so that the streets in Midtown were full of twenty-foot mounds of uncollected garbage that first weekend of August 1981. Other than that, it had pretty much gone according to plan. I had told them about Tommy long before and had showed them a photo to get them prepared. Through work, I had managed to get four tickets to *The Pirates of Penzance*, which had opened earlier in the year and was a huge Broadway hit, sold out for months. I hoped my mother would be so excited about that, it would eliminate (or at least cover up) any of her apprehensions about my settling down with a hot Puerto Rican boy instead of a nice Jewish girl.

We went to meet them at Grand Central, Tommy wearing one of my dress shirts, which now barely fit his shoulders, as he had started going to the gym at the college before classes when he could squeeze it in. He looked great; I couldn't imagine Herb and Lillian not liking him.

We just had time for introductions and small talk before the Sunday matinee, which was just as well—I was really nervous. Afterwards, when we went out to dinner, my mother kept talking about the costumes and the production numbers, as I had predicted. My father was more curious, asking questions of Tommy about his parents. When Tommy told him about how he had been thrown out of the house at eighteen, leaving out the specifics about being caught in the act with Eddy, my father looked genuinely pained.

I was just thankful—for them and especially for Tommy—that it had gone so well. He had been really tense all week and made it clear he was doing it for me, but I could tell, just from the way he was actively involved in the conversation, that he was enjoying the dinner.

More than once I had rubbed my leg against Tommy's under the table. It seemed a bit unreal to be there at the restaurant with Tommy, with my mother and father across the table. As Tommy and I walked them back to Grand Central, I thought that Herb and Lillian had come a long way in the three years since the Thanksgiving inquisition.

At the station Tommy gave my mother a kiss and then my father a hug. Tommy was very physical like that—with everyone—in a way I could never be. I guess it was from the way his mother had been with him as a child, plus the wrestling at school and all his other ... let's say, activities, he was just used to physical contact; it came to him totally naturally. I watched Tommy hug my father and realized I couldn't then just shake his hand good-bye. I went to put my arms around Herb, the way Tommy had, but it felt incredibly awkward, so I patted him on the back and pulled away quickly. Still, I could tell my father noticed.

By the end of that year we had settled into a life of domesticity that

178 // JEFFREY SHARLACH

I thought was probably not too unlike the life my parents had in the two years they were alone before I was born. The apartment on Ninth Street, which had always seemed small, even when I was there alone, somehow accommodated the two of us comfortably. In the miniscule kitchen we had managed to choreograph a dance so we could both be there at the same time. And when we did brush against one another, it usually just led to kissing and caresses and then sometimes a quick detour to the bedroom.

In the mornings, Tommy still got up early, setting the alarm for 7:00 a.m. so he could have time to stop at ZZZ for his $1.99 eggs-bacon-toast-and-coffee special before he went to work at Atlantic. He would take his books with him and sit there sipping his coffee, reading for school, for an hour.

I stayed in bed and watched the *Today* show or sometimes would finish reading the *Times* I'd bought the day before, because it was still impossible to get it delivered up the four flights of stairs. I knew it was best not to try to talk with Tommy too much before he had his coffee in the morning. While I was lying there in bed, I would already be thinking about what we'd do that night when we both got home, planning out the evening in my mind.

It wasn't often that we argued during those first couple of years, and when we did, it was usually because of my insistence on planning everything out in advance, and Tommy, for whom planning had never seemed to lead anywhere except disappointment, just ready to take things as they came.

"We're different people," Tommy told me. "You'll never be like me, and I'll never be like you."

"Thank God," I said. "I don't think I could stand living with someone like me."

We kissed. If I started to annoy him with my constant planning, Tommy usually still could silence me by simply putting his finger to his mouth like he had done that first night. And if that didn't work, a strong hug and pressing his lips against mine were pretty much guaranteed to succeed.

I admired the way Tommy was so certain everything would work out okay, but there were still those moments—in bed after Tommy fell asleep, or in the mornings when I awoke before him—that my feet would be going back and forth under the covers, worrying about our future together.

๑ 20 ๑

Tommy didn't have a phone at Atlantic in the room where he sat at the editing machine, so we had arranged that he would call me every day around three o'clock. At 2:45 I would begin looking at my watch. If a meeting was scheduled, I would tell him in advance, "Call me at 2:30 today. I'll be tied up after three." Or if something unplanned came up, Rita, who usually answered my phone at CBA, would either try to find me or ask Tommy to call back.

Sometimes, unexpectedly and for no particular reason, I would feel overcome by anxiety as I waited for Tommy to call. There was never any reason for it—I thought maybe it was because it reminded me of years back when I would wait, powerless, for Tommy's phone calls—but when he finally called, and we would talk, I would feel relieved, like a drug rushing through my veins, making every limb relax. All was well with our world. After those calls with Tommy, I usually felt energized. Sometimes I would be listless all day and then, right after the call, I'd sit down to write something that had been lingering for a week or more. I joked with him about it. "After we talk, it's like a rush from coke," I said. "A Tommy high."

The conversations themselves were identical to the domestic arrangements I used to hear my mother talking about with my father—

when he'd be home, what time we'd have dinner, and who would stop at the drugstore to buy more toothpaste.

We had gone out to Fire Island together a few times over the past two summers. Sometimes we stayed in an empty bedroom at Randy and Gerard's. There, one weekend, we all gathered around the TV to watch the wedding of Prince Charles to Diana Spencer, with Gerard and Bernice re-enacting the key scenes later that night after a joint and a couple of bottles of wine.

Another time, we rented a bedroom for a week from a friend of Gerard's. One weekend last year we even stayed with Jim and John, who half-jokingly tried to convince Tommy to go back to Manhattan Men.

"Yeah, what's the going rate these days?" Tommy asked, and I turned red, feeling the heat rising to my face.

Jim noticed it—I guess I wasn't very good about hiding what I was feeling—and said, "Tommy, forget it. You're with Josh now. It's not worth it."

"I was only kidding," Tommy said, and it was all over in a matter of seconds. Still, I felt uncomfortable even being there and decided that going back to that house hadn't been a good idea—too many memories of the past. But the weather was great, and maybe, in some ways, Tommy was having a positive effect on me. We were each becoming a little more like the other: me, a tiny bit less controlling and more carefree; and Tommy, more organized and willing to plan—he even had an agenda now where we wrote out appointments.

July 4 was a Saturday in '81, so we both were off work on the Friday. In my single days, I would have made plans months ago to be sure I had somewhere to go for the three-day weekend, but now I was content to relax in the city with Tommy. We went out for breakfast together at ZZZ on the corner, and then I picked up the *New York Times* on the way back to the apartment. I had been skimming through it when I got to a small story inside, reporting that forty-one gay men had come down with cases of a rare cancer, Kaposi's sarcoma, and that eight had died, all within twenty-four months of diagnosis. I read parts of it aloud to Tommy.

"Most cases had involved homosexual men who have had multiple and frequent sexual encounters with different partners, as many as ten sexual encounters each night, up to four times a week." I looked up from the paper. "It's strange," I said, "how something could only affect gay men."

"Josh, please," Tommy said. "Don't start worrying about that, okay? It's nothing. It's only forty-one people in the entire country. It's got nothing to do with you, and there's nothing you can do about it."

I started to say something else, but Tommy put his finger to my mouth. "Shhh." And he kissed me. We ended up in the bedroom.

Financially, things had gotten a lot easier. I had received a number of salary increases at CBA and that, combined with some nice year-end bonuses and the fact that Tommy was earning enough now to pay for all his own expenses, including school, made it easier for me to save money. I was still making a lot more money than he was, and I paid for our trips and usually our dinners out, but Tommy covered his tuition, half the rent, and all his own clothes, which actually amounted to almost nothing because he loved to wear the same stuff over and over again until it fell apart.

"People always tell me I look great in that shirt," Tommy would say when I'd try to show him it had already been laundered one time too many.

"Tommy, they tell you that because of the way you look," I said, "not because of the shirt." Tommy didn't say anything. Before we lived together, he always would dress showing off his body with tight T-shirts and jeans. Now, the jeans were still tight—they just didn't make them with a 32-inch waist with enough material to comfortably accommodate Tommy's thighs—but he had taken to wearing bulky sweatshirts and or my extra-large T-shirts, which would hang down well below his waist. Still, they didn't really hide his pumped-up chest and, with time, his face had gotten more angular and handsome. So I was pretty confident I was right that it wasn't the shirt eliciting the compliments he was getting.

"Let's get a share on Fire Island," I said over dinner one night in April. "We've got the money now, and we could get our own house together."

"*You've* got the money, Josh," Tommy said. "*We* don't. I don't." It wasn't the first time he brought it up. I knew he sometimes felt uncomfortable when I paid for stuff he couldn't afford. But he had grown up in the city and was used to spending summer weekends here. For me, having grown up with the beach nearby and walking barefoot in the grass during July and August, it felt strange being stuck in the city, especially with CBA shutting down early on Friday afternoons.

"Josh, I don't want to be out there like your kept boy," Tommy said. "It makes me feel like crap."

"I had a lot of things you didn't have growing up. My parents paid for me to go to school, and I've had a good job for years," I said. "You're just starting out. I'm not supposed to go backwards, right?"

"Why do we have to go out there, though?" Tommy asked. "Why can't we go somewhere else, where people don't spend all day talking about everyone else?"

"Where, Tommy?" I asked. "We don't have a car, and that's the only place near the city where we don't need one and can hang out at the beach."

"I don't know, Josh."

"Just fuck 'em," I said. "You're still hot. Let them drool over you and just forget about whatever you think they might be saying behind your back."

We found a small three-bedroom house, not far from Randy and Gerard's, at the west end of the Pines. It was away from the ocean—"on the wrong side of the Boulevard," as Randy would say—and although there was no pool, it had a large deck in the back and was surrounded by trees so that the neighboring homes were barely visible.

Elliot and his friend Franklin from NBC ended up taking one of the bedrooms. Elliot still helped Jim and John with the phones occasionally over the weekend to make extra money, but Rick had a boyfriend now who planned to share the other bed in the Manhattan Men phone room. I tried to talk David into taking the third bedroom, but he pleaded poverty, saying he was having a hard enough time just paying the rent. "Anyway, I don't want to sit there all summer watching the two of you make out like teenagers," he told me.

"David, we're not like that," I said. "And Elliot and Franklin will be there, and they're both single."

David promised to think about it and to see if he could find someone else to share the bedroom, but in the meantime I put up an ad for the share on the bulletin board at the gym. Two days later I had a call from Stuart, a young guy working as a designer on Seventh Avenue, and Tommy and I arranged for him to come over for an interview. Elliot joined us too, but Franklin was away for work.

I smiled when I saw how nervous Stuart seemed, and I tried to put him at ease, remembering my own Fire Island share interview five years before. "Do you want to smoke a joint?" I asked Stuart as we sat down.

"I thought it was a nonsmoking house," he said. I glanced over at Elliot with an *I-don't-think-this-is going-to-work* look. "It is," I said. "We just smoke pot."

"And usually outside on the deck," Elliot added.

"Great," Stuart said, pulling out a perfectly rolled joint from his shirt pocket. "Let's smoke this; it's killer weed I just got."

That was all it took. About ten minutes later, we all agreed that Stuart would fit in quite well.

Being together with Tommy that summer on Fire Island was a completely different experience from my single years back in '78 and '79. "We've become an old married couple, like you and Gerard," I joked with Randy. And in many ways it was true. We went to dinner parties and invited other couples over. I had brought my VCR out from the city for the summer and lots of nights, we stayed in and watched movies while the single guys—Elliot, Franklin, and Stuart—would get ready to go out to the Sandpiper at 1:00 a.m., after it got crowded.

My favorite time was when everyone else was at Tea Dance, and we would go for walks, holding hands along the deserted beach, bathed in the soft light of the setting sun. It was an incredibly peaceful feeling; a sense of contentment settled over me as I watched the day end, secure in the knowledge we'd be spending the evening together—and the days and evenings that followed.

❧ 21 ❧

At the end of that summer of '82 we went out to San Francisco for a long weekend; it was the first Gay Olympics, although it wasn't called that because the U.S. Olympic Committee had won a court order to stop the use of the word "Olympics." Later that fall, about a month after we got back from California, Randy came down with a bad cough. It was constant and sounded like it was from deep inside his chest. I had tried numerous times to get him to stop smoking but now, even with the cough, Randy kept puffing away. Just before Halloween it got so bad that Randy needed to stay home from work.

I spoke with him on the phone after he came back from seeing the doctor.

"He thinks it could be pneumonia so if it's not better by Monday I might need to go into the hospital so they can run this intravenous drip for a few days and get rid of it once and for all," Randy told me.

"And you're still smoking?" I could hear him taking puffs of a cigarette in between coughs.

"I have to build up the nicotine in my system in case I have to go into the hospital next week," Randy argued.

After the weekend, he showed no improvement, and on Tuesday,

Randy went into the hospital, to NYU, just a few blocks from his apartment. I called him by phone that afternoon. "I can come by and visit you on the way home, and we'll have our own happy hour," I said. "Just like Company."

"Except without the two-for-one," Randy said.

"And no Tony in his T-shirt."

"That would certainly cheer me up," Randy said. "You can drag him over. Or have Tommy bring over a couple of his old buddies from Manhattan Men."

"He's not in touch with them anymore," I said. "We never even really talk about it."

"Well, he can call me whenever he feels like talking about those days," Randy said.

"I'm glad your wit is still intact. Do you want me to bring you anything?" I asked.

"Don't come," Randy said. "Seriously, I don't want anyone to see me here. I'll be home Friday night and then this will all be over with."

"You sure you don't want me to come by?" I asked.

"Definitely," Randy said. "I don't want to have to fix my hair. Gerard will come by each night after work. I've got my book and my TV. It's like being on vacation."

I talked to Randy each afternoon that week. Fortunately, with most of the people at CBA having been there so many years, there were a lot of older employees and being home sick for a week or even being hospitalized wasn't as remarkable as it might have been, had the office been filled with younger people. In any case, Carole was the only other person who knew Randy was actually in the hospital—the official word was that he was still at home. Randy sounded better each day, as the drugs in the intravenous drip seemed to be getting rid of the pneumonia. I was relieved when he told me that, but for Randy, there never seemed to be any doubt.

That Thursday I went by Company after work and was surprised to see Gerard. "How's Randy doing?" I asked.

"I'm just getting ready to go over," Gerard told me. "But first things first. A couple of cocktails make it much more pleasant."

"Is it that bad?"

"As hospitals go, it's probably as good as it gets," Gerard said. "And he's in a private room because of the pneumonia. But there are better ways to spend the evening."

"He's coming home tomorrow, right?"

"Hopefully."

"Oh, I thought it was for sure."

"Well," Gerard said, "to Randy, the whole thing is nothing; a little diversion on the road of life."

I guess Gerard was trying to stay calm too but, like me, we all had been seeing the news about the gay plague.

"Is it something more serious?"

"They don't really know," Gerard said. "The doctor said it might even be related to GRID."

"The new gay cancer?" I asked. I was scared and worried but tried not to show it; Gerard seemed so calm about it all.

"Now it's GRID—gay-related immunodeficiency disease," Gerard told me. "It's all these strange infections in the body they haven't seen before, at least not in people under fifty."

"But Randy doesn't do any drugs using needles," I said. "And he definitely doesn't have dozens of sex partners."

"They don't know anything. Nothing's for sure," Gerard said. "The doctor just mentioned it as a possibility."

"Does Randy know?" I asked.

"Yes, of course, he was sitting there for the whole discussion."

"And what did he say?"

"The doctor didn't make a big deal of it; just that there might be some connection," Gerard said. "Randy didn't take too much notice. He's just dreaming about that first cigarette when he gets out."

Randy came home on Friday, and I was glad to see him looking so well when he returned to work on Monday. He had lost some weight in the hospital, but he had been a little chubby before so, to me, he actually looked a bit better than when he went in.

"Yes, rested and relaxed and ready to deal with Harriet after my two weeks in bed," Randy said.

"It's nice to talk to you without cigarette smoke in my face," I said.

"Don't get too used to it," Randy told me. "I'm just cutting back. Not stopping."

A temp had been filling in for Randy—actually, a series of temps, as Harriet rarely put up with any of them for more than a couple of days. She was notorious in her lack of patience, and it wasn't unusual for a temp to end up leaving before lunch, following a crying bout in the women's room after being subjected to one of Harriet's tirades. Probably no one was more relieved than Harriet that Randy was fine and back to work at CBA.

On Christmas Eve, Tommy and I went to Randy and Gerard's for dinner. Like every holiday, "the family" had gotten together, but this time the mood was somber. Marc, Sam's lover, was in the hospital with Kaposi's sarcoma, the cancer that we'd first read about in the *Times*. None of us spoke much. Every time I started to say something, it seemed so unimportant and trivial compared to everyone's hospital and doctor stories. I guess the rest felt the same.

Kaposi's caused purple lesions on the skin, and as word spread about the disease, I would check my skin daily for any suspicious signs—I worried about every black-and-blue mark. I guess I had always been somewhat of a hypochondriac, but this was a disease tailor-made for people like me. No one knew exactly what caused it, and there was a long list of possible signs of infection that changed monthly.

Now it was important to scan your skin regularly for unusual purple marks and then determine whether they were bruises or budding lesions. The *Native* published a helpful guide on how to tell the difference between a bruise and a Kaposi's lesion. So when I pressed on it and the color lightened, that meant it was only a bruise.

Tommy saw me doing it once in the bathroom. "You're too funny," he said. "Just pressing on your skin like that, you're bruising it even more."

"I know we're together now," I said seriously, "but before, you had sex with a lot of guys."

"And you were a virgin before I seduced you?"

"No, but I'm still in the low double-digits when I count the different guys I fucked with over the course of a year."

"Josh, I'm fine," he said. "And you are, too."

I had to admit that Tommy looked great—even better now than he did that first afternoon on Fire Island five years earlier. With our regular eating routine, Tommy weighed about ten pounds more, but it was all muscle, and he had gained it in all the right places.

"You read the paper all the time, Josh," Tommy said, "so you should know. We're not using needles, and we've been together for three years now, so we're not even at risk."

It was true. There had been a blood drive at CBA and although I had donated previously, I was worried that maybe I shouldn't this time. But there was a lot of pressure for each department to get the highest participation. When I went, the Red Cross worker asked me to fill out a card, answering specific questions: if I used drugs, had gay sex with multiple partners in the last thirty-six months, or was Haitian, another group that had been identified at high risk. I answered no honestly to all three and had been cleared to donate. There was no way to actually test the safety of the blood, so it depended on the honesty of each person donating.

Sam stopped by Randy and Gerard's after visiting hours ended at the hospital that Christmas Eve. He looked shaken when he arrived. It was the first time I had ever seen him without Marc. Everyone gave him a hug, and Randy brought over a glass of scotch. Sam told us about the experimental treatments they were using to try to shrink the lesions.

"He's fortunate that the six of them are all on his legs," Sam said. "No one really sees them."

"He can just wear linen pants on the island this summer instead of shorts," Gerard added, trying to be helpful. "How's Marc taking it?"

"They're not painful," Sam said, "but psychologically, it's very rough being there. The other guy in his room has them all over his body, including his face. And he told Marc that a year ago, he started with just a few on this leg."

"But that was before the interferon treatment, right?" I asked.

"Yeah," Sam said. "So hopefully it'll be different with Marc."

I put my arms around Sam's shoulder. "I'm sure it will be." I hoped I sounded more convincing to Sam than I did to myself.

One morning just before Labor Day, I awoke to find we'd forgotten to set the alarm. Tommy was still asleep next to me, and when I nudged him, he smiled sleepily and kissed me on the neck.

"It's almost seven-thirty," I said.

Tommy rolled over and put his arms around me. "Don't worry," he said. "I'll skip my bacon and eggs. Let's just lie here for a while."

I pressed my body closer to Tommy's, and Tommy hugged me tightly. I loved lying there in the mornings like that. Sometimes on the weekend I could lie there for an hour or two in Tommy's arms, drifting in and out of sleep. When Tommy hugged me, I felt so safe and protected, like nothing could hurt me.

I stroked Tommy's hair. "One of us better get in the shower," I said.

"I'll go first," Tommy said, but he didn't move.

I clicked on the TV. The logo starting the eight o 'clock segment of the *Today* show came on the screen with the date, September, 1, 1983, fading to Jane Pauley and Bryant Gumbel.

"You really want me to get out of bed," Tommy said, burying his head under the pillow. He hated watching TV in the morning but I had my routine. I liked to at least know the news headlines when I got up in the morning, even if I couldn't get the *New York Times* delivered. A Korean Airlines 747 from JFK had been shot down by the Soviet Union.

"The Russians shot down a 747 that took off from JFK last night," I told him, pulling the pillow away. "More than two hundred people were killed."

"That's why I don't turn on the TV in the morning," Tommy said. "Who wants to start their day listening to that shit?"

"We could be at war with Russia by this afternoon."

"There, you're all set," Tommy said. "You've got something to worry about all day." He rolled over on top of me and gave me a long kiss before getting out of bed.

Occasionally, there were more stories about the strange disease,

GRID, which had been renamed AIDS, for acquired immune deficiency syndrome. No one knew very much for sure, and there was no treatment available, but now it seemed that it wasn't limited to gay people so "gay-related immune disease" no longer made sense. And there seemed to be a wide range of levels of infection, so "syndrome" had replaced "disease" to cover all possibilities.

The *Native* reported the news regularly, explaining that there was ARC, or "AIDS-related complex," which covered those who had symptoms of some unusual infections but not the more serious, full-blown life-threatening AIDS.

That June, the *Times* reported that the Centers for Disease Control, the CDC, has tracked more than fifteen hundred cases of AIDS, with more than six hundred deaths. Noting that more than 75 percent of the victims were homosexuals, the *Times* report said that CDC officials "emphasized their belief that the vast majority of people are not in danger of contracting the deadly disease."

We'd sit around and try to calculate our own odds. There was no test or any way to find out whether someone was infected, other than to spot the purple lesions or come down with some other signs of illness. Every time Tommy or I got a cold, I would worry. I didn't say anything, because I knew Tommy would just laugh at me or get angry. But still, I was pretty sure that even Tommy couldn't help but wonder each time one of us started coughing if maybe—just maybe—it was the beginning of the end. And if I happened to cough in a meeting at work, I would notice other people looking at me, probably thinking the same thing.

❧ 22 ❧

At Thanksgiving my parents told me that Craig Bloom, the son of their best friends and a guy who had been in the Boy Scout troop with me at the Scarsdale Jewish Center, had also come out.

"Now you won't have to worry about what the Blooms will say about your having a gay son," I told them. I had actually run into Craig Bloom a few years back at the Saint but because Craig hadn't told his parents yet, I had promised not to say a word to my own.

Like the year before, Tommy came with me to Scarsdale for Thanksgiving. That first year I had been so tense that I smoked half a joint in the lavatory on the train after we left Grand Central. Tommy, as usual, had been cool and calm and once we arrived, his charm and cute smile won everyone over quickly. My parents couldn't have been more welcoming if he had been a woman whose last name was Horowitz. Annie was especially warm and friendly with Tommy, giving me a big hug good-bye that year. And Toby—well, Toby had his Walkman now and was too busy listening to his cassettes to even take off the earphones for more than a few minutes.

This Thanksgiving, everything felt more natural to me. My father picked us up at the Scarsdale train station on Thanksgiving morning, and

Tommy and I both gave him a hug. The house was only about ten minutes from the station, and Tommy had bought flowers at Grand Central, which he gave to my mother when we arrived. She kissed each of us on the cheek.

"It smells great," I said.

"I'm glad you come up to have a home-cooked meal once in a while," my mother said.

"I'm sure it will be really delicious, Mrs. Silver," Tommy told her.

I just smiled to myself, remembering his "tough guy" talk with his "posse" when we first met. I'd known it was an act, even that first day after we talked in the ocean.

"We actually eat at home, too, most nights," I said. "Tommy's a great cook." In reality, we usually would buy food and heat it up during the week. But I thought it could be good to give my mother some images of domesticity of me and Tommy to keep in her mind.

We were still standing in the kitchen, watching my mother getting things ready for dinner. I couldn't tell if she was really busy or just distracting herself to avoid listening to the conversation. Although I felt my father had truly accepted my being gay and was genuinely welcoming of Tommy in their home, I wasn't sure my mother had overcome her long-held dream of my arriving in a station wagon with her imaginary daughter-in-law and grandchildren.

The last time we had been together, two months earlier, it seemed like every sentence from my mother was about something she had read about homosexuality, and I was angry about that.

"I realize it's hard for you to imagine, but it's not something I think about every hour or every day," I had told them. "Tommy and I talk about our monthly expenses, the weather, Reagan—probably most of the same things you two talk about."

My father said, "We know, Josh," before I cut him off.

"It's not just gay-gay-gay all the time," I said. "I spend a lot more time thinking about work and my career than I do about being gay."

"You made your decision, so you're comfortable with it," my mother said.

"It's *not* a decision," I said. "I've already explained that a hundred times. The only decision was whether to be honest with myself and everyone else about who I was."

My father changed the subject and that was the end of it. I just hoped spending time with me and Tommy would help them realize what our lives were like.

The Thanksgiving dinner went fine—maybe I had finally gotten through to them—and when Toby excused himself as my mother started to clear the dishes, Tommy stood up and started to help her. "You don't have to do that," she said. "You're a guest here."

"I want to help. I feel like you're all my family now," Tommy said. "I don't want to feel like a guest."

I stood up and helped out too, along with Annie, so the table was cleaned quickly. "Let's go down to the den," I suggested to Tommy, and when we sat down on the leather sofa, I leaned over to kiss him. "It really means a lot for me to have you here," I said. "I get chills in my spine when I see you sitting at the table with my mother and father, Annie, and Toby.

"It means lot to me to be here," Tommy said. "You're really lucky. I wish my parents could be like yours."

On the coffee table I spotted the copy of *Newsweek* from earlier that year, with the AIDS story on the cover. It was the first time any of the news magazines had done a story about AIDS and although I didn't have a subscription, I had bought a copy, trying to read what little was offered about the disease in the mainstream media. I had to conceal it in my briefcase the way a high school student might hide a copy of *Playboy*. I knew Tommy would be angry if he saw it. I read how the head of the U.S. Public Health Service claimed AIDS was "no threat to the public because only 1,450 people are infected, all of them gay and bisexual men or IV drug users."

The *Times* had already run a dozen articles about AIDS, one of them on the front page, so I was sure my parents had seen them, although that subject hadn't come up in our conversations.

"I hope there isn't going to be another post-Thanksgiving-dinner ambush, like the year they asked me if I was gay right after the pumpkin pie," I said.

"They're worried," Tommy said. "It's natural. Just make it easy for them, and tell them we're both fine."

My father came down to the den and sat in his usual chair, on the side of the couch.

"I see you saved that *Newsweek* issue on AIDS," I said.

"Your mother's pretty worried about it," my father said.

"Generally worried, or she's worried about me?"

"Both."

"And you're not worried?" I asked.

Tommy jabbed his elbow against my ribs. "We're worried too, Herb," Tommy said, taking over. "Everyone should be worried. No one knows how you get it or how you get rid of it. But Josh and I are both fine. We've been together now for four years, so we're not even at risk."

"It is scary, though," I said. "We know people who've had some of the symptoms."

"It's mostly just in New York and San Francisco," my father noted.

"At least that's where the doctors know enough to diagnose it," I said, relating some of the stories from the *Native* about the problems people were having getting decent care—or any care—outside the big cities.

"It seems like such a crisis," my father said, "but there's hardly ever anything about it in the *Times*."

"No one cares," I said.

"Well, we care," my father said, standing up and putting a hand on each of our shoulders. "Be careful. I hope you're right that you have nothing to worry about."

We both stood up and gave him a hug.

Later that night, in bed back in the city, I marveled again at how strange it was that Tommy seemed more at ease hugging my father than I did. "No one ever hugged when I was growing up," I told him.

"My mother, my aunts, my uncles, cousins—everyone except my father—was always hugging and kissing." Tommy said.

"That's why you're so good at it," I whispered in his ear as we began to make love.

❧ 23 ❦

I froze when I found the card. It had been six years since that first summer on Fire Island, but I knew those yellow index cards Rick kept so carefully filed in his little metal box with the dates and amounts for the workers each month. It was the last Saturday in March, and the temperature was supposed to be in the seventies that afternoon, about twenty degrees warmer than usual for this time of year. The sudden arrival of the warm weather had energized both Tommy and me, and we had decided to clean up the apartment in the morning and then go out in the afternoon for a lazy walk down Christopher Street to the pier. Tommy had gone downstairs to get the paper, coffee, and some cleaning supplies.

I stared at the card in disbelief. There was Tommy's name and the dates with initials of the clients, the last one just two weeks before: 3/14/84. There were a total of three for March, and I could still recognize Rick's handwriting where he summarized the January and February totals on the back of the card. I sat down on the bed, reading it over and over again, as though somehow if I stared at it, the information on it might change. Maybe another name would appear. Or maybe the dates would go back to 1974 instead of 1984. I was still staring at it when I heard Tommy unlocking the door.

For a second I considered putting it back in the drawer with Tommy's T-shirts where I had found it. But I couldn't. I knew in that instant that everything had changed between us and trying to pretend it hadn't would never work. I wasn't that good an actor. I took the card and walked into the living room.

Tommy handed me the newspaper. "Here, babe, you're all set with new things to worry about." He could probably already see from the look on my face that it wasn't going to be the beautiful day we had envisioned when lying in bed together just an hour earlier. "What's up?" he asked.

I pulled the yellow card out of the pocket in my sweatpants. "What the fuck is this?"

Tommy's usual grin disappeared. "Calm down," he said. "Let me explain it to you."

"You don't have to explain," I said. "I'm not an idiot. I lived with these guys, remember? I knew Tommy Hawk before he was a film editor." I felt the blood rushing to my face. Tommy reached over and put his hand on my shoulder. "Fuck you, Tommy, just don't touch me. You usually get paid for that now anyway, right?"

"Josh, what do you want? You want me to explain what's going on, or you just want me to leave?"

I had tears in my eyes. "No, I don't want you to leave."

"Then calm down and let me explain it to you."

"I can't believe that with everything going on, you're fucking around like this," I said. "You're going to kill both of us."

"Are you going to keep talking, or are you going to let me talk?"

"Okay, go ahead. Let me get some water."

"Come sit here on the sofa with me," Tommy said.

I got a glass of water and sat down.

"Look, I love you," Tommy said. "More than anything. I love being with you, I love what we have together, and I love the way your family has accepted me." He shrugged almost dismissively. "I'm seeing a few of the old clients I used to see regularly. It's extra money, Josh. That's it. I love you."

"And you're going to get AIDS, and we'll both end up dead."

"I don't fuck them."

"Right, and they just pay you to come over there and look beautiful."

"Basically."

"Basically what, Tommy? I'm not an idiot."

"I strip for them, pose, I let them rub my chest, feel my arms. And they jerk off."

"Tommy, you're a fucking liar."

"Okay, yeah, and maybe they touch my dick. I'm trying to be honest with you; that's it. No penetration either way," Tommy said. "Zero risk."

"Why is anyone going to pay a hundred bucks—or whatever you charge these days—for that?"

"These are guys who hired me before. Rick mentions to them that I'm back and tells them my rules," Tommy said. "It's not like before. Most of these guys are scared shitless, and they don't want to take any chances either."

"And how long has this been going on? Did you ever actually stop working, or has that all been a big lie?"

"Since last fall," Tommy said. "Maybe a couple of times a month."

"Well, not this month," I said, waving the card. "You're already up to three for March."

"Rick kept calling me, leaving messages about how clients were asking for me," Tommy said.

"But why?" I asked. "I still don't understand why you'd do it. Just to have other men tell you how great you look?"

"If you think that about me, Josh, you really haven't learned much about me in four years of living together."

I just stared at him. I was too upset to speak.

"You can't understand what it's like for me," Tommy said.

"What are you talking about?"

"I didn't have my parents to pay to send me to a fancy private college," he said. "And I'm not making the big bucks like you are—and I probably never will."

"So what? We're a couple," I said. "We share. We do things together. You just went to get me the paper, right?'

"But you don't understand what it's like, always trying to keep up with you financially," Tommy said. "I don't make the kind of money to go to the Pines every summer or out to dinner or buy memberships to the Saint. That's not my life. I'm living your life."

"You know I always help you out," I said. "I don't make a big deal about it; I just pay for it."

"I know," Tommy said. "You're great about it. But still, it makes me feel like shit when I don't have the money to pay for myself. I'm always under this pressure to live the lifestyle you and Randy and Gerard and all your fancy friends have."

"How come you never talked to me about it before?" I asked. "Instead of just lying to me and going back to hustling?"

"I don't know," Tommy said. "I guess I thought it would just be too hard."

"But it was easy to lie to me, right?" I said. Now the initial shock had passed, and I was getting pissed off.

"It's a second job, Josh. It's a way to make money. That's it."

"And everyone knows about it except me, right? Jim, John, Rick. I'm sure Elliot knows."

"I don't think so."

"How do you think I feel that my lover is fucking with strange guys to make extra money?"

"I'm not fucking, and I told you it's nothing to me. It's work. They get off, they pay me, and I come home to you."

I stood up. "You know, I can't believe you. You walk in the door here, all sweet and innocent, telling me you had to stop in the library after class, and really you have some old guy feeling you up," I said. "The whole thing makes me feel like crap."

"Your best buddy David has done it," Tommy said. "And you don't think any less of him."

"David?"

"Yeah, your friend David has sex for money," Tommy said as he stood up too. "You can ask Rick for the records." He started to go to the door. "I'm going for a walk."

"I thought we were going to talk," I said.

"We talked. I'm not good enough for you, Josh," Tommy said. "I'm a fucking call boy, remember?"

"Tommy," I said, but he just put his finger to his lips before he walked out the door and down the stairs.

I listened to the sound of his footsteps fade and then when I heard the front door to the street slam shut, I went to the window and stood on the balcony that was bolted to the side of the building. Maybe this would be the day it finally fell off, but I didn't care. I watched Tommy cross Fifth Avenue, walking west toward the river. It was too late to even call after him. I wanted to get dressed and run downstairs to catch him, but I felt paralyzed. I sat down on the window ledge and looked at all the people passing by on the streets of the Village, enjoying the weather.

I sat there for nearly an hour. Finally, I picked up the phone to see if it was working in case Tommy tried to call. I was going to call Randy or Elliot. But Randy would just say "I told you so." And Elliot—what if Elliot knew and had never told me? So much for being friends. And David. I just shook my head.

It must have been three o 'clock when I decided I needed to get out of the apartment. I hadn't eaten anything; I'd tried to read the *Times* but gave up after re-reading the first paragraph of the lead story about seven times; and I was mostly walking back and forth between the living room and the bedroom. The yellow card sat on the kitchen counter, but I couldn't even look at it again. When I put it back in the drawer, I started to sob when I saw the stacks of Tommy's T-shirts in there.

I wanted to go out, but I was afraid Tommy might call or come back and I wouldn't be around. I wrote out a note on one of my notepads from work that sat on the kitchen counter. *Went out for food. Back soon. Wait for me. I love you.* We always used one of these CBA notepads I had brought home from work to write one another messages. I looked at the paper with my name and my new Client Service Manager title imprinted on top, crumpled it up, and threw it away. I put the pad away in one of the drawers and ripped off half a sheet from a plain yellow legal pad and wrote out the same note, adding *xoxo* after the *I love you*.

I put on my jeans and a sweatshirt and walked down the steps. My eyes were still red, but I had on my sunglasses. I was praying that Irving wouldn't open the door to chat.

I made a clean escape from the building and turned left at Fifth Avenue to head to Washington Square Park. On a Saturday afternoon with good weather, it was packed. Everyone seemed to be in couples. Was it always like this, I wondered, and I just didn't notice? Or was the warm weather making everyone particularly romantic?

I sat on a bench and played through the conversation with Tommy in my mind. If only I hadn't found the card. If only I had put it back in the drawer without saying anything. But no, that never would have worked.

After all our time living together, it was easy to tell when one of us was out of sync with the other, the millisecond break in timing that lovers pick up from each other. Tommy would have kept asking me what was wrong until I finally told him.

I took a pack of matches from my pocket, pulled out a freshly-rolled joint and took a few hits. Normally, I would have walked around the park to be more discreet while smoking pot instead of just sitting here, but today I didn't care. *Fine, let them arrest me.*

I got up to walk; I was going to go down Christopher Street. Maybe I'd run into Tommy. But the afternoon light was already starting to dim, and I went back to the apartment. From the street I could see that none of the lights were on. When I got upstairs, I walked over to the answering machine, and the red light wasn't flashing. Maybe the light was broken. But when I turned the dial, the double-beep meant the tape was still at the beginning.

❧ 24 ❧

I sat down on the sofa and lit a candle. I had to talk to someone. David was still my closest friend, even though we hadn't spent much time with one another since Tommy and I had gotten together. But we had known each other long enough and had been through so much together in those early years that when we did meet, we would connect as though it had only been a night or two since we last saw one another.

Randy had been my adviser and mentor, not only through the gay world but also through the landmines at CBA. But Randy was older, and I wasn't prepared to hear a lecture from him on how he had warned me that people don't change. Still, it was comforting to know that if David wasn't around, I could call Randy and surely be invited over for dinner to forget my worries in a fog of booze, pot, and cigarette smoke. But in thinking about it, I could see what Tommy meant. When we were there, Gerard and his friends were always talking about expensive clothes and trips to Europe and the latest new restaurants.

I dialed David's number. It rang five times, and I was about to hang up when he picked up. He was out of breath. "I was just coming up the stairs and heard the phone ringing," David said. "If I had known it was only you, I wouldn't have rushed."

"Thanks."

"I was hoping I might have another gentleman caller tonight," David said, mimicking one of the lines in *The Glass Menagerie* from his storehouse of refrains out of his favorite classic movies.

"I *am* a gentleman caller," I said, imitating David's exaggerated accent.

"I meant a single gentleman caller," David said. "An eligible young bachelor."

"I might be," I said.

"What happened?" David asked.

I told him about finding the card, the argument, Tommy leaving, and my moping around all day.

"He'll be back," David said.

"I know he'll be back; all his stuff is here," I said. "But I don't know if we can ever get back to where we were. Plus, he was justifying it. It wasn't like he said he was sorry and would never do it again."

"Do you want me to come over?" David asked.

I thought about that but when—or if—Tommy came back, I definitely didn't want him to walk in on David and me sitting there talking. "Let's just meet at Sandolino for coffee," I told him. That was still one of my favorite places, and I thought the familiarity would be comforting.

I looked at the untouched note for Tommy sitting on the desk. It still worked. I added in the time, *7:30 p.m.*, on the bottom under the *xoxo*.

When I got to Sandolino, David was already waiting for me outside. We sat down and both ordered coffee. David put his hand on my knee under the table.

"I'm sorry, honey, I really am," David said. "What do you want?"

"I love him. I want to be with him," I said. "But I don't want him to keep hustling."

"Did you tell him that?"

"Sort of," I said. "In the end I was getting angry, so it didn't really come out that way."

"Well, he's angry, too," David said. "He's angry that you found out but mostly probably angry at himself."

I looked up at David. He still looked so handsome with his golden-brown hair. I wondered what things would have been like if we had been lovers—or if we became lovers. I was getting ready to ask David about Manhattan Men, but he saved me the trouble.

"You know I did it once," David said.

"What?" I asked, feigning innocence.

"Manhattan Men."

"Really? When?"

"Years ago, after that summer on Fire Island when I first met them."

"And you only did it once?"

"Maybe a few times."

"That's okay. I'm used to people lying to me."

"Josh," David said, "c'mon. It's not easy to talk about."

"I know. I'm experienced with call boys."

"Josh," David said as he squeezed my knee again under the table. "Behave, or I'll get a cigarette from someone and start blowing smoke in your face."

David told me about how he had been short of money one month. "I needed fifty dollars more to pay the rent and had Jim's card in my wallet, so I called him," David said. "I didn't even think about it much before I called. And then when I did it, it was easy. It was a nice hotel—the Waldorf—and the guy was some big executive from Dallas who kept telling me how gorgeous I was."

"I don't need to know the details," I said.

"Well, even Blanche Dubois had to depend on the kindness of strangers," David told me.

"Very funny."

"It was painless and easy and an hour later, I walked out the door with the seventy-five dollars plus a twenty-dollar tip," David said. "Jim told me the client was really happy and asked me if I'd do it again, and I told him no."

"So what happened?"

"A few months later the same guy is back at the Waldorf, and he tells Jim he'll make it worth my while if I'll see him again," David said. "I went over, and this time it's over before I know it, and he gives me a fifty. After Jim takes their cut, I still made over a hundred dollars in less than an hour.

"And you're still doing it?"

"No, that was it," David said. "And it was with this guy, Bob, or one of his friends from Dallas."

"From Texas, huh?" I asked. "You're sure it wasn't Billy Bob?"

"I can see you're feeling better, Josh," David said. "Anyway, I'm not proud of it but just wanted you to know I did it. And it is possible to do it, like Tommy told you, and not have it feel like anything other than a way to make money."

We ordered hamburgers—I was hungry; I hadn't eaten anything all day. At 9:30, when we finished, I told David I wanted to get home to see if Tommy had called or come back in the past couple of hours. "What are you going to do tonight?" I asked.

"The usual," David said. "Go out to look for trouble. You want to come with me to Uncle Charlie's for old time's sake?"

I had liked going there, and now Uncle Charlie's had expanded and in addition to Uncle Charlie's South, North, and the restaurant, there was now an Uncle Charlie's Downtown on Greenwich Avenue, right there in our neighborhood, and Uncle Charlie's Village, which was really more of a dance club, down at the end of Christopher Street in the River House Hotel, a gay hotel with a restaurant on the top floor looking out over the Hudson.

I turned down the offer. I just wasn't going to be very much fun at a bar. "No, I really want to get home to see if Tommy's there," I said.

But there was no Tommy and no flashing light on the answering machine. I took a few hits from the rest of the joint that I had started that afternoon in the park, opened the windows on to the balcony, and sat again on the window sill, my feet on the balcony, looking down at Ninth Street. It was warm out for March, definitely the warmest night of the year so far. At eleven o 'clock, I took two Tylenol PM, got into bed, and passed out asleep.

It was 4:15 in the morning when Tommy crawled into bed next to me. Mercifully, I had slept the whole time. He kissed me and told me he was sorry.

"I'm going to stop. I'm calling them tomorrow, and you're going to be standing next to me, listening to the call," Tommy said. "I'm getting rid of the answering service for good."

"I've heard it all before," I said.

Tommy kissed me. "Please, Josh, I don't want to fight," he said. "Let's just turn the page." He wrapped his arms around me and that was the last thing I remembered before I fell back to sleep.

I woke up as the sun first began to slip through the space along the edge of the window shade. The hum of the air conditioner was drowning out any noise from the street, and Tommy was still asleep next to me. I was still as seduced by Tommy's beauty as I was that first afternoon I saw him in his yellow tank top in the Pines; that image still stuck in my head six years later. Usually, if I jerked off thinking of Tommy, it was the hot, unapproachable Tommy of 1978, not the one lying here next to me, sharing my bed.

I kissed his neck, and Tommy smiled, his eyes still closed.

"I love you," I said, but I still felt shaken from all that had happened in the past twenty-four hours.

"Me, too," Tommy said, and he pulled me closer, wrapping his arms around me so our chests were pressed up against one another. As I felt Tommy's body, the muscles in his arms, I started to get hard. Tommy rolled on top of me and opened his eyes. We looked at one another and started to kiss.

Afterwards, I thought that had been the most passionate lovemaking we'd had together.

❧ 25 ❦

Seven weeks later we headed out to the Pines again for the first weekend of the season. Elliot wasn't going to be coming this year; he was taking a class on Saturdays, and it was just as well. I wanted Manhattan Men out of my life completely. Tommy did offer to let me listen in when he called Jim that Sunday morning, but I had told him I didn't want to hear the call; that Tommy should just take care of Jim and the answering service, let me know when it was done, and then not speak about it again.

That Monday afternoon, a box of red roses arrived for me at CBA. The note just said one word: *Done*. Rita got a vase from under the sink in the lunchroom and filled it with water for me. "Who sent the roses?" she asked, and when I told her I didn't know, she smiled like it didn't matter if I admitted that I knew or not. Randy, on the other hand, didn't have discretion in mind when he walked by before lunch.

"Big fight with the hubby over the weekend?" he asked, flicking his cigarette ashes into my wastebasket. I refused to keep an ashtray in my office in the hope it would discourage visitors from smoking. But Randy just used the wastebasket, despite my admonitions that he would start a fire. "Look who's talking about playing with fire," Randy had said, chuckling.

Randy wasn't big on following most of the rules at CBA, but because he worked for Harriet, one of the top executives in the office, he was pretty much untouchable. Although Randy kept threatening to quit, saying he couldn't stand to work another day for Harriet, it was pretty much the same thing he'd been saying for the past five years, since we first met.

"I'm sure Harriet will be presenting you with the gold watch at your retirement party in thirty years," I told him. "You can't live without each other at this point."

"What was the fight about?" Randy asked.

"What makes you think we had a fight?" I asked.

"Ahem," Randy said as he looked over the flowers and then pointed the cigarette at them for added emphasis.

But I wouldn't give him the satisfaction of hearing any details. "It's fine now," I told him.

After that Saturday night at Sandolino, David and I had become closer, and I was really happy when he agreed to take the smaller bedroom in the house back on Fire Island. It was our third summer back in the same house. Tommy and I had the master bedroom, and Stuart, who now had a boyfriend, took the larger of the other two rooms.

CBA had just won the Johnson Wax account—I had worked hard on the pitch and had been assigned to manage the business. I was still working for Scoot, who now had a number of big clients under his responsibility. In any case, I was sorry that I would no longer be dealing with Gordon, as after a few months of dancing around the subject, we had finally come out to one another. He had told me about his partner, Ron—together for twenty-two years—and I told him about Tommy. It had been great to have another gay man as my client, but I was excited to move on from GM after seven years of rhapsodizing over the joys of power-assisted steering and intermittent windshield wipers.

Along with the rest of the account team, I had gone out to the Johnson Wax headquarters in Racine, Wisconsin. It was actually a step down from Detroit, a totally boring Midwestern town, although the Johnson Wax headquarters had been designed by Frank Lloyd Wright, so that made up for the cheerless motel by the highway where we had to stay overnight. The famous architect had even designed the interior of the headquarters building, including the desks and the chairs, although those had to be retrofitted after Wright's original design for three-legged chairs proved to require too much of a balancing act for the middle-aged secretaries to master.

Back on Madison Avenue, the company sent each member of the team a gift box filled with products. I stuffed the Raid, Glade, Edge, Pledge, Off, and other monosyllabic symbols of American domestic life into a large shopping bag to take out to the house on Fire Island that first weekend.

Tommy and I each took that first Friday off from work so we could get out to the Island early and get the house opened up for the season. That first night was cool, and after everyone arrived we built a fire in the red metal fireplace that stood in one corner of the living room. We had gone out among the trees behind the house to gather branches, and I rolled up newspapers to get the fire going. We smoked a joint, listened to Wham singing "Wake Me Up Before You Go-Go" and marveled at how we had gathered the wood and built the fire. "So butch," David said. "It's like being on a camping trip."

It was a fun group at the house that year. I was glad to not have to listen to any stories about Manhattan Men from Elliot, and Stuart could always be counted on for a steady supply of high-quality marijuana. His boyfriend, Alex, worked for Home Box Office, and the two of us enjoyed talking about the TV business. Plus, David and Stuart could spend endless hours discussing the latest gossip from the fashion world, for which there never seemed to be a shortage of new material.

Maybe it was because we were all getting older, but that year we ended up just staying at the house more nights than not. The five of us would alternate making dinner, each trying to outdo the other with some gourmet recipe that we had found during the week and written down, occasionally even bringing the more exotic ingredients with us from the city.

Tommy and I never had time to watch movies at home during the week, so I took the VCR out to the Pines. Alex sometimes brought tapes of the movies that were airing on HBO that month, as there was no cable service at the house. Once in a while we would go over to Randy and Gerard's after dinner, but I tried to be sensitive to how Tommy felt about being there, always alert to a yawn or other sign of waning interest that would prompt me to ask if him if he wanted to leave.

It was hard to think anything good had come from the whole incident with the yellow card, but it had brought us closer together. Tommy had told me how he felt in what he called "my world," and now I was more sensitive to it.

Marlon and Rafael, two of the original group of four—the Latino contingent that first Labor Day barbeque seven years ago when I first met Tommy—now had shares in their own house for the summer. Tommy hadn't kept in touch with them, and he seemed genuinely excited to see them again when we all met up at Tea Dance. The two of them had both stopped working for Manhattan Men when they moved in together in '79. Marlon was now an architect, and Rafael worked in a veterinarian's office near where they lived on Eighth Avenue. They had two cocker spaniels that they brought out with them every weekend. I liked going over to their house with Tommy. Even though Marlon probably made as much money as anyone working in the garment industry—the *schmata business* or *rag trade*, as David would say—to Tommy, they weren't as pretentious as Randy and Gerard and their friends. And they were his world, not mine.

At the end of August Randy was home sick from work with a bad cold. I talked to him on the phone. He sounded terrible. "I'm not going to go out to the Island," he told me. "I'm just going to rest here in bed."

"That's probably a good idea," I told him, although it was the first time that I could remember Randy ever not going out to the Pines on a summer weekend.

"Do you think he has AIDS?" Tommy asked me in bed that night.

"No, I don't think AIDS. Maybe it's ARC," I said, using the acronym for AIDS-related complex. According to the news reports that summer, 10 percent of those infected with the virus were likely to develop ARC, and 10 percent of those were predicted to progress to full-blown AIDS. "Even if he's infected, the odds are ninety-nine to one that it doesn't progress to AIDS," I said.

But that next week, Randy was hospitalized once more. At first he insisted that he didn't want any visitors again, but when he was still there for a second week, he relented. I walked over to NYU Medical Center from CBA that same day, still in my suit and tie. Gerard had told me that Randy wasn't responding that quickly to the medication this time, that the pneumonia was more persistent, but seeing Randy there in the bed, with the IV drip and the oxygen tubes running to his nose, I struggled not to sound shaken as I went over to say hello and kissed him on the cheek.

He was in a double room—alone, fortunately—and I sat down in the chair next to the bed. Randy said the doctors didn't seem to know why the treatment wasn't working; they thought perhaps it was because he'd developed some sort of resistance after the prior therapy. And now,

Randy told me, he had these sores in his mouth that made it difficult to eat and even to talk. His face, which had always been full and round—even showing traces of baby fat at forty-five—now looked narrow and gaunt. He must have lost more than ten pounds in the two weeks.

Randy closed his eyes, and I sat there in silence, looking out at the lights of the city. The view was amazing through the large glass windows. I could see the Empire State Building, the Chrysler building, and, looking down, the cars, the buses, the people all rushing home from work or going to meet friends for drinks. It seemed surreal to me, like I was with Randy suspended in a glass bubble, watching the world pass by outside.

Gerard came in with a bag of food from a Chinese restaurant. Randy opened his eyes for a minute and then closed them. "He hasn't been eating so I brought him some of his favorite dishes," Gerard whispered.

"What are the doctors saying?" I asked him. Gerard tilted his neck toward the door, motioning for me to follow him out to the hallway.

"It's not good," Gerard said. "The drugs aren't working, and he's not eating, which is making him even weaker."

I left shortly after that. I stopped at the pay phone in the hall and called home; Tommy was already there. "I'm on my way; see you soon," I told him. On the way out, going down the hallway, I had been shocked to see that nearly all of the rooms seemed to be filled with young guys. The entire floor apparently now had been set aside for people with AIDS and ARC. I walked home from the hospital, still dazed from the experience.

I rang the buzzer under the Silver-Perez nameplate as I got to the building. It was a habit Tommy and I had adopted to let the other know we were on our way up the stairs. When I walked in the apartment, this time I was the one who didn't feel like talking for a change.

"Just hug me," I told Tommy, and as he wrapped his arms around me and pulled me close, I kissed him with tears in my eyes.

"He's bad, huh?"

"Yeah," I said. "I don't know whether he's ever going to come home from that place."

"I'll go with you next time," Tommy told me.

"Thanks. I love you," I said, and then our lips locked together.

❧ 26 ❧

Randy did come home from the hospital, right after Labor Day, but he never went back to CBA. He told Harriet he had been diagnosed with Hodgkin's disease, but neither Randy nor Carole, who also knew the truth, thought that Harriet or anyone else believed that. Randy's T-4 cells, the cells that fight infection in the body, had dropped below 200 which was the dividing line between being classified as having ARC and full-blown AIDS. Supposedly, anything below 500 meant the immune system was compromised, and you were likely to develop some symptoms of ARC.

It was strange being at CBA without Randy. But other than Harriet, who was running through at least one assistant a week as she tried to find a replacement, probably no one besides Carole and me noticed he was gone. I busied myself in my work, though now there were a lot more stories in the *Times* about AIDS. It seemed like there was at least one article a week, each one sounding more terrifying than the one before.

"I think we should have our T-cell counts measured," I told Tommy. "I have to go for my checkup anyway next week. I'm going to ask Dr. Rothstein."

"You can spend your life worrying about whether you have AIDS," Tommy said. "I'm not going to."

"We should know, though," I said.

"Why?" Tommy asked. "Why should we know? There's not one fucking thing we could do if the count is low—other than worry."

"I guess," I said.

"We're fine, Josh. We've been together for five years and haven't slept with anyone else," Tommy said. "We both look great, we go to the gym, we go running. Just stop torturing yourself."

When I went to Dr. Rothstein that next Tuesday morning I asked him about measuring my T-cells. Dr. Rothstein, Joel Rothstein, was gay, and I had started going to him shortly after I came out. He was a doctor I knew from the Pines, and Randy had recommended him. And he was Jewish. That was a plus, because I knew Lillian would approve of my having a Jewish doctor. Tommy had never had a regular doctor, but he had seen Dr. Rothstein a few times, too, over the years for minor things, like a tetanus shot.

While he was drawing my blood for the other standard tests in the physical, I asked him about the T-cell test. "Unless there's some other abnormality in these tests, I wouldn't run the T-cells," he told me. "It's an expensive test, and the insurance isn't going to pay for it."

"Well, what if I wanted to pay for it?"

"Still," Dr. Rothstein said, "it's not going to tell us much. There's very little data of what T-cell counts should look like in healthy people—they've never been tested in large numbers. It might vary by time of day, stress, whatever—we just don't know. Your lungs are fine, Josh; everything checks out great. I know it's hard, but try not to worry about it."

I didn't mention it to Tommy when I got home. He would have been pissed off at me for bringing it up.

The fall went quickly, as it did every year. It was always a busy time for me at work, because clients were trying to use up their budgets before year-end and start the planning for next year's campaigns. At the production house, things were also busy for Tommy. Most of the work was on video now, and the changeover from film had leveled the playing field. Because everyone was starting fresh with the new equipment when it came in, it no longer mattered that Tommy was so young; with the video equipment he was as experienced as anyone else there. Plus, the company had started to make music videos, and Tommy spent more time editing those than the usual thirty- and sixty-second commercials. He was working on a video of "That's What Friends Are For," which Elton John had written and Dionne Warwick, Gladys Knight, and Stevie Wonder performed— all the profits were being donated for AIDS research. I had never heard Tommy so excited about his job.

We didn't renew our membership to the Saint that fall. "Too much bridge and tunnel crowd," I said.

"Like me?" Tommy said. "You weren't going to say that anymore, remember?"

"Sorry," I said. "You know what I mean."

It was hard to tell exactly when the excitement had worn off but the thrill of dancing at the Saint was gone. "I'd rather spend the money on theater tickets," I said.

"Me too," Tommy said, and I couldn't help thinking about how we were both getting older.

When we went up to my parents' for Thanksgiving dinner and my father picked us up at the station, he seemed particularly enthused when he greeted each of us with a hug and told us, "You both look great!"

I could only imagine how hard it was for them out there in the suburbs, hearing the stories on TV about AIDS. The media sensationalized it all, and after decades of invisibility on television, now gay men were on view nightly—usually covered in Kaposi's lesions, in wheelchairs and stretchers, or jumping out of hospital windows.

Herb and Lillian and most people in the country never saw the thousands and thousands of healthy gay men that Tommy and I were surrounded by in the city each day, going about our lives as we had before.

No one said the word AIDS during dinner, but I was sure, as they looked at me and Tommy, listening for any telltale cough or checking for unusual marks on our skin, they worried if the two of us were both okay.

I took Tommy to the CBA Christmas party for the first time that year, introducing him as "my partner." Everyone at Tommy's studio knew about me; he even had a picture of the two of us in a small frame sitting on top of his editing console. But at CBA, although I didn't pretend to have a girlfriend, I hadn't talked about Tommy or advertised my sexual orientation. But now, after repeatedly reading in the *Times* that the so-called "general public" wasn't at risk for AIDS, I decided I wasn't going to keep Tommy invisible any longer. It was time for people like me to start showing the world *we* were part of "the general public."

I was surprised by how friendly people were to Tommy at the party. Scoot brought his wife over and talked to us for ten minutes. Harriet gave Tommy a big kiss, saying, "I've been wanting to meet you." I wasn't sure that was true—I didn't remember ever mentioning Tommy's name to Harriet—but after all, I figured, she had gotten where she was by knowing how to say the right things to people. I watched Carole and Tommy dancing together and thought about Randy. Randy would have loved watching this with me.

That Monday I took the framed photo of Tommy and me, together on the deck at Fire Island, which had been on the shelf in our living room, and placed it on my desk at CBA.

There was no Christmas Eve party at Randy and Gerard's that year. Tommy had gone with me to visit Randy the weekend before, and we told him about the office Christmas party. Randy had gained some of his strength back, although it seemed like the fat was gone from his face, probably for good. "It's great," Randy told me. "I really admire what you've done. And you're a lovely couple together." He squeezed my hand.

The words sounded strange coming out of Randy's mouth. I was used to his sarcasm, his grimaces, and his cigarettes. It didn't sound like Randy; more like some alien being that was occupying his body.

He was fortunate that Gerard was there to take care of him; he certainly wasn't able to take care of himself. Tommy and I both knew other people, ones who were single and lived alone, without anyone to take care of them at home, who got sent to Goldwater, an old polio sanitarium from the 1930s that was isolated on Roosevelt Island; the city had reopened it to house AIDS patients.

Tommy and I bought a couple of fake logs and spent Christmas Eve at home. I put on the record of Minnie Riperton singing, "Lovin' You" as we lay on the rug in front of the fireplace.

"I'm lucky to have you," I said.

Tommy wrapped his legs around mine. "We're lucky to have each other."

> *Lovin' you is easy 'cause you're beautiful*
> *Makin' love with you is all I wanna do*
> *Lovin' you is more than just a dream come true*
> *And everything that I do is out of lovin' you*
> *La la la la la la la ... do do do do do*

Christmas morning we left for a week in Key West. I had been to Miami Beach to visit my grandparents a few times and to Fort Lauderdale in my single days but had never been to Key West. Marlon and Rafael had gone last year and told us it was a great place for gay couples. We rented a room at a gay-owned guest house, Alexander's, flew down to Miami, and changed planes there to a propeller-powered DC3 for the thirty-minute flight to Key West. *David would definitely enjoy this*, I thought, as the plane, sitting at an incline as we boarded, looked just like the plane in the last scene in *Casablanca*, a scene reenacted many times in the living room at Fire Island after a long night of drinking.

Key West was quieter than we expected, but Tommy and I were both a lot quieter than we used to be, too. It wasn't so important to go out dancing, although when we did, I could see Tommy definitely still got into having people look at his body, as much as he insisted he didn't. There was a tea dance poolside at one of the guesthouses, La-Te-Da, and we got ready to walk over there.

"I don't care that you enjoy it, Tommy. It still turns me on to look at you in a T-shirt," I said. "But just admit it—that you like people looking at you."

"Don't hate me because I'm beautiful," he joked, mimicking a Pantene shampoo commercial that ran incessantly on the television that winter.

"It's funny the way you work so hard to pretend you don't like the attention," I said.

"I can help you find a short, fat boyfriend if you want." Tommy pushed me down on the bed. He flexed his arms and pretended to kiss his biceps, looking at his arms in the mirror. I reached up and pulled Tommy down to kiss me.

"It's not easy to live with an egomaniac," I said.

"Yeah, Josh; everyone feels really sorry for you," Tommy told me.

"Bring a little package of Kleenex with you when we go out tonight."

Exactly two months after we got back, on March 4, Randy died. He had been at home, pretty much in bed all the time since he had gotten out of the hospital. I had been stopping by at least twice a week, and Tommy had come with me the last time we saw him at home, two days before he died. The next night he had gone back to NYU, in an ambulance Gerard had called after Randy had trouble breathing, and in the morning he was gone.

I left work when Gerard called me at CBA. I told Scoot that Randy had died and didn't have to say anything more. "Go ahead; leave and just call me later," Scoot said putting his hand on my shoulder. "Take tomorrow if you need it."

Although Randy had stayed in touch with his family, his parents were both in their seventies and in poor health. Neither of them knew he was gay, that Gerard was his lover and not his roommate, or that he had AIDS. Randy had told them the Hodgkin's disease story, saying that at the time, no one in Metairie, Louisiana, wanted to talk to anyone whose son had AIDS. His sister, although she was aware of his relationship with Gerard and knew he was sick, never came to visit from Arlington, Virginia, a three-hour train trip away. She said she couldn't leave the kids, but Randy was sure it was because of the AIDS and nothing else. "She's terrified," he had said at the time. "And I don't blame her."

Gerard organized the funeral three days later at Redden's on West 14th Street, one of a handful of funeral homes in the city that even accepted people who died of AIDS. Tommy went with me, holding my hand. Harriet and Carole were both there from CBA. The group from the house at Fire Island was there, except for Marc, who was home sick—still alive, but barely. Gerard's friends and business colleagues attended, including the owners of the label for which he designed—two middle-aged Jewish couples from Westchester who reminded me of my parents. There were about twenty-five people all together. When we walked outside, the bright sunlight took me back to that day in March two years before when Tommy and I had that big fight. It seemed like so long ago now. I squeezed Tommy's hand hard as we walked back home.

After Key West we had decided not to go to Fire Island that summer and instead to spend the money on a trip to Europe together later in the fall. I had been in London for one semester of my junior year when I was at Cornell and had traveled around after that, but Tommy had never been out of the country. And my head was filled with romantic fantasies of sitting together with Tommy at some little café in Paris. "We can go to Europe for ten days, go away for a few weekends over the summer, and even with the trip to Key West spend less this year than Fire Island costs us," I had told him, calculating the expenses on a yellow legal pad.

So that was what we did. Over Fourth of July weekend, which spread over four days that year, we went to Provincetown, a small fishing village at the tip of Cape Cod that had always had a small, gay artists colony. It was where Tennessee Williams wrote most of *The Glass Menagerie* and *A Streetcar Named Desire*. When we had been in Key West over New Year's we had met another couple from Boston, who had a house there and had invited us to visit.

Provincetown was smaller than Key West and, I thought, considerably more charming. There were no hotels or motels, only small bed and breakfast inns. It was all surrounded by the Cape Cod National Seashore, our tax money at work supporting another gay resort like Fire Island.

But this was different from Fire Island. During the day it was filled with straight tourists driving up the Cape for their whale watches and jamming the streets pushing baby strollers and buying ice cream cones.

That's when the gay men headed to the seashore. Tommy and I rented bikes and rode them on the trails through the dunes to Herring Cove, the gay beach. At night, the gays would take over as the tourists headed back to their motels and cottages farther down the highway. Before and after dinner, we'd stroll up and down along Commercial Street, and with the town library, the post office, the town hall, and the church, it looked like Main Street USA at Disney World but the real thing. We bought a stuffed purple moon with a face etched on it to hang in our bedroom on Ninth Street. Tommy liked the way the face looked. "It'll watch over us and protect us," he said.

At the beginning of August, we did go out to Fire Island for a weekend, staying with Marlon and Rafael. Sitting on the deck there, the four of us, I couldn't help but smile when I remembered back to how we had all first met at the Manhattan Men barbeque eight years before. Now Marlon was becoming well known as an architect, Tommy was making music videos, and Rafael was about as domestic and loving a partner as anyone could find.

"I'm glad we decided not to get a share on Fire Island this summer," I told Tommy, sitting over lunch at Sandolino. "It's just not the same." More than 2,300 people had died last year from AIDS, and it seemed like a lot of them were from the Pines, or at least everyone in the Pines seemed to know someone who had died or was sick. At Tea Dance, we would hear people having a prolonged coughing bout, marking them as the infected, and we'd try to avoid looking over to see who it was. Some had the telltale purple spots or that same gaunt look I had seen on Randy's face that night in the hospital. The talk on the deck of the Blue Whale had turned from T-shirts to T-cells.

❧ 27 ❦

I needed something to think about that would distract me from worrying about whether Tommy or I—or both of us—was going to get sick, so I planned the vacation to Europe over the Labor Day weekend, detailing it carefully on a grid so that Tommy and I could be away for ten days and each only use five vacation days from work. It was a beautiful trip, and we shot six rolls of film—more than two hundred pictures. I loved taking pictures of Tommy. And Tommy? Well, let's just say Tommy liked to pose. We went to London first, then to Paris, and then to Madrid—three nights in each before flying home. When I had the photos developed, the picture of the two of us in front of the Eiffel Tower came out great, and I took it to work to replace the one of us at Fire Island that was on my desk. David came over one night to look at the photos. "You guys are really lucky to have each other," he said. "It's no fun being single these days."

Gerard invited us over for Christmas Eve. "Randy would have wanted us to all get together," Gerard said when he called. "And we need to keep going—we're still alive." Marc had died during the year, and Sam was going to help Gerard get everything organized for the dinner. All of us were trying to cling to some semblance of normalcy, but that was getting more difficult every day.

Of course I knew Gerard, and we had spent a lot of time together over the years, but the link to him and the whole crowd had been through Randy. That evening, it was pretty clear to me—and probably everyone else—that Randy's being there in spirit was definitely not as much fun as having him there in person. And Sam was with a new boyfriend, less than three months after Marc had died. It felt disorienting, like the world was spinning slightly off its normal axis.

"It was strange to see Sam kissing another guy," I told Tommy afterwards. "He was with Marc when I first met him, and I had never seen him with someone else."

"Well, if anything ever happens to me, I don't want you to sit home, alone and miserable," Tommy said.

"Don't worry; I'm already making a list of prospects," I joked, but it hardly perked up the mood.

We went back to Key West over New Year's, and it felt good to get on an airplane and out of New York. "I just can't stop thinking about it when I'm in the city," I said as we took off.

"It?" Tommy asked. "Thinking about AIDS?"

"What else?" I said. "I just feel surrounded by it. The television every night, the *Times* every morning."

"That's why I told you to stop reading the *Times*. And the *Native*," Tommy said.

"What good does that do, burying your head in the sand?" I asked.

"Because there's nothing you fucking can do, Josh—that's why," Tommy said, raising his voice. "You get sick, you die. There's nothing they can do to treat it, and no one can even tell you what to do to avoid getting it."

"Well, no drugs or fucking around," I said.

"Yeah, right," Tommy said. "And on Thursday, sucking is supposedly safe and then by next Tuesday, you read somewhere that it's the worst thing you can do."

I nodded. It did seem that way. Every week there was some safe-sex recommendation or medical finding that seemed to contradict one from the week before.

"You can just make up your mind that you're going to live your life and—like my grandmother walked around saying, *Que sera, sera*—whatever will be, will be." Tommy told me.

Tommy put his arm around me on the plane and stared to sing *Que Sera, Sera* into my ear.

"Let's take an AIDS break for the week. We don't watch TV, we don't read the newspaper, and we don't mention the word," Tommy said. "If someone else brings it up by the pool, we walk away."

"Okay, deal," I said, shaking Tommy's hand.

"And that includes examining yourself for any suspicious marks on your skin when you get out of the shower."

Tommy had been right. I did feel better not listening to the TV, reading the newspaper, or talking about AIDS. Getting away from the phone was great—no one called us with reports on anyone else being sick—and Tommy and I spent the week lying by the pool, making love, and holding hands as we walked down Duval Street together to watch the sunset from Mallory Square. We rented bikes and had someone take our picture together in the exact same spot as the year before, in front of the concrete marker of the southernmost point in the United States: "150 miles from Miami, 90 miles from Havana," the sign beside us read.

When we got back home, though, the Christmas card I had sent to Elliot in Indiana was sitting in my mailbox, stamped in purple ink with an illustrated purple finger and the words *Return to Sender*. Underneath, in the list of reasons, the box next to *Deceased* had been checked. I stared at it, thinking they must have just checked the wrong one but realized they probably hadn't. Elliot had written to me that fall but had never said anything about being sick. We hadn't spoken by phone in a while, though. I had just sent him a postcard from Key West.

I ripped open the envelope and took out the returned card. Tommy and I had both signed it. I put it back on the desk, where it had sat for most of December before its round trip back and forth to Indiana. Tears were running down my cheeks. Tommy hugged me. "It'll be okay," he said, but even Tommy—super-confident, never-down Tommy—sounded like he had his doubts. I went in the bathroom and closed the door, sobbing. My whole body was shaking, and I didn't want Tommy to see me like that. I splashed cold water on my face, and then Tommy knocked, so I opened the door.

He wrapped his arms around me and held me tight. "I told you; it's going to be okay." And I wanted so much to believe that.

In May, Tommy got his degree. I took the morning off from CBA to attend the graduation, and two of Tommy's friends from work were there as well. I shot a roll of pictures of Tommy outside, holding the diploma, with his wide grin. He was twenty-nine now but certainly didn't look any older than twenty-one in his cap and gown. That night I organized a party at an Italian restaurant in the neighborhood to celebrate. David came, and Carole was there, as were Tommy's pals from Atlantic, and Marlon and Rafael. But Randy and Elliot were gone. I had tried to call Franklin, but the home number I had was disconnected, and when I called NBC, they said he didn't work there anymore. Maybe he just got another job. At least, that's what I would have automatically assumed a few years before—now, of course, I couldn't help wondering if he was even still alive.

That winter the Food and Drug Administration, the FDA, approved a test that detected HIV, the human immunodeficiency virus, which French scientists at the Pasteur Institute in Paris had discovered years earlier and was supposedly responsible for AIDS. But there was a lot of controversy over the test and whether people should have it done.

There were still no drugs approved for treating the disease, so even if you did test positive, there was nothing to do except worry. And there was still a lot of debate within the scientific community as to whether HIV alone caused AIDS, or it was just one of the contributing factors.

The *Native* and most other gay publications all advised against being tested. Word had already leaked out that there was discussion in the Reagan administration to begin testing all visitors coming to the United States and permanently barring any of those who tested positive. Leaders of the gay community were warning that despite promises of anonymity, the Republican administration could compile lists of everyone who tested positive, which could even lead, one day, to quarantine camps for everyone positive.

I was torn. I hated not knowing. But like Tommy said, there wasn't anything I could do differently if I did test positive. And it was scary. People were terrified of AIDS; by now sixteen thousand had already died, including the Hollywood star Rock Hudson, whose decline, including nighttime evacuation from Paris by stretcher when a last-ditch experimental therapy there failed, had been televised live. There was no treatment and no definitive word on how it was spread. *Newsweek* ran another cover story on AIDS, calling it "one of the most difficult challenges ever faced by modern medicine." But still the odds seemed good: the *Times* was still reporting that only a small percentage of those infected actually developed AIDS, and Tommy and I would celebrate our seventh anniversary that Christmas, so we'd been together long past the three years they said it usually took to show symptoms.

Every day now, it seemed that the two New York tabloids, the *Daily News* and the *New York Post*, managed to come up with terrifying headlines. I didn't read them, but the huge letters on the front page were impossible to avoid. The phone rang with news about people Tommy and I knew being sick or in the hospital. Or dead. We heard that Franklin had died alone at Goldwater. Gerard told me that Sam had committed suicide, using instructions provided by PWAC, the People with AIDS Coalition. GMHC, the Gay Men's Health Crisis organization, was trying desperately to provide the care and education in the community that the government didn't. Tommy and I were both okay, but we felt like survivors from the *Titanic*, huddled in our lifeboat, surrounded by the dead and near-dead floating beside us.

It was in June of that year that I felt first the lump in Tommy's neck as I was caressing him one lazy Sunday morning while we were lying in bed. I rubbed my hand over the spot again. "It feels strange right there," I said. "A bump I never noticed before."

"Yeah, that's it," Tommy said, looking at the ceiling. "Measure me for a coffin. Call the funeral home."

"Don't joke," I said. "It could be swollen lymph nodes; that's one of the warning signs."

"Josh, I feel great," Tommy said. "I'm bench-pressing three hundred."

"I know," I said. "But could you at least check it out? Maybe we should get tested."

"I'm never getting tested until there's something I can do about it if

I'm positive," Tommy said. "I told you that."

"You should still see what's causing that swelling," I said.

"Here's the deal," Tommy said. "We don't say another word about it all week, and then if it hasn't gone away by next weekend, I'll call Joel Rothstein on Monday, okay?"

"You and your deals," I said, shaking his hand. "Deal."

Maybe I wasn't going to talk about it, but that certainly didn't mean I wasn't going to think about it. Think about it; research it; learn everything I could. There were two computers in the research center at CBA that could be used to connect to different electronic bulletin board systems, called BBS. I had saved an article from the *Times* about a BBS in San Francisco that had been launched to exclusively cover AIDS topics.

I got Carole to arrange for me to use the computer at night; after Randy's funeral, she and Harriet ended up going out for coffee, and she had replaced Randy as Harriet's full-time assistant. Harriet was now head of the entire New York office at CBA and, fortunately, I was one of her favorites, but it didn't really matter. Carole, as her assistant, got nearly as much respect as Harriet, as she was the one who controlled access to Harriet's office and calendar. And although most people didn't know it, Carole's opinion of who should be moving up and who should be moving out at the CBA New York office counted as much or more than the opinions of any of the senior managers reporting to Harriet.

After that Sunday morning, I spent hours looking through the articles on the BBS. In the end, I just shook my head and gave up. Some of the articles said that swollen lymph nodes could be the first signs of ARC; others said it was a positive sign that HIV had once attacked the body but that the person's immune system was still strong enough to fight it off.

Over the next few weeks, the bump under the skin in Tommy's neck hadn't gotten any bigger, but it hadn't gotten any smaller either. I couldn't notice it unless I put my hand on his neck.

"You're going to call Rothstein, right?" I asked.

"Yeah, I will. This week."

"If there's something going on, you shouldn't wait," I said.

"I said I'll call," Tommy told me. "I'll take care of it."

But he never did, and I knew there was no sense pushing. The more I told Tommy he should make an appointment, the less likely it was that he would ever go. And anyway, Tommy did seem fine. He was going to the gym and seemed to be as full of energy as ever.

Three weeks later I woke up in the middle of the night. The bed was all wet. First I thought it was a dream but rubbing the palms of my hands along the sheets, I realized they were soaked. Tommy was covered in sweat. "Tommy, wake up."

Tommy felt the sheet. "Shit. What happened?"

"I think it's a night sweat," I said. "It's all just perspiration." We both got out of bed and looked at the covers. The sweat had drenched the bottom sheet so much that it had soaked through to the mattress cover. Tommy wiped himself off with a towel. I changed the sheets, and we got back into bed. It was already five o 'clock. I never fell back to sleep that morning.

Tommy called me at the office just before eleven.

"Is everything okay?" I asked.

"Josh, you gotta calm down, okay?" Tommy said. "I'm fine. I know you were worried, so I just wanted to tell you that I called Rothstein and got an appointment for five-thirty today."

"Oh, that's great," I said. "Do you want me to come with you?"

"Noooo," Tommy said, dragging the word out for emphasis. "I want you to get dinner so the two of us can have a nice relaxing evening together."

At home, I was pacing the floor, waiting for Tommy to get back. Maybe Rothstein had sent him right to the hospital. Maybe he had collapsed and died right there in the office. It was nearly 8:00 p.m. when the buzzer rang and I heard Tommy walking up the stairs. He wasn't exactly light on his feet but still made it up the stairs in about half the time it took me or anyone else. He walked in, kissed me on the lips, and put down his backpack.

"So?" I asked.

"So, what?"

"What did Rothstein say?"

"He said it could be nothing, or it could be something, or I could be dying," Tommy said.

"Really, Tommy, don't joke. What did he say?" I asked.

"Josh, they don't know anything. They don't know what anything means. Rothstein said half the gay men in New York are walking around with swollen glands," Tommy said. "They're not all going to be dead in five years."

"And did you tell him about the night sweats?"

"It was once, Josh," Tommy said. "One sweat. Singular." He started to hum "One Singular Sensation" from *A Chorus Line*.

"Okay, what did Rothstein say about the one, singular night sweat?"

"The same bullshit," Tommy said. "It could be something, it could be nothing. It could be my body successfully fighting something, or it could have just been too much to drink."

"We hardly had anything to drink that night," I said. "It was during the week."

"Whatever," Tommy said, just about shouting. "The bottom line is they don't know a fucking thing."

"Did he do the HIV test?"

Tommy pulled back and looked at me.

"Okay, well, did you let him do any tests?" I asked.

"He tested the T-cells. But he told me that like he explained to you last year, *when you asked him about testing yours*, they don't know a lot about what that means either, and even if they did, there's nothing to do about it, whatever the numbers are."

"Let's open a bottle of wine," I said.

"Good idea."

↬ 28 ↫

The T-cell tests showed some abnormality, but no one was exactly sure what the numbers meant. At year-end, Tommy still seemed perfectly healthy. If anything, he looked better than ever, as he was putting extra effort into working out and his body looked more pumped up than before. Tommy had asked me not to tell anyone about the symptoms, whatever they might be symptoms of. "I don't want every conversation to start with *How are you feeling?* and *What did the doctor say?*" Tommy had said, so I hadn't told anyone, not even David, or Carole, who, with Randy gone, had now become my closest friend at the office.

Tommy had his T-cells tested every three months, and I had made a chart on which I tracked the T-4 cells that were supposedly the good, so-called "helper cells," and the T-8s, the killer cells. The AIDS articles now talked about the most important measurement being the ratio between the two, so I would pull out my calculator, dividing the number of T-8 cells by the number of T-4s. Every gay man in Manhattan was becoming well versed in molecular biology. That is, every man except the one who dutifully reported the numbers to me after each visit but then paid no attention when I tried to show him whether the trend was up or down.

"It's fucking meaningless, Josh," he said. "There are guys I see at the gym who get sick and then three months later they're dead. And there are others that I know were in the hospital one time two years ago, and today they're fine."

For Christmas that year we flew out to Southern California. Tommy made me promise the same deal, saying otherwise he wouldn't go: no watching TV, no reading newspapers, and no mention of AIDS. There had been a lot of news stories about people going to Mexico to get a drug, riboflavin, that was sold there and supposedly helped to prevent the onset of AIDS in those infected by boosting the number of T4 cells. When we went to Tijuana for the day, I mentioned it to Tommy.

"If you say another word, you're spending the rest of the vacation alone," Tommy said.

"Well, I just thought since we were here ..."

Tommy put one hand over my mouth and his finger in front of my lips. "Stop thinking, Josh," he said. "Just do that for me. Okay? Don't think again until you get back to work on January second, okay?"

"Okay, deal," I said, sticking out my hand. Tommy shook my hand and squeezed it back so hard it hurt. Tommy grinned

"I just wanted to show you, I'm not losing any of my strength."

"Yeah, Superman," I said, mimicking what one of the little kids who lived next door on Ninth Street always called Tommy. "You've still got to watch out for the kryptonite."

The day we flew back to New York, the front page of the paper announced that the United States had banned any travelers who tested positive for HIV from entering the country. There were reports that gay couples risked being picked out of line, forced to undergo testing, and waiting for the results, or they would not be allowed in. The *Advocate* recommended gay travelers sit separately on planes and go through immigration and customs without acknowledging one another.

The vice president called for mandatory HIV testing. "Next stop, Guantanamo," Tommy said, referring to articles that said the U.S. was considering reopening the old military base there to use as an AIDS treatment center. "Yeah, what are they going to treat them with if there's no treatment?" Tommy said. "It's basically a concentration camp. Same as Hitler, except this time the pink triangles will outnumber the Jewish stars."

"Tommy," I said, exasperated, "I'm not allowed to talk about it, and you can go on your rants whenever you want."

"Except you, Josh; you'll get a pink Jewish star."

"Enough, Tommy." This time I was the one who put my finger on his lips.

We had decided to skip Fire Island again that summer. I hadn't really kept in touch with Gerard now that Randy was gone. Tommy and I got together in the city one night with Marlon and Rafael, who told us they were getting depressed from going to Pines each weekend and were thinking of selling their house.

"All everyone talks about is who's sick, what treatments are working, which doctors are incompetent or sick themselves," Marlon said. "Some of the houses are completely empty for the summer, just dark with the curtains drawn."

"It was a lot more fun when all everyone talked about was sex," Rafael said.

"Yeah, yeah," Tommy said. "Let's all have a good cry about the good old days."

"Or we could just smoke a joint and have an orgy right here, and then we can all talk about that," Rafael said.

"Yeah, now *that's* a good idea," Tommy said.

I knew he was joking, but I had to admit I had fantasized about the four of us in bed together. I couldn't think of any three hotter guys I'd rather do it with than Tommy, Marlon, and Rafael.

There was silence after Tommy's suggestion. *Maybe they're all considering the possibility*, I thought. The music had stopped, and Rafael put in another of the CDs he had started to buy to replace his cassette collection. He turned up the volume, and the four of us stood up and started to dance to Whitney Houston singing "I Want to Dance with Somebody." Marlon lit up a joint and passed it around.

By that fall of '86, Manhattan, too, had started to seem like a city of ghosts. When I went by NYU Hospital on First Avenue, I thought about Randy. Whenever I went to the Upper West Side, I thought about Elliot. And of Franklin. I made a list of all the people I knew had died. There were twenty-eight. I was only thirty-three years old. Probably my parents in their fifties or even my grandparents in their seventies couldn't make a list of twenty-eight people they knew who were already dead. Every restaurant, every shop, every block of the city was filled with memories.

With the experience of the past five years, the doctors had gotten better at treating the various infections, but there was still no way to halt the decimation of the immune system for those with full-blown AIDS. Victims had started to suffer from AIDS-related dementia as the virus attacked the brain, and a story in the *Native* speculated that it was much better for the mind to go before the body. According to the article, it was more difficult for the onlookers, but much easier for the patient, unaware of the terrible death he was dying.

"What time is it?" Tommy asked, rubbing my shoulder as we lay in bed. "I just heard the buzzer." I always slept with earplugs to try to block out some of the noise from garbage trucks that arrived every morning before dawn and started chomping through the previous day's debris.

I looked at the clock. "It's three-thirty." The buzzer rang again. "It must just be kids."

"I'll go open the window and yell at them," Tommy said.

"Go ahead, and bring a flashlight so you can show them your muscles and really scare them."

"Yeah, how 'bout I just show you," Tommy said, and he wrapped his arms around me and started to squeeze. The buzzer rang again.

"God damn it," Tommy said. "Those kids are dead."

He stepped over me and bolted into the living room. I heard him open the window.

"Josh, come over here," he said.

"What is it?" I asked. "I'm asleep; just tell me."

"Come over."

Downstairs on Ninth Street an ambulance was parked in front of the building. There were two police cars in front of the ambulance, one with its doors wide open. Judy, whose apartment was right by the front door, was standing out on the sidewalk in her bathrobe, talking with two policemen.

"What do you think happened?" Tommy asked.

"I don't know," I said. "Something in our building. Let's get some clothes on."

I put on my sweats and a T-shirt and opened the door. There was a lot of commotion in the hallway, and I walked down to landing where Beverly, one of the other tenants, was standing.

"It's Irving," she said. "I don't know what it was."

I went up to tell Tommy, and we watched out the window as Irving was carried on a stretcher and loaded into the back of the ambulance. Irving's eyes were closed, and he had an oxygen mask on his face, which seemed drained of any traces of color. We both walked downstairs and saw everyone had gathered in Irving's living room.

The police were still talking to Judy, writing notes on clipboard. "They said they think it must have been a heart attack," Judy said to us.

"Is he going to live?" I asked, somewhat concerned about Irving but actually more worried about what would happen with our rent-stabilized apartment if Irving died.

"They don't know. He had a faint heartbeat when they took him away. Do any of you know his relatives or anyone to call?" Judy asked.

"In the morning I can look up the name of his attorney in the city records," Beverly's husband offered.

In the meantime, we realized none of us had a key to lock the door to Irving's apartment.

"What do you think they're going to steal first?" Beverly asked. "The twenty-year-old TV or the forty-year-old toaster?"

I walked back upstairs with Tommy. It was already 5:00 a.m. and after we got back into bed, I couldn't fall back asleep. I lay there thinking about how Irving looked on the stretcher, with his eyes closed and the plastic mask. When the alarm went off at seven o 'clock, thoughts were still darting through my head at maximum velocity.

"You're running in bed again," Tommy said.

I smiled. I felt better just hearing Tommy's voice.

"I love you and your overactive imagination," Tommy said before he gave me a kiss. "But try not to think so much all the time, okay?"

❧ 29 ❧

Irving came home from the hospital less than two weeks later. It had been a heart attack, but he had called 911 himself as soon as he had felt it coming on and that, plus being able to get to Saint Vincent's Hospital in less than three minutes, helped him to survive. For me, it was strange to think that people dealt with all this stuff—hospitals, getting sick, dying—before AIDS. I mentioned it to Tommy.

"Well, Josh the one thing we know for sure is that even after they find a cure for AIDS, you'll have something else to worry about," Tommy said.

Tommy's editing of "That's What Friends Are For" had won several awards and was getting a lot of attention in the industry. A lot of music producers wanted to work with him and at Atlantic, they knew he was in demand and had made him a senior editor and had given him a big raise. He was starting to make good money but was getting restless.

"I'm not used to staying still so long," he told me. "I've never had so much stability in my life." He still always teased me about my stereotypical suburban upbringing in Scarsdale, the three kids, the wood-paneled station wagon, and the swimming pool in the backyard.

"I thought I wanted it, everything nice and planned out, like you," he said. "But now stability seems boring to me."

I nodded, though I wondered whether it was just work or if maybe our home life had started to bore Tommy too.

"I want to start my own thing," he said. "It's me the producers want to work with—it doesn't matter to them if I'm at Atlantic or out on my own."

We were sitting in a booth at the Knickerbocker, one of our favorite restaurants on University Place. Above us was a framed Al Hirschfeld caricature from the *New York Times* Sunday Arts section. The first time we had gone there to eat, I had shown Tommy how to look for the word "Nina," the name of the artist's daughter, hidden in the inked line drawings. I had explained how every Sunday morning, my sister and I used to try to find them—the number next to the artist's signature indicated how many times the word Nina appeared in that particular week's drawing.

Maybe inspired by that illustration above, I pulled out a pen. I always carried one in my pocket, even when we went out to dinner, so I could write down things I might think of that needed to be done the next day. I started to sketch a logo for Tommy Perez Productions.

"I think you should go for it," I told him. "I'm making enough now that I could support us for a few months if I needed to. And you're right; this whole music video thing is exploding."

We sat back and listened to the piano player, a young guy named Harry Connick Jr., accompanied by a bass player.

"He's really good," I said. "We should remember his name so we can watch for the next time he's here."

The plans for Tommy Perez Productions started to take shape. Gabriel, who'd helped me with the invitation for my first-anniversary-of-being-out-of-the-closet party eight years earlier, was now the chief creative director at CBA, and he put together a final design for the logo and laid out the business cards and stationery. I helped Tommy write a business plan using the new computer software at the office, Lotus 1-2-3, to design a table showing how much money would need to come in each month to pay for the rent, the loans on the equipment, and other expenses.

We decided that we would take a vacation over Christmas and New Year's and then when he got back to work in January, Tommy would talk to his bosses at Atlantic and tell them he planned to resign. The original owner, the one who basically had given Tommy his first job there as a favor to me, had retired the year before so, although I still felt a little guilty about helping Tommy plan his exit, I was able to rationalize it all. Tommy, guilt-free as always, was full of excitement, counting the days until he was out on his own.

We planned a trip to Italy, stretching it to two weeks: a few days in Rome, then Naples, Florence, and Venice. We both had the money to go and as Tommy said, once he started the business, it would be a while before he could take any time off, so I agreed now was a good time to splurge. On New Year's Eve, we welcomed 1987 by holding two plastic cups of Prosecco and kissing under fireworks at the Piazza San Marco in Venice.

One night at the end of January, we were walking up the stairs on our way back from dinner the Knickerbocker, and Tommy stopped at the landing before ours. I was already unlocking the door when I looked down and saw him stopped, with one arm resting on the railing.

"You okay?"

"Yeah," Tommy said. "Must have been something I ate."

But once I got in the apartment and sat down, I could hear Tommy struggling to catch his breath. I looked over at him; we were probably both thinking the same thing, but neither of us said a word. Almost thirty now, Tommy still looked like the athlete he had always been. It was hard for me to picture him any other way, but lying in bed that night, I, who had never really prayed from the heart, just always mindlessly repeating Hebrew words that I had learned in bar mitzvah class, put my hands together under the covers and made a request of God.

Tommy had spoken to the partners at Atlantic about his plans to resign and go out on his own on January 5, right after we returned from our trip. He told them he'd remain until the end of the month as he hadn't signed the lease for the space yet and still had to arrange for the telephone lines and equipment to be ordered. They asked him to stay on until the end of March but finally compromised on February 28. They offered Tommy a $5,000 spot bonus—one month's salary—if he'd stay the extra month, but as he told me, he was ready to move on to the next chapter. And eager to get started.

Monday, February 2, Tommy Perez was in the hospital for the first time ever. He had gone to Dr. Rothstein, who listened to his lungs, diagnosed it a probable case of Pneumocystis pneumonia, and wanted to admit him that day so they could start the intravenous drip to treat it right way. Tommy had called me at work; I told Carole and left to meet him at the apartment.

"What do I tell Stephen and John?" Tommy asked. They were the partners at Atlantic.

"Just call and tell them you weren't feeling well and went home," I said. "We'll figure out the rest later. One day at a time."

On the way downtown to meet Tommy, I was terrified; my hand shook as it held on to the pole in the subway. But then once I was with Tommy, trying to be strong for him and protective, I managed to calm down, helped him pack a bag, and we went downstairs and hailed a cab.

If it weren't for the wheelchairs outside the doors at the NYU Medical Center, with its beige-wallpapered corridors and soft incandescent lighting, I could have imagined we were checking into another luxury hotel, like the Hassler in Rome, instead of a hospital. Tommy had brought home a photocopied sheet of instructions from Dr. Rothstein's office that explained it all: he'd be in a new wing called Cooperative Care, where the patients stayed in private rooms and ate together in a cafeteria on the top floor. The "cooperative"—or "co-op," as it was called—part of the "Co-op Care" was that the patient had to have a care partner—-husband or wife or lover or friend—stay in the room to help out, so I had packed a bag too, planning to stay overnight with Tommy.

By the time Dr. Rothstein came to check on Tommy around seven o 'clock, he was already on the IV drip. "You should be home by the weekend," he told Tommy.

"And then what?" he asked.

"There are lots of people who have just a single case of pneumo," he said, using the abbreviation that was now common, "and then they're fine for years. There are a lot of new drugs in the pipeline. We'll have it licked soon." He sounded incredibly optimistic, so I tried to be positive, too, for Tommy's sake. Tommy was sure he'd be fine, Rothstein didn't seem worried, and I made up my mind to try to do the same.

We walked to the cafeteria for dinner and were surrounded by other gay men wheeling along their intravenous tubes and catheters. "The new tea dance," Tommy said. Most of the people wore sweatpants and sweatshirts like Tommy. Some had on jeans and flannel shirts, like they had just drifted over from Christopher Street by mistake and ended up here instead of at Ty's. Others had the purple lesions, sometimes camouflaged, mostly unsuccessfully, with makeup. I pretended to eat, moving the food around on the plate so Tommy wouldn't notice, but I wasn't hungry.

Back in Tommy's room, there was a chair that converted to a single bed for the care partner. But I crawled into bed with Tommy and held him tight, sticking my hand under the plastic tube that wound down to Tommy's forearm. "Don't worry; it's going to be fine," Tommy told me, stroking my hair. I was trying not to be scared, not saying anything, but I was sure he could feel my body trembling. "Take a deep breath, Josh. Breathe."

In the morning, we decided I should go talk to Steve and John at Atlantic. They both knew me from my visits with Tommy at the studio. I went home to put on a fresh suit, called Rita to say I'd be late, and went over to Atlantic. Steve and John arrived together; they drove in from Bellmore, somewhere on Long Island. They were surprised to see me sitting there in the reception area.

"Josh, what's up? Is Tommy okay?" Steve asked.

"Not exactly," I said. "He's in the hospital, NYU."

"Wow," Steve said. "He seemed fine yesterday morning, didn't he, John?" And then, not waiting for John to answer, he asked, "What is it?"

"Pneumonia," I said. "It's a virulent form that needs to be treated with IV."

"But he's okay, right?" Steve asked.

"It's a four-day course of antibiotics, and then he should be out Friday," I said.

"So he'll be back at work on Monday?" John asked.

"Should be," I said. Thankfully, they didn't ask any more questions, but unless they lived in a state of total media avoidance, like Tommy insisted I do when we went on vacation, they had probably figured out it was likely to be AIDS-related. The *Times* now had stories pretty much every day about the disease, and it was the focus of one horror story after another on TV.

"Just give him our best," Steve said, shaking my hand. "And let us know if there's anything we can do."

When I got to the hospital that afternoon, I opened the door to the room to see Tommy was doing pushups on the floor with the IV line stretching to the metal hook, which he had adjusted to its lowest setting.

"What are you doing?" I asked.

"Gotta keep my strength up," Tommy said.

"You're crazy," I said. "Just get into bed and rest."

Tommy stood up, pulling the IV hanger up with him while I watched, shaking my head. He was breathing heavily. "There's no way that can be good for you," I said.

"It's good to have you here to tell me what to do since my mother's not around," Tommy said.

I kissed him. I was doing my best not to let any of the terror I was feeling show, because that wasn't going to fit into Tommy's script of what was going on—he had been sick, the treatment was making him better, and all would be well.

"Did you call them?" I asked. Last night, I told Tommy I thought he should tell his parents.

"No," Tommy said. "And I'm not going to."

"They'd probably want to know," I said.

"Why?" Tommy asked. "So my father can enjoy watching me pay for my sins while my mother stands there crying? No thanks." I put my hand on Tommy's shoulder. "Believe me, they don't want to hear from me. It's been ten years."

"Things have changed. You're older. They're older," I said. "They probably would like to know about you."

"That's your version of loving parents, not mine," Tommy said. "If you want me to get better, stop talking about my folks, okay? Just don't remind me of them. As far they're concerned, I've been dead for ten years already."

Dr. Rothstein walked in, cutting short the conversation. He looked at the charts and listened to Tommy's lungs with his stethoscope. "Your lungs are already much clearer than yesterday," he said. "You're responding well to the medication."

"Still Friday?" Tommy asked.

"Looks good," the doctor said.

He did come home on Friday; I left CBA early to help take him to the apartment from the hospital. Tommy called Steve and John. They had sent over a collection of helium balloons with a teddy bear that wore a sweater with *Get Well Soon* inscribed. He told them he was home but wasn't sure about whether he'd be okay to come in Monday. The doctor had suggested he wait until Wednesday before going back to work.

But on Monday morning at 6:30, Tommy was up and ready to head to the shower.

"You're sure?" I asked.

"It's not like I dig ditches all day," he said. "I'm sitting at a chair in front of television screens—the same thing I'd be doing at home." He promised me that if he felt tired he'd leave early and come home but I—and Tommy, too, probably—knew that was never going to happen.

He was already weeks behind schedule with TPP, Tommy Perez Productions. I told him I thought he should talk to Steve and John about putting his departure on hold for a while. "Let's see what happens over the next few months," I told him. "Because you're never going to get insurance if you leave there."

I knew how our friends without insurance struggled, waiting hours in public clinics to see a doctor. People got care, but there was a big difference between being stuck at Goldwater and being in Co-op Care at NYU Medical Center. And Dr. Rothstein had become one of the city's top AIDS doctors, frequently on TV and on the board of directors of AmFAR, the American Foundation for AIDS research.

Tommy was never one to give up, probably from his wrestling background, and I admired his tenaciousness. He met with Steve and John to lay out the proposal that I suggested: he'd stay on at Atlantic with the understanding that he could give them two months' notice in the future if he wanted to leave and in the meantime, for any producers he brought in, he could work on the project and get a credit as Tommy Perez Productions. Steve and John agreed and gave him another thousand-dollar-a-month raise. Tommy was definitely a star on the editing equipment.

I tried to keep my attention on work but it wasn't easy; every day there was more grim news. I had stopped buying the *Times* but that only lasted for three days—I was always looking over people's shoulders on the Lexington Avenue subway to try to read the latest headlines, so instead of having the full background, I was getting bits and pieces from what I saw on the subway or from the front pages of the tabloids. By Thursday of that first week I had given up and was back to making my usual stop at the newsstand on 14th Street before getting on the train.

In March the *Times* ran a full week's series on AIDS, with major stories every day on how the disease was impacting New York and the people who lived here. Some scientists now believed that nearly everyone who was infected with HIV would at some point develop AIDS and die. I called David, and we talked about it, as Tommy wouldn't let me mention a word about it at home. "It's impossible," David said. "We're probably all infected at this point—we're not all going to die."

David told me that Russell had been diagnosed with Kaposi's lesions on one of his feet. "He's freaking out," David said. "You know Russell— Mr. Vanity." Russell was still officially David's roommate, but he hardly ever stayed there, as most of the past couple of years he'd been at his boyfriend's apartment on the Upper East Side.

"And what about Chuck?" I asked about Russell's boyfriend.

"He was already in once for pneumo," David said. "I don't think he's doing too well."

"And you're fine?"

"We're stars, darling," David said. "Nothing's going to happen to us." I wanted so much to believe him.

Tommy seemed to be doing great. He was back at the gym and on some of the summer weekends, we would rent a car and drive to upstate New York or Connecticut; sometimes to visit friends, and other times to just rent a room at an inn or a motel. We'd go back to the city, tan and relaxed, on Sunday. I was glad we hadn't gone to Fire Island for the summer; from what I heard it sounded pretty depressing. I didn't need to sit around all weekend and hear about who was sick and what the latest underground treatments were; I heard that all week.

Tommy, as always, wouldn't let me say a word about AIDS. No newspapers and no TV when we went out of town. Once, in Litchfield, Connecticut for the weekend, we saw a young guy with the purple lesions on his neck being pushed down the sidewalk in a wheelchair by an older woman, probably his mother. I looked over at Tommy; he was staring straight ahead.

But the blinders could screen out only so much. David called me at work one steamy Monday in the middle of August with the news that Russell and his lover, Chuck, had been found dead in Chuck's apartment. Chuck had started to get lesions on his face and Russell, seeing what was coming, decided he would rather be dead, too. "They committed suicide together," David told me.

"How do you know?"

"He had been talking about it," David said. "Not like he was going to do it but that if it ever got bad, he'd rather end it on his own terms. And he had told me that Chuck's doctor had given him a bottle of barbiturates that, if taken with a significant amount of scotch, lying face down on a pillow would just end it right then and there."

I sat at my desk and rested my head on my hand as I listened to David. It was only 9:30 in the morning. How was I supposed to spend the day sitting in meetings, figuring out how to get people to buy lemon-scented furniture polish?

"Chuck's neighbor Holly found them," David said. "She had a key. Maybe she knew they were going to do it. I don't know. She said it was beautiful; they were both dressed in white robes and had lit candles. The CD player had Mozart's 38th Symphony playing on repeat mode when she walked in.

The newspapers the next day reported that the Broadway choreographer Chuck Chapman, thirty-four, and Russell Meyer, twenty-nine, had been found dead of drug overdoses in Chapman's apartment.

When Tommy came home, I told him about it and showed him the story I had torn from the paper.

He didn't even glance at it. "Where are we going for dinner tonight?" he asked.

❧ 30 ❧

We spent life waiting. Waiting for new drugs. Waiting for the cough. The lesions. The unstoppable diarrhea. Whatever symptom might be an indication that another infection had taken hold. I dreaded every ring of the phone. When Tommy went to the doctor for T-cell tests, I started to get panic attacks, waiting for the results. We decided that Tommy wouldn't tell me when he was going to get tested, only after he came back with the results, which I dutifully recorded at home.

We had gotten a home computer, a TRSDOS-80, at Radio Shack that now covered most of the white Formica desk; it was where I kept the records of Tommy's tests in an electronic file. Using CompuServe, I was able to connect by telephone from home to the AIDS bulletin boards that had the latest information. Tommy would never look at them and got mad when I did, so I usually connected to read them in the mornings after Tommy left or when I got home before him in the evenings.

Back at work, just after Labor Day we had an off-site meeting for the entire agency. All of us had crowded into a ballroom at the Roosevelt Hotel across the street; it was the first time since I joined nine years before that I remembered the entire company together, other than for the annual Christmas parties.

Our CEO stood at the podium and announced that CBA had been acquired by a large publicly traded British advertising group that planned to combine CBA with other agencies they had purchased to create the world's largest advertising agency. The CBA offices on Madison Avenue were going to be closed down, and the company would be merged into Huntley & Dwyer, another agency headquartered in the Chrysler building.

"I know you're all worried about your jobs, and our plan is that everyone will continue to have a position in the merged company," the president of the acquiring British group said to a collective sigh of relief. "We're still working out all of those details, and your managers will be meeting with you in the next couple of months to fill you in." He went on to talk about all the new opportunities for expansion and career growth as part of the new enterprise.

Like a lot of plans that year, nothing quite worked out as expected. With all their talking and first-class airline tickets back and forth to London, no one had thought to sit down with the clients to see what they thought about being shuffled around among the agencies. Some, among them Johnson Wax, decided to take matters into their own hands. They notified CBA that they were putting the account into review immediately, and the new merged entity would not be invited to participate. By the end of September, Scoot, my protector, was out, along with me and the rest of the J-Wax account team. Our last day would be October 31.

"What are you going to do?" Carole asked.

"I don't know," I said. "It's probably for the best; I'm ready for a change."

"Harriet can find you something somewhere," she said. "I'll talk to her."

"For as long as she has a job," I said.

"She's the only woman in management at either agency," Carole said. "They're not going to get rid of her."

Carole was probably right. Harriett would probably try to find me something, but I was thinking it was a good chance to look around and see what else might be out there for me. I was getting nine months of severance pay—a month for each year I'd been there—so I didn't have to rush.

I decided not to tell Tommy over the phone, so when he got home from the gym that night I told him to get dressed. "I'm taking you to dinner," I said. "To celebrate."

"Celebrate what?"

I put my finger to my lips. "I'll tell you when we sit down. After a glass of champagne."

We walked over to the Knickerbocker, which was still our favorite.

"We lost J-Wax. More than a hundred people were laid off, including me, and Scoot, too."

"That's why we're celebrating, because you're unemployed?" Tommy said, pretending to check to see if I had a fever with the back of his hand.

"Look, I've been thinking about it all day, and the way I see it, it's an incredible opportunity for us to get out of here."

"What?" Tommy asked.

"Out of that apartment, out of New York, out of this sinking ship," I said. "I'm tired of it. I don't want to be in the middle of 'AIDS Central' anymore. I want to be someplace where everyone isn't dying, where people talk about stuff besides T-cell counts and catheters and home intravenous kits."

I pulled out a sheet of paper I had folded and stuck in my back pocket. I showed Tommy how my nine months of severance pay could cover nearly all of our expenses. Tommy had already been hospitalized once and under the new rules, that made him eligible for Social Security disability payments as well as Medicare.

"You can start Tommy Perez Productions and run it from our home."

"And where's that going to be?" Tommy asked. "And what are you going to do?"

"Well, I was thinking we could go to Florida, maybe Fort Lauderdale," I said. "We both like the sunshine and being tan. You can show off your body year-round."

"And you?"

"I'll show off my body all year too, although I guess I won't get much attention walking next to you."

"Besides showing off your body," Tommy asked. "What are you going to do with your hyperactive brain that can't be still for two seconds?"

"I don't know for sure," I said. "Maybe I won't be so neurotic once I get out of New York."

Tommy laughed. "Yeah, right. And there's another subway train right behind this one." That was our verbal shorthand whenever one of us heard something very unlikely to come true; it was something we heard all the time in the New York subway whenever conductors wanted to try to get people to stop squeezing into the train so they could close the doors.

"Maybe I'll write some short stories," I said. "Or I can go work for a small ad agency down there. It'll be good just to take a break and clear my head."

We talked about it more over dinner.

"Tommy, I'm not trying to be pessimistic, but just be realistic," I said. "If anything happens to either one of us, we're not going to be able to stay in that apartment. Even if we could make it up, no nurses or home attendants are ever going to climb the four flights of stairs."

At the end of the evening we decided to fly down to Fort Lauderdale for a long weekend two weeks later to see how we liked it. I walked over to Hotaling's, a newsstand on West 42nd Street that carried out-of-town newspapers, and bought a copy of last Sunday's *Fort Lauderdale Sun-Sentinel* to look through the real estate section.

That night, I went through the listings with Tommy half-watching, circling the ones that looked like they might be possibilities. A new two-bedroom, two-bath apartment was $350 a month or less. "We could set one bedroom up as an office for the two of us," I said. "And we'll each have our own bathroom."

The weather was beautiful the entire weekend in Fort Lauderdale. By Sunday afternoon, we had found a place we both loved. It overlooked the Intracoastal Waterway and had a big terrace facing west over a park. We'd be able to sit on the terrace and watch the sun set behind the palm trees. Both Friday and Saturday nights we had gone out to the Poop Deck, poolside at one of the oceanfront hotels, and it was crowded with a mix of gay men and women. Everyone was friendly. Tommy met someone who worked at a production company who said he could use some freelance help during the winter season, and Tommy was excited about that.

It all seemed so clean and bright. New York, by comparison, even on a sunny day—or maybe especially on a sunny day—felt depressing and dirty to me. It was still warm in October, but with the ocean breezes and in our shorts and T-shirts instead of a suit, it felt a lot more comfortable than a warm day in New York. "We'll buy a car," I said. "No more squeezing on to the #4 train." We had rented a car for the weekend—a convertible—and it felt good driving around, something I had rarely done since I moved to the city. I felt like a teenager who had just gotten his license.

That night, on the outside deck of a disco, the Copa, we sat at a wooden picnic table that reminded me of the one from that first summer at Fire Island Pines. We tapped the tops of our beer bottles together. "Deal?" I asked.

"Deal."

Back in New York, we made plans to move the first week in December, right after Thanksgiving. Tommy spoke to Steve and John, and they agreed to let him present himself as the Florida affiliate of Atlantic, which was quickly becoming the largest producer of music videos on the East Coast. He got out the artwork for Tommy Perez Productions and met up with Gabriel to insert the new address and phone number.

I wanted to go up to Scarsdale to tell my parents about the move in person before everyone was together for Thanksgiving dinner. They were already shocked when I told them on the phone about losing my job, and in addition to the move, I felt like I should tell them about Tommy's having been hospitalized, even though now he was doing fine.

I also decided I would go for an HIV test—for my parents' sake. There was really no other reason to know; nothing had changed and there was still no treatment. All the drug therapies being tested still had huge side effects, so it made no sense for anyone healthy to try them, assuming they could even get into a treatment protocol. But going to tell my parents about Tommy, I felt I needed to know so at least I could spare them a lot of unnecessary angst. If it was positive, I would just tell them I hadn't been tested. I discussed it with Tommy. We had already talked about telling our friends and family—well, my family at least—that Tommy had ARC before we left, but still I was surprised when all Tommy said in response, when I told him I had set up the appointment for the test, was that it probably was a good idea.

"Do it for them," he told me.

Once I decided, I wanted to go right away, but the earliest appointment was two days later on Thursday morning. Dr. Rothstein gave me the consent forms to sign and showed me how the blood sample would be sent to the lab only with a number—he kept the cross-reference names on file only at his office. He went on to explain that New York State law required that the results be delivered in person with appropriate counseling, but because I had been a patient for years and Dr. Rothstein knew I was well versed in the ramifications of HIV infection, he agreed he'd give me a call. "If it's negative, I usually get the results back in twenty-four hours," he told me as I left. "So you might even be hearing from me tomorrow."

Tommy and I had both stopped smoking marijuana since I had read some articles that mentioned it might be a possible co-factor in the destruction of the immune system, but that night I was so anxious, I wished we hadn't given away all the pot we had left when we decided to quit. We were both drinking more, and Tommy's washboard stomach was no longer as taut as it used to be. Tommy suggested we go to a movie to take my mind off the test results, so we walked over to the Waverly and saw *Moonstruck*, but other than Cher, I couldn't even tell you who was in it, let alone what it was about.

Wednesday had been my last day at Carlton Bennett, so Friday morning I kept busy at home, cleaning out the file cabinet under the desk and searching for any new information posted on the AIDS BBS—and waiting for the phone to ring. At two I called Joel Rothstein's office and got the service. "He's gone for the day, but we'll leave him a message," they told me.

"Can you ask him to call me? I'd really like to speak with him," I said, remembering the many calls to Tommy's service. It was only nine years before, but it seemed like centuries; another planet inhabited by different people. Tommy was still at work, and when I got home I told him that Rothstein had never called. "I guess it was positive," I said.

"We knew that it probably was before you went," Tommy said. "It would be a miracle if you were negative."

"I don't know whether I can go through the whole weekend, not knowing," I said. Tommy came over and put his arms around me and kissed me. I had tears in my eyes, thinking how brave Tommy was, how he could show me compassion when he was the one who had been hospitalized, and he was the one walking around with swollen lymph nodes. "I love you," I told Tommy.

"I love you, too," Tommy said, wiping away my tears. "We'll get through this. We're together." That only made weep more, and I buried my head on Tommy's chest so his T-shirt would absorb the tears.

We went out to dinner together to Cinco de Mayo, a Mexican restaurant in SoHo that served pitchers of frozen margaritas, guaranteed to get us drunk as quickly as possible. Marlon and Rafael came down to meet us, and we had a great time. When we got home it was around midnight and we staggered up the stairs, laughing. Tommy unlocked the door, and the red light was flashing on the answering machine.

"I actually forgot that I was waiting for Rothstein to call me back," I said as I went over to the desk.

"See?" Tommy said. "Like Randy always used to tell you, alcohol solves everything."

"Are you ready?" I said, getting ready to turn the black knob on the machine to the play position. My legs were shaking, and I didn't wait for Tommy to answer.

Josh, it's Joel Rothstein. I'm sorry I didn't call you earlier, but the results hadn't come back before I left the office. I stopped in because I knew you'd be anxious, but everything is fine. Your test was negative.

❧ 31 ❧

Tommy sat with me on the train up to Scarsdale. It was Sunday afternoon, two weeks before Thanksgiving, and the leaves were still on the trees in the bright red, gold, and yellow colors that somehow never appeared on the trees in the city. I had called to tell my parents that Tommy and I wanted to take them out for their wedding anniversary, which had been the week before.

"That's the only way I can be sure my mother won't turn it into another big family event," I told Tommy. "And we can be alone just with the two of them."

My father picked us up at the train station, again remarking how good we both looked, as if he might have been anticipating otherwise. When we arrived at the house, my mother was still in the bedroom getting dressed for dinner. Tommy and I were both wearing slacks and button-down shirts. I caught a glance of us in the living room mirror as we walked through to the den. I loved looking at the reflection of me and Tommy together.

My father sat down in his usual chair; the TV was tuned to his favorite show, *60 Minutes*. He never had figured out how to set the VCR timer, so he would just leave it taping at the slowest speed when he left the house and at some point over the six hours, it would capture the program he wanted to watch. I picked up the remote and turned off the TV. Tommy and I both sat on the same white couch that had been there since I was a child.

My mother walked in. "Come on in and sit down so we can talk with both of you before dinner, okay?" I asked. She sat down on the other side of the L-shaped couch next to my father. She didn't look at either of us as she sat down.

"We know you're both worried about AIDS," I said. Tommy reached out and held my hand. "I went and got tested this month, and I'm negative."

"Thank God," my mother said, still looking down at the hands in her lap.

"And Tommy?" my father asked.

"I haven't been tested; I don't want to be, but actually we can be pretty sure I'm positive," Tommy said. "I was already in the hospital once with a pneumocystis infection."

"When?" my father asked, looking at me. "Why didn't you tell us?"

"It was at the beginning of the year, right after we got back from Italy. We didn't want you to worry, and Tommy didn't want anyone to know," I said as Tommy nodded.

"Once people know, everything changes—you become a 'person with AIDS,' a P-W-A." Tommy said.

"Actually, Tommy has ARC—AIDS-related complex," I explained. "So hopefully, he'll never go on to actually develop AIDS."

"I'm feeling fine now, and the doctor told us that he has a lot of patients who have Pneumocystis once and that's it," Tommy said. "And then they never have any other symptoms." We talked about it more, and my father surprised both of us with how much he knew about the disease and the available treatments.

"What about the AZT?" my father asked, referring to a failed cancer drug that had recently gotten a lot of media attention as the first anti-HIV drug approved by the FDA.

"Our doctor—Dr. Rothstein—doesn't think it's a good idea." I said. "There are a lot of side effects, and you have to take a pill every four hours, setting the alarm clock for the middle of the night."

"He says you're better off resting and getting a good night's sleep," Tommy told them. "Besides, I haven't had any problem since the one time in January."

"So is there anything we can do?"

We explained there was really nothing to do at this point but wait. "The odds are in my favor, and I just have to hope for the best," Tommy said.

"Dr. Rothstein is one of the best in the city," I added. "He's a professor there at NYU Med School."

"Let's stop talking about it," Tommy said. "I'm doing fine now, and that's what's important."

So my father helpfully changed the subject, asking, "How's the job hunt coming?"

"That's the other thing we wanted to talk to you about tonight," I said. "We're going to be moving to Florida."

"Why?" my father asked. Now my mother finally looked up.

But before I could answer, my mother asked, "When?"

"Right after Thanksgiving. The first week in December," I said.

I explained how we had already rented an apartment in Fort Lauderdale, close to the beach. I told them how I wanted to take a break for a month or two and then maybe write or go to work for an ad agency in Florida. Tommy told them about his plans to do freelance production and still work with Atlantic from there.

Over dinner in an old bank building that had been converted to a French restaurant, we spoke about more details of the impending move.

I told them we planned to buy a car as soon as we got to Florida, and my father asked about Tommy's disability payments and the insurance. When we left, he even joked about how they'd be the only parents flying down to Florida from Westchester to visit their children, instead of the other way around.

Tommy tried to get in touch with his own parents, whom he hadn't seen since high school, more than ten years ago, after the family priest had advised Tommy's mother and father to consider him dead when they caught him with Eddy. "Act as though he never existed," the man of God counseled, and Tommy's father did just that.

After he had moved in with me, Tommy had called his mother secretly once a month when he knew his father was away at work. But then, according to his mother, five years ago his father found out about the calls and ripped the phone cord out of the wall and beat her with it like a strap. She had told Tommy all this when he was finally able to get the new phone number from an aunt. When he called his mother, she pleaded with him not to phone again. "He'll kill me," she told him. "You know he will."

"Just leave him," Tommy begged her. "Please. I'll help you, Mom." But he knew she never would and that was the last time they had spoken.

I persuaded Tommy that we should try to go up to the Bronx and talk to them before we left. "Maybe they've changed," I said. Back in September, Tommy and I had gone to an AIDS Mastery workshop in the city run by Louise Hay, who was the author of some popular self-help books. In the workshop she talked about clearing disease from your life by eliminating any part of your existence where you felt uneasy, or at "dis-ease," as she put it. That had been one of the things we talked about on the flight down to Fort Lauderdale. Tommy decided to give it a try.

He didn't want to call anyone to announce the visit in advance. This was the first time I had been to this part of the Bronx. About the only time I had even been to the borough at all, other than passing through on the Metro North train to Westchester, were childhood trips to the zoo or Yankee Stadium. As we walked from the subway station, it looked a lot different at ground level, with empty lots and homeless people huddled around burning trash in empty drums to keep warm. It was slightly better when we got to where Tommy had grown up, a collection of three twenty-story brick buildings built around a center courtyard.

The lobby was clean, but the lock on the front door was broken, and the elevator was out of order—a cardboard sign that looked like it had been used far too many times was wedged in the door announcing that. "How do they build buildings like this with only one elevator?" I asked.

"Welcome to the Bronx," Tommy said.

As we headed for the stairwell, I told Tommy, "You're an amazing guy. Be strong and remember, whatever happens, I love you and I'm here with you." The hallways were on the outside of the building, and we stepped outside again into the cold to walk to 11D. I saw the Perez nameplate in its rusted mount on the blue metal door. "They're still here," he said, and then hearing the TV on inside, "and they're home."

Tommy's mother answered the knock on the door and lunged to hug him. "*Mi hijo!*" she screamed. She saw me standing in the breezeway and pulled back. "*Pero tu padre.*" I could hear Tommy's father's voice in the background. He was standing behind Tommy's mother in the door. He wasn't the powerful presence that Tommy had described, but I could see where Tommy got his broad shoulders.

"Get out," he said. "You're not welcome here. You're never welcome here." He pulled Tommy's mother into the apartment and told her to go to the bedroom. She started to cry, stepping backwards out of the way. Tommy started to argue with his father in Spanish at the doorway; his mother was crying inside the apartment. Tommy made a fist, but I put my hand on Tommy's arm and pulled it back.

"Go with your boyfriend. Get out." His father slammed the door shut. We walked down the stairs, and Tommy was shaking when we got to the lobby. I hugged him, and we walked to the subway. Someone yelled "*Maricones!*" out an open window. We headed back downtown on the #2 train in silence.

❧ *32* ❧

I bought a bottle of champagne, and we sat drinking it together on the terrace in Fort Lauderdale, watching the sunset. It was Christmas Eve 1987. "Happy eighth anniversary," I said as we clicked the glasses together. Like most gay couples, we had our pick of dates on which to celebrate our anniversary. It could have been the day we met, the day we first had sex, when we got serious, or when we moved in together, although I'm not sure how we would have figured that last one out. Tommy and I always celebrated it on Christmas because that was that snowy morning in 1979 when he rang my buzzer with his bouquet of roses. I could close my eyes and remember every detail of that day. In some ways, it felt like it was so recent, and in others, a millennia before.

We had been in Fort Lauderdale for nearly a month and were both still adjusting. I had bought a used car, a 1982 Camaro with a glass T-top that could be removed so that driving around, it felt like a convertible. The neighborhood where we lived, near Las Olas Boulevard, had a lot of gay residents. Sometimes we walked over to the Poop Deck at the Marlin Beach Hotel. It was nice to be around gay people who didn't talk about AIDS constantly.

Neither of us was working, and although Tommy's weight was back to around 180 and he didn't look as pumped as before, he still turned heads at the beach and at Tea Dance—and unlike before, when he used to pretend he didn't care but really did, at this point I don't think he paid any attention to whether anyone was looking at him or not. The winter sun warmed us both. Tommy, who had never shown much interest in reading anything he didn't have to read for school, started to go through my old books, all of which I had packed and shipped down to Fort Lauderdale. Except for an occasional paperback I might have given to Elliot, David, or one of my other friends, I had held on to nearly every book I had read since high school.

I luxuriated in the freedom of not having to go to work every morning. I started writing a short story on the big Radio Shack computer. The newer computer screens now usually came with amber or green characters, which were supposed to be easier on the eyes than the white on black, and I was thinking about buying one. And new ones had the screen separate from the actual computer. Meanwhile, it felt satisfying to be writing about subjects other than the benefits of floor wax and insect repellent.

Herb and Lillian had decided to spend their year-end vacation in Miami Beach, and on New Year's Day they drove up to see the apartment and take me and Tommy out for dinner. My mother stood on the terrace and talked about how beautiful the view looked, but as I stepped inside to get everyone drinks, I could see tears in her eyes. I figured she still dreamed of the imaginary house nearby in Westchester, filled with my imaginary wife and their imaginary grandchildren.

Now, late that February morning, I sat on the terrace looking at a large pelican sitting on a post that anchored a dock behind our apartment building. That particular dock never had any boats, so I thought that was why the pelican always liked that perch. Actually, I wasn't sure it was the same pelican. They all looked alike to me.

"Two months, and I'm still sitting here on the terrace," I said to Tommy as he walked out in his shorts, carrying a paperback of *Dancer from the Dance*, a finger holding his place in the novel. "I guess I should get off my ass and do something," I said. "This is probably the first time since school that I've had more than two weeks of not working."

"Why don't you just enjoy it?" Tommy asked. "You've got the money coming in as though you're still employed."

"That's not going to last forever," I said. "And it feels weird not having anything to do all day."

"Weird in a good way or a bad way?"

"It's just different. Everything for me was always programmed," I said. "When school ended, there was summer camp; after high school came college; and after college, a few weeks later I was working at CBA."

"So just enjoy doing nothing for a change," Tommy suggested. He went to lie down on the hammock, which was angled against one side of the terrace. I looked over at him. He didn't seem like the exploding bundle of energy he had been in New York, the Tommy who could never sit still, his knees usually moving back and forth whenever he sat in a chair for more than five minutes. Now he could lie in that hammock for hours. Maybe it was the warm weather, maybe the humidity. The pace was slower in Florida, that was for sure. And a lot of the people in the apartment complex, the supermarket, the drugstore were all retired. Probably the same age as my grandparents, I figured.

When I looked over, Tommy had closed his eyes. I wasn't sure if he had dozed off as soon as he lay down or if he was just thinking, listening to the birds. It sounded as though he was sleeping, and I could see his chest going up and down. It was still beautiful, a work of art the way each one of his pecs was shaped so the nipples on his chest stood out just at the point the muscle curved around underneath. He hadn't been to a gym in months, not since we moved, and his body wasn't as hard or tight as it had been.

"I like it better," I told him one morning, resting my head one side of Tommy's chest and rubbing the other with my hand until the nipple stood erect. "It's softer; makes a more comfortable pillow."

Tommy had definitely been losing weight, but I wasn't sure how much. We didn't have a scale and if the new doctor, Dr. Fusardo, told Tommy his weight when he went for the first blood tests in Florida a few weeks before, Tommy didn't mention it to me when he got back. Dr. Fusardo had been recommended to us by Joel Rothstein, who had called him to talk about Tommy's case even before we moved down. We had gone over together in December for initial visits and now, Tommy went back himself for the bi-monthly exams, just walking the few blocks down Las Olas Boulevard.

In the hammock, Tommy turned on his side as though he was shifting around intentionally to give me a better view, and I could hear from his breathing that now, yes, he was definitely asleep. Tommy's hair was longer now, still beautiful, and it hung down over his forehead and eyes. Those great cheekbones, which Tommy had always attributed to his Indian blood, reflected the afternoon light, and his nearly hairless skin was still as smooth as it had always been.

We rarely left the apartment, other than to walk over to the beach, usually in the afternoons after most of the people had already left, as we had done in the Pines. It was quieter then, and we both liked the light at that time of the day. Just like on Fire Island, the sunset was behind us, but the reflection of the sky on the ocean as day became night always brought on a feeling of tranquility.

It was another Tuesday, a month later, when the phone rang as I was waiting for Tommy to get back from the doctor. My heart was pounding as I got up to go to kitchen to answer it. The ring of a phone was usually never good news these days. Either someone was sick, dying, dead, or being commemorated in some memorial service in New York that I wouldn't attend.

But now, with Tommy at the doctor ... *Shit. Please let it be nothing*, I bargained.

It was Tommy.

"Is everything okay?"

"Calm down," he said. "Not really."

"What is it?" I asked. "Are you still at the doctor's?"

"Yeah, I'm here. He's filling out some forms. I have pneumo again."

"How?" I asked. "You're not even coughing."

"Coughing's just one symptom, he said," Tommy told me.

"Is he sure?"

"Not really, but he says we should start the IV right away," Tommy said, "without waiting for the test to come back."

"So you have to go into the hospital?"

"Yup."

"Shit. That sucks," I said. "I'll come over and meet you at Fusardo's so we can walk back together."

"No," Tommy said, "just wait for me there. I'll be back in twenty minutes or so. He's just filling out the admission paperwork."

"It's the same thing?" I asked. "The four days of IV?"

"I guess so," Tommy said. "He didn't really explain the treatment."

"See you soon," I said. "I love you."

Tommy drove me crazy the way he would never ask the doctor

any questions. Not that he would have known what to ask—he had stopped reading news about AIDS years ago and wasn't interested in hearing whatever I had happened to learn about the latest experimental treatments from checking the electronic bulletin boards.

I went back to the terrace. It was 1:30 in the afternoon on a crystal-clear Florida winter day, bright sunshine reflecting off the water and creating a rippling pattern on the roof of the terrace. I lay in the hammock, hypnotized by the changing design above me.

I was jolted awake by the sound of Tommy, trying to open the door. The keys we had gotten from the landlord required a lot of twisting and turning. I had called him to get new ones, and the landlord was supposed to drop them off right after the holidays, but when Tommy was coming in, I didn't mind the advance warning; it reminded me of how we used to ring the buzzer to alert one another before heading up the stairs on Ninth Street.

I went to meet him as he walked through the door, wearing his sandals, shorts, and T-shirt.

"I don't know how anyone who looks that good can have to go into the hospital immediately," I said as Tommy hugged me. It wasn't the strong hug that used to get me immediately aroused, but the embrace felt great, and I didn't want it to end.

"He said it's fine as long we get there before five-thirty," Tommy said. "Let's go to the beach." He saw my eyes were red. "C'mon babe," Tommy said. "Don't cry. Okay? It's Tuesday. I'll be out by Saturday."

Maybe if I had been through what Tommy had been through in my thirty-one years, I might be able to handle uncertainty the way that he did. He talked about going to the hospital as though it was no more of a disruption than a business trip, the outcome as definite as the red carbon print impression on the return plane ticket.

Back in New York, at NYU Medical Center, there had been the separate floor in Co-op Care for patients with AIDS symptoms, mostly gay men because they were the ones with the good insurance plans to pay for a private medical care. The drug addicts were at the public hospital, Bellevue, down the street.

Here at Broward General, they were probably a few years behind New York in terms of the caseload, and so the AIDS cases were mixed in throughout the hospital. Tommy spent the first night in a room with an older black man. He was a former nurse who knew many of the other people who worked in the hospital and drew a constant stream of visitors. When he didn't have anyone there with him, he would sing hymns.

I closed off the curtain and got into the bed with Tommy; I was experienced now as to exactly which way to position my body among the plastic tubes and wires. The sheer white privacy curtains shimmered in the breeze from the air conditioner duct. I thought it felt like we were in heaven together. Tommy said it made him feel like we were on the camping trip he had always wanted to take with me but we had never arranged.

"We'll do it when you're better. I promise," I told him.

Visiting hours ended at eight, and I left to drive back to the apartment. It was the first night I had spent alone in Florida. We hadn't smoked pot at all since we'd been in Fort Lauderdale—I didn't even know who I'd buy it from here—but I still had a plastic bag with some I had been saving for emergencies that Stuart had given me as a going-away present before we left New York. I rolled one and went to lie in the hammock, bringing out a glass of scotch with ice. It was dawn when I woke up.

I went back to the hospital later that morning and, like the days that followed, I stayed until the end of visiting hours. Sometimes Tommy and I would play board games—the ones I used to play with Annie and the rest of my family, sitting on the floor on Sunday afternoons in front of the fireplace in Scarsdale. I had taught Tommy how to play Scrabble and Monopoly, and sometimes a game would spread over several afternoons because we would take a break whenever Tommy happened to doze off.

When Tommy was sleeping, I would sit in the visitor chair and try to sleep myself; other times, I would close the door and lie there in bed with Tommy, although I had been admonished by one of the nurses that I would be barred from visiting if I did it again. I had learned how to read the schedules posted on the bulletin board by the nurses' station to know when that woman was working; none of the others seemed to care. For many of them, this—the AIDS epidemic—was probably the first time that most had ever dealt with anyone openly gay, and I was surprised—really surprised—at how sensitive and caring nearly all of them were.

Those days at the hospital in Florida were surprisingly peaceful for me. Before we moved, the thought of being there at a hospital in Florida, alone with Tommy, with none of our friends or family around for me to lean on, had seemed terrifying. But now, caught up in the middle of it, I surprised myself with how calm I was.

❧ 33 ❦

Maybe the doctors were better in New York, maybe this was a particularly virulent strain, maybe Tommy had built up resistance to the one antiviral the doctors had available for treatment, but he didn't get better in four days this time. It was a full two weeks, April 7, before he could leave. Tommy waited on a bench by the main entrance as I got the car and pulled around to the driveway. Even then, he was still so weak, I had to go over and help him into the car.

He had lost nearly fifteen pounds in the two weeks, some from the medication, some from not eating, although I often brought take-out food for him when I went to the hospital at noon after visiting hours started. Tommy had been moved to a private room after that first night; in order to accomplish that, Dr. Fusardo had indicated to the nurses that he suspected a tuberculosis infection, which, because that was easily communicable to the so-called "general population," required mandatory isolation.

The weather was warming up, and we kept the air conditioning on more often, but Tommy usually spent most of his time outside in the hammock. The pneumonia was gone, but he was still in a lot worse shape than the day we had gone to the beach together before he checked into the hospital. It was hard for him to eat—he now had sores in his mouth and throat—and when he did eat, sometimes he'd throw up. I had gotten a scale, but Tommy refused to weigh himself. It didn't matter. After years of looking at Tommy's body, of knowing every curve and bone, I could tell that the pounds were disappearing.

I watched him in the hammock, a paperback resting on his stomach, his eyes closed. His old 501 cut-off shorts had been washed so many times that the blue was nearly gone, and the light color made Tommy look even more tan than before. I remembered how Tommy's thighs had been so big that the seams had split and opened up about an inch on either side when he first started wearing those shorts. It had been the sexiest one inch of skin I could imagine. Now the fabric hung loosely, draped around him more peacefully, without the body struggling underneath to be free.

Dr. Fusardo came over to see him one night the next week, as Tommy wasn't able to go out to the office. He examined Tommy in the bedroom while I sat on the terrace. Fusardo pulled open the sliding glass door. "C'mon in, Josh," he said while Tommy was in the bathroom getting dressed. "I want to talk with both of you."

Fusardo explained that there were at least five separate infections going on simultaneously. "You could go back in the hospital, and we can try treating them, one by one," he said. "But every treatment is going to have side effects, and your immune system is so weak that even if we manage to get one other control, another one is likely to take hold."

"So what do we do?" I asked.

"There are drugs coming; other drugs that actually help to rebuild the immune system," Fusardo said. "I'll try to see if there are any test protocols with openings nearby. I think there's one starting at University of Miami. In the meantime, Tommy's better off here than at the hospital, where he'd be exposed to so many different people and lot more germs and viruses all day. And he'll be more comfortable."

"I don't think I can take care of you alone, though," I said to Tommy. "Both our families are up in New York," I explained to Fusardo, although I didn't go into detail that Tommy's parents had pretended he was dead for the last eleven years and realistically, even Herb and Lillian were unlikely to help with emptying my lover's bedpans, no matter how accepting they now were of the two of us.

"There's this great hospice program in town," Fusardo said. "Very gay-friendly and very AIDS-knowledgeable."

I swallowed hard. I felt hot, like I had with the shocks from Radofsky's machine. "A hospice?" I asked. "Isn't that for people who have less than six months to live?"

"In theory, yes," Fusardo said. "But right now, it's the only way to get home care like Tommy needs that can be paid for by the government programs." He explained that it would require him to fill out forms that said Tommy likely would not survive more than six months, but then after that, there would be a social worker assigned and a full cadre of doctors, nurses, physical therapists, and psychologists on call to come to the apartment. We could even get help with the shopping and cleaning. "Since you're not married, Tommy is officially single, so they'll pay for a level of care as though he's all alone."

Kenneth—or Ken, as he insisted we call him when he first met us—was the social worker assigned to Tommy's case by the South Florida Hospice Association. He was tall, probably close to six feet, and had dark blond hair, lightened in streaks by years of Florida sun, and piercing blue eyes. Ken was handsome and in good shape, not pumped-up like Tommy had been but with more of a swimmer's body. I had always loved guys with deep, dark brown eyes like Tommy, but Ken's were a grayish-blue that seemed to reflect whatever image they were taking in. That, combined with a habitual chuckle that seemed it could be instigated with the least likely of comments, put us instantly at ease that first day.

"This is going to be one of my success stories, I'm sure of it," Ken told us, and he seemed so confident that we both felt like we should believe it too. Ken arranged for a hospital bed to be moved into the bedroom. The bed we had moved down from New York was dismantled. I put the mattress on the floor in the living room, moving the dining table against the wall to make space for it.

Each morning, a home-care aide arrived at ten o 'clock to help clean and prepare meals. She was supposed to help bathe Tommy, too, but I made a deal with her that I'd do that and in exchange, she could go to the Publix and buy the groceries with the cash I gave her—I'd much rather bathe Tommy than go to the supermarket. A nurse came at midday to take his temperature and pulse and replace the IV bags of nutritional supplements and morphine.

At night we were alone in the apartment since we never really had time to make friends in Fort Lauderdale. There was hardly anyone to even speak with by phone, because so many of our friends in New York had already died or were dealing with their own health problems—or had their hands full with the health problems of their friends.

Tommy had lost so much weight I couldn't even guess what he was at now. I trimmed his hair myself, which was still just so naturally beautiful that even my amateur skills couldn't really mess it up. The cheekbones were still there, but now they only accentuated how much weight he must have lost. Still, if it got to him, and I'm sure it did, he didn't say a word about it, and if I tried to talk about it, I got the familiar finger in front of the lips.

One night during the second week after the program started, we invited Ken to stay for dinner after his daily visit, and Tommy managed to get out of bed and sit with us at the table for an hour. Like us, Ken was from the Northeast and ended up in Florida, running away from his problems. He told us the story of how one morning, after eight years of living together, his partner had told him he wasn't in love with him anymore. They lived in a small town, Newark, Delaware, where they had both gone to school at the University of Delaware, and Ken just wanted to get out of town. "So I came to Fort Lauderdale for a week's vacation and never left," he said.

Tommy and I smiled at each other. Tommy had been sure Ken was gay, but I hadn't thought so.

"We weren't sure you were gay," I told him.

"I'm still not sure," Ken said as he chuckled. "I like to keep them guessing. It never came up until about six months ago. The clients in the program were mostly old Jewish people," he said.

"That's perfect, then," Tommy said. "You'll be all set for Josh when he's ready."

We all laughed, but I wasn't sure why. Was Tommy already thinking of my life without him?

Evenings, I crawled into bed with Tommy to watch TV or to read together, but once Tommy fell asleep, I would go into the living room to sleep on the mattress, leaving the bedroom door open so I could hear if Tommy called me. Sleep came fitfully, and often I lay there on the mattress, listening to Tommy's breathing, which was now unusually loud and pronounced. More than once in the middle of the night, I woke up, didn't hear it, and ran into the bedroom, scared, only to be relieved when I saw Tommy's chest moving up and down under the covers.

I spoke to my mother and father by phone, but they never came down to visit. "We'll just see you both when you come up for Thanksgiving," my mother said, and Herb offered to buy the tickets.

"That seems so far away," I told them.

"It's a busy travel time. It's good to buy them in advance," Herb told me, he and my mother both on the phone at the same time. "If you don't use them, we'll just get the money back." Herb was always very practical.

"Give them a break, Josh," Tommy said when I complained. "They're dealing with everything a lot better than most people's parents."

When Tommy had first been hospitalized in March, I had called Tommy's aunt, his mother's sister, to tell her the news and give her the phone number at the apartment. Since then, Tommy's mother had called nearly every day. I explained to her as best I could, with what I remembered from my high school Spanish, what the doctors were saying, but it was already so confusing in English that it was tough to translate. Plus, she had to go use a pay phone on the street so his father wouldn't see the calls on their bill, and it wasn't easy to hear with the noise in the background.

"Just tell her to call us collect," I told Tommy when he got back from the hospital, but she was so scared of his father that she was sure he would still find out somehow if she used the phone at home. I listened to Tommy talking to his mother on the phone in Spanish. Sometimes the calls were so emotional that Tommy started to cry, which scared me. I had never seen him cry. Tommy had always been the one who hugged me and made the tears dry up.

Some days, Tommy didn't want to talk with her and just had me tell her that he was asleep, which was often true. He slept most of the day now, the breathing heavy and labored, each breath a chore. One morning around nine, I was in the bed with Tommy—he had fallen back to sleep while I watched the last part of the *Today* show. Suddenly, he propped himself up against the pillow. "I had a dream last night," he told me. "I want to call my mother."

"Why don't we just wait for her to call this afternoon?" I said. "If your father hasn't left for work yet, he'll beat her senseless when he finds out she's been talking to you."

"No, I really want to talk to her," Tommy said, his voice hoarse and raspy.

I dialed the number for him. Luckily, it was Mrs. Perez who answered. I handed the phone to Tommy, but he was too weak to even grasp the receiver this morning. I held the handset up against his ear.

"*Mama, es el fin,*" I heard him say. Tommy cried and said nothing, listening to his mother. "*Te amo también.*" He motioned for me to hang up.

"How do you know it's the end?"

"I know."

❧ 34 ❧

It was at seven the next morning when his chest, that beautiful chest, became still. I had spent the night in the bed with Tommy, our bodies next to each other, with the plastic tubes in between us. I had lain there, half-awake, half-asleep, listening to Tommy's breathing, which I could tell was becoming increasingly difficult.

The nurse had come the afternoon before as Tommy drifted in and out of consciousness and had told me that many times, she had seen patients accurately predict when death was approaching. She had called Ken, and he had come over an hour later.

"Do you want me to stay here with you?" Ken offered.

"No, we'll be alone," I told him. "That's the way it always was—the two of us together against the world."

"Always *is*," Ken had reminded me. "You're still together." He hugged me before he left.

That night in bed, just before midnight, I had whispered in Tommy ear, stroking his hair. "It's okay to let go. You're not giving up."

I sat there for about fifteen minutes, crying softly that morning, wiping my tears with the white sheets. I went to the refrigerator and pulled down the card with the pager number that Ken had given me. A couple of weeks before, while Tommy was sleeping, I had told Ken the story of how Tommy and I had met. "To this day, every time I get an answering service, it reminds me of the agony of that first winter, trying to get in touch with him," I told Ken. And because Ken always had a solution for everything, he had pulled out his pen and written down the two numbers. "When the office is closed, just call me at home or on my pager," he had told me.

I didn't have to say anything when Ken answered the phone. I guess he just knew.

"I'll be right there," Ken told me. "Just cover him and wait for me to get there."

When Ken arrived, he hugged me and held me tight. "You guys were beautiful together," he said. "Sometimes success isn't staying alive but just getting through the experience. You may never be this close with another person in your entire life—believe me, a lot of people go through life without ever having this kind of connection."

Ken took charge of everything; he had been through it all before. The police, the funeral home, the nurse, the bed rental agency. The entire morning seemed to be a blur of people in and out of the apartment, even after Tommy's body had been taken away in the hearse. I couldn't call Tommy's mother. I didn't have the energy to get through it in English, let alone in Spanish. Ken, who was fluent in Spanish, called her. "*Cálmate*," I heard him say.

"She needs a tranquilizer," he said when he hung up.

I gave him her sister's number. "Call her, and she'll get her to a doctor or something. Otherwise, the father will get home and probably just hit her until she stops crying."

Ken had to go to the office and stop by to check on other patients, although I realized he never mentioned any of the other patients—or "clients," as Ken insisted on calling them—when he had been with us. He always made me and Tommy feel that we were the only ones that mattered when he visited.

"I'll come by at the end of the day," he said.

"You don't have to. I'll be okay."

"Josh, I'll see you around six o 'clock," Ken said. "It wasn't a question. That's about when it's going to hit you, and I don't want you to be alone. And beep me during the afternoon if you need anything or just want to talk."

Ken had told me not to clean up, to just relax, but I couldn't sit still. I called my parents and told them. I heard my mother gasp. I called Annie, who offered to fly down from Boston, but she was teaching now at Harvard and it was the end of the semester, so I knew how hard it would have been for her. I talked with David, who had tested positive years before but had no symptoms, and with Gerard, who, like me, seemed to escape infection despite years of unprotected sexual encounters before we knew of the danger.

I had thought about doing a memorial service in the city, but after I talked with both of them, I realized that there weren't enough friends of ours left in New York to attend. And even for those who weren't infected or for straight friends, I knew it still took a toll on people to constantly be visiting hospitals, attending funerals, and going to memorial services. Joel Rothstein had given up his medical practice and had bought a vineyard outside of San Francisco. He was now mixing grapes instead of IV solutions, having become totally burned out from taking care of thousands of young men, most of them now dead, with no cure in sight and only the eternal promise of drugs in the pipeline. Another train right behind this one.

I started to clean up the bedroom against Ken's instructions. I put the old bed frame back together and dragged the mattress back in from the living room. Ken had taken all of Tommy's leftover medications to give to other clients who weren't able to afford the latest drugs, none of which seemed to work anyway. I went in the bathroom with a black plastic garbage bag and threw away Tommy's toothbrush and razor and most of the other stuff I didn't use—except Tommy's hair gel, which I decided to leave in the medicine cabinet.

Ken came back at the end of the day as he had promised.

"I couldn't just sit here," I told him. "It felt good to be doing something."

"Everyone's different," Ken said. "But you have to let yourself grieve and deal with the feelings; otherwise, they'll keep coming up in your life in different ways—ways you probably won't even realize at the time."

"I don't know. I guess it will hit me when I get back to the city."

"You're definitely going to go back?" Ken asked. "You shouldn't make decisions like that right now."

"No, it's nothing I decided today," I said. "I'm a New Yorker. I'm never going to be happy down here. Especially not alone. I'd been thinking about it a lot the past few weeks—what I'd do after Tommy died."

❧ 35 ❧

Over the next few days I packed up Tommy's clothes. I kept his leather jacket from the high school wrestling team. Tommy had gotten so much bigger since high school that it hadn't fit him for years, but he never wanted to part with it. I tried it on for the first time; it was way too short but it fit around my shoulders. Ken made arrangements for hospice to pick up the clothes. I saved Tommy's rosary and the Bible that a visiting nun had given him when he was in the hospital in March and which I planned to give to Mrs. Perez, somehow, when I got back to New York. Tommy had held the rosary a lot that last week, and I thought maybe it would comfort his mother to know that.

I sold the Camaro to a used car dealer and after I left, Ken was going to arrange to have the furniture taken to a thrift shop run by the Hospice Association to raise money. I packed up my books, my photo albums, and videotapes, along with most of my clothes and Tommy's leather jacket, and sent them to my parents' home. They had offered to keep them in the garage in Scarsdale until I got settled back in the city.

I was going to stay at David's on the fold-out couch in his living room. "I don't think it'll be very comfortable," David had warned me.

"I've been sleeping on a mattress on the floor the past two months," I said.

I still had three months left of my severance pay and that, along with what was left of my savings, meant I'd be able to pay the rent until I found a job. My father had offered to help with the security deposit, but I told him I was sure I could handle it myself, once I found an apartment. The economy had recovered quickly from the market crash the year before, and I was pretty sure I wouldn't have any trouble finding work.

Ken picked me up on Friday morning and drove me to the Fort Lauderdale-Hollywood airport. In the trunk were my two suitcases and a small carry-on black tote bag that held my diary, the rosary, and the Bible, along with a small rectangular cardboard box, not much larger than a soda can if had been squared off. Inside was a maroon velvet bag with a black drawstring on top, and inside that were Tommy's ashes in a plastic bag wrapped with a white tie wire. The red-faced man with the round face at the funeral home had opened it to show me before closing it up, demonstrating how the interlocking tabs held the box closed.

"They're not actually ashes," he explained. "It's more accurate to say remains, more like a coarse dust."

Ken had insisted on going with me. "Trust me, Josh," Ken had told me. "These next few weeks you never know when something is going to hit you, and you'll break down."

Ken and I hugged at the curb, with the suitcases sitting on the sidewalk.

"Thanks for everything, Ken," I said. "It's been rough, but you really helped me through it—Tommy, too; both of us."

"You know, you guys were really special. You get used to people dying when you do this job," he said. "But ..." And at this his voice trailed off. "Now I'm the one who's going to break down," he said. "Go. And call me tonight, and let know you arrived safe."

"I'm going to miss you," I said, still holding the tote bag in my hand, and we embraced.

When I got on the plane, I puzzled over where to put the bag with the cardboard box. It didn't feel right to put it in the overhead bin and definitely not on the floor. So I took the box out of the tote bag and held it in my hands for the entire trip. It was the first plane flight I could ever remember where I didn't read a book or a magazine.

Over time the disarray subsided. The bold grid of New York City returned to its rightful numerical order. Years later, as he walked through Manhattan, the blocks were still filled with ghosts, but they were less haunting now. He would see new things, things he had never noticed before, even on streets he had walked down hundreds of times.

It might be the engraved heads over a brownstone doorway or the glass-rooftop addition on the top of a building. Before, he hadn't looked up as much. Maybe his eyes had been on Tommy. Or before that, looking at passersby, hoping to find his Tommy.

Now, freed from those burdens, he could be more open to the rest of life's bounties. He had loved and been loved. He had learned how little that mattered could actually be controlled, no matter how much he worried about it in advance. When the announcement came, now in the recorded sound of a professional speaker, "There's another train right behind this one," he smiled, and waited patiently for it to arrive.

In the mornings, lying there under the sheets alone, occasionally he would anxiously rub his feet against one another—but less intensely and with not as much urgency. He was still running. But it was no longer a race.

ACKNOWLEDGMENTS

This novel had a particularly long gestation period and hence a lot of people helped along the way. After my partner Ken and most of my friends died during the first decade of AIDS, I left my full-time job in New York City and moved to Florida in 1993 with the intention of taking a break and writing a novel about that exhilarating, and ultimately terrifying, time from the late 1970s through the 1980s. From my home I started doing some business consulting at the time to pay the bills and that unexpectedly grew into a relatively large firm not unlike the one I left New York to get away from, albeit this time with an ocean view. That delayed my being able to dedicate time to the novel for many years much to my dismay. However, I now think the passage of time added much to my being able to look back at that era from a greater distance and with a more nuanced view. Most of the manuscript was written during the summer of 2007 which I was fortunate to spend in the Mediterranean seaside village of Sitges, Spain. To those friends who painfully slogged through the first draft and gave me feedback after that summer I owe a special debt of gratitude. My editor, David Groff, who I'm sure got tired of arguing with me, can be satisfied that in the end I admitted he was right and accepted his recommendations. Finally for all of the Joshes and Tommys out there, the pursuers and pursued, the dreamers and the lovers, thanks for the inspiration.

Although this is not a memoir, I've tried to be as faithful to the period as my memory permitted. You're invited to share your own recollections of life in New York City and Fire Island during the 1970s and 1980s at **www.runninginbed.com**

ABOUT THE AUTHOR

Jeffrey Sharlach was born in Connecticut in 1953. He's trained as a journalist and an attorney, runs a communications consulting firm, teaches at the NYU Stern School of Business, and lives in New York City, where he moved in 1974. *Running in Bed* is his first novel. **www.jeffreysharlach.com**